100

WILL O' THE WISP

H . BEDFORD-JONES

WILL O' THE WISP

H. BEDFORD-JONES

ALTUS PRESS • 2015

EDITED AND DESIGNED BY
Matthew Moring

PUBLISHING HISTORY
"Will o' the Wisp" originally appeared in the November 28–December 26, 1936 issues of *Argosy* magazine (Vol. 269, Nos. 1–5). Copyright 1936 by The Frank A. Munsey Company. Copyright renewed 1964 and assigned to Steeger Properties, LLC. All rights reserved.

THANKS TO
Everard P. Digges LaTouche and Gerd Pircher

TABLE OF CONTENTS

CHAPTER I

SPY IN LONDON

MID MAY and bitter cold, with a fine mist blowing in the London streets. A chill May afternoon, with destiny astir over Europe like the wind whistling here around the London chimney pots. May of 1778.

Brian Desmond sat scratching away with his quill pen, near a window of his rented London room. A coal fire blazed cheerfully in the fireplace. Desmond was enveloped in a quilted dressing gown that hid everything save face and hands. The hands were long and slender and deft. The face was long and lean-jawed, alert, with a whimsical touch to the blue eyes under their black brows and hair.

A low tapping sounded at the door. Desmond rose and unlocked it. A man, wrapped to the ears in greatcoat and muffler, came in, crossed to the fire.

"I have the information," he said at once, "but it cost me twenty quid." He spoke in English, with no trace of an accent. Then at a gesture from Desmond, he switched to French. "The lugger *Merlin* is waiting at Dover for her. She has ordered her carriage for midnight, with relays of horses on the road. Therefore, she will reach Dover about dawn."

Desmond went to his secretary and took a purse from one of the drawers. He tossed it to his visitor.

"For your expense and trouble," he said cheerfully. "You talked with a servant?"

"Her groom. Rather, the groom of the house where she's staying. Some English lord—I forget the name."

"Lord Stormont." Desmond nodded. "I'm to see him at six. You had no trouble, you made no slips? But I shouldn't ask that. Other men might make slips, mistakes, errors. You're a sharp rascal, though."

"Not a soul around, except a dirty fellow with a wooden leg."

Desmond started, stiffened, lost his smile.

"Good lord! It can't be—it must be! Quick, man; did he have gray hair?"

"Yes, m'sieu', hanging long, and a gray mustache—"

"And you came straight here? Then get out at once. We're lost, both of us. That man was Constant, the cleverest spy in the English service—go, go, damn you! Take the back way and you will have a chance. They'll let you go, to grab me...."

The door slammed, the visitor was gone. Desmond went to

*He sent the horse at the
nearer man and fired.*

the window, his gaze flitting along the street below. Well, too
well, did he know that man of iron, Constant. As he looked,
his brain was racing.

Upstairs, Major Medbury and his family. On this second
floor, opposite him, two elderly ladies, sisters. On the first, the
school teacher and his family. Yes, the trail would come straight
to him; no escaping it. Fool that he had been!

"Faith, I might have known she'd have Constant working
with her, protecting her!" he murmured. "And—by the poker!
I'm caught."

A figure moved, there across the street. A man with a wooden
leg, nearly hidden by the greasy coat covering him, grayish hair
dragging about his shoulders, mustache drooping over his lips.
Constant, yes; Desmond knew the disguise. And in the street,
soldiers.

Caught! They would have the back way stoppered, the street
blocked at both sides. A thorough fellow, Constant.

All this in one mental flash—then Brian Desmond was at work.

The papers from the desk he flung into the fireplace. He whipped off his dressing-gown and darted to the trunk in the corner. Everything here was lost; but this possibility he had long foreseen. And Constant did not know him by sight. No one knew Will o' the Wisp by sight, except the woman who was leaving Dover in the morning. But the landlady would be on the stairs, would come up with them; and that shrill-voiced virago knew Brian Desmond by sight. There was the danger to evade.

This flamed through his brain even while he stooped to the trunk—every detail, every possibility, every slim chance. And now he must risk everything, life itself, on one dice-cast. For a French agent, prison; but for a French agent in English uniform as he meant to be, death....

The trunk flew open. Desmond's brain hesitated, though not his fingers, weighing the chances anew. No; the woman would be on the stairs. He must risk all, even the death of a spy. And to have such a crisis come at this time, of all others! It was maddening. Still, such was life—his life.

His fingers were flying now. One chance—play it strong, at all costs! His face he must risk. Powder dashed on brows and temples, changing black to gray; it was dim enough in those accursed stairs. And the eyeglass would help, must help. And the voice.

Deuced lucky he had another den ready to shelter him! Not luck—shrewd calculation. The sort of work that made Will o' the Wisp the most dreaded secret agent in Europe.

Boots, breeches, gorgeous coat, sword—as by magic, the uniform grew upon him. He could hear voices below stairs now, the scrape of boots in the street. They were getting the land-lady out and inquiring. More powder on the hair and brows. He buttoned up his tunic and adjusted his sword-belt, slapped on the cocked hat with regimental cockade, and inspected himself in the glass. Then a monocle, a single eyeglass, screwed into his eye and changing the whole set of his face. By heaven, it might do!

A muffler, wound about his neck; he tucked his chin into it and flung a heavy greatcoat about his shoulders, loosely open to reveal the splendor of scarlet and gold. One last glance about the room. A few things tucked into pockets—pipe and tobacco, money, watch. Then to the door, opening quickly, stepping outside.

DESMOND CLOSED the door softly, turned the key in the lock, and pocketed it. Steps and voices below; they were coming up. He heard his own name, in the shrill accents of the landlady. He heard what he dreaded more—the ominous *tap-tap-tap* of a wooden leg. Constant was with them, then.

Stepping quietly, seeking the sides of the steps to avoid tell-tale squeaks, Desmond mounted to the landing above. He stood there, waiting. The pound of boots stormed along to his own door, in the hall below, and stopped there. A sharp knocking. A shake and a shiver at the door.

"Break it down!" snapped a voice. "Egad, we know the fox is in his hole...."

Then a brief silence....

Desmond chose the instant unerringly. His voice boomed out in a deep and hearty bass.

"Until tomorrow, Medbury! Show up at a good hour. *Au revoir.*"

He tramped heavily, coming down the stairs. Then, toward the bottom, he came to a halt of surprise at sight of the uniforms, the staring faces turned toward him. With a snort, he put a monocle to his eye and glared.

"What's this? What's all this?" he barked.

An officer turned to him. "On His Majesty's service, sir. We've run a French spy to earth. Captain Holland of the Somerset foot. Your name, sir?"

"My name, is it?" rasped Desmond. The gawking woman, the gaunt hair-draggled face of Constant, seeped into his consciousness. "Sink me! Things have come to a pretty pass—harumph! Your duty, no doubt. Colonel Fitzgerald of the Yeomanry. Visiting my friend Major Medbury above stairs."

The captain saluted. But the greasy cloaked figure reached forward to finger Desmond's greatcoat. The voice of Constant rang like a knell.

"Dry wool, sir, and rain i' the street—"

Desmond's fist drove down full force. Struck by that hammer-blow squarely between the eyes, Constant crumpled and sprawled on his face, one arm quivering spasmodically. Desmond put hand to sword. The spy's words had escaped all of them; none were as quick-witted as Constant.

"Why, damme! Put filthy hands to His Majesty's uniform, you dog?" came the deep rasping voice. "Who's in charge here? Who's responsible? You, Holland? Sink me, but I'll have your commission for this! Out of my way, d'ye hear?"

Through them, past them, tramping on down the stairs, went the choleric figure, and on past the staring guards below, who saluted the half-glimpsed uniform. As Desmond left the house and passed more guards, he heard the smashing, rending noises above where the door was being broken in. With a chuckle, he drew his coat close and strode away.

"Faith, a miss is as good as a mile!" he muttered gaily, his spirits rising on the instant. He lifted bleeding knuckles to his lips and his blue eyes danced. "The rat will have something to remember me by, eh? Pity it wasn't a bullet. My life's not worth a farthing while that fellow's alive."

Safe enough for the moment. Only the landlady knew the features of Brian Desmond. And thought of that imp of hell asprawl under his feet was comforting.

He had only three blocks to go, and went unhurried, pocketing the monocle and wiping his black brows clear of powder. Constant would guess the truth, too late; the hue and cry would be out for Colonel Fitzgerald—too late. In another few hours, Fitzgerald would be spurring out of London town for Dover; but first, he had work to do.

Work, yes; work and peril went hand in hand these days. For France had recognized the struggling American colonies; Lord Stormont, English ambassador to France, had come home to London, and war was on. No war of tramping armies in Europe, but a war fought on the high seas, in far corners of the world. A war of finance, of intrigue, of diplomacy, not a war of nations at each other's throats. France was not anxious for war. And it was no secret that George III, erratic and heading into later insanity, detested the very thought of war.

None the less, there was war, and stern work for Brian Desmond.

FOR THE moment, he was Fitzgerald; here were the quiet lodgings where Colonel Fitzgerald lived. He entered, greeted his landlady, accepted some letters that had come in his three-day absence, and went on up to his bedroom and parlor. Colonel Fitzgerald was home again; but not for long.

He lighted the ready-laid fire, and then stripped. Attention to detail was one of the things that kept Will o' the Wisp plaguing half the courts of Europe, instead of rotting in a dungeon or a grave. This greatcoat was just the thing for a gallop to Dover and a Channel passage; but Desmond was too wary. These clothes had served their turn.

He inspected the letters and tossed two of them into the fire. The third he opened out and inspected at length. Orders from Paris, in reality from the Comte de Vergennes who ruled France as minister. Desmond sat down to his table, dipped a quill, and took time to decipher the coded message that a French agent had left for him. Then he crumpled up the papers and laid them on the flames.

"Bah! Old stuff," he muttered, and leaped to his feet. His body was lean and trim, tapering like a sword, incredible in its agility. A flash of exultation blazed in his eyes. "Tonight Will o' the Wisp sups with a king! There's triumph for you. Not that I'll get much to eat," he added ruefully, with a glance at his watch. "So I'll sup first and talk with His Majesty later—and ere morning, praise be, I'll bring tears to the eyes of lovely Jane Warr, who's worth all the kings on earth. Well, it can't be helped. If she serves England, I serve France. And now to be off, away from this place forever!"

He shaved hurriedly; time pressed, and somehow there rattled in his brain that sinister *tap-tap-tap* of a wooden leg. Strange, he thought, how a man such as Constant could be so clever. A man from the depths of life, apt at disguise, at foreign tongues, at home anywhere in Europe, even able to ape the gentleman—handicapped, moreover, by that wooden limb. Yet there lay the most deadly and inhuman rogue going, and the shrewdest to boot.

Desmond dressed carefully in rich garments—the finest of lace at throat and wrists, fobs and seals dangling, clothes tailored by the best in London. In his pocket, passports and papers, for the Colonel Fitzgerald he seemed to be, and for the Colonel Desmond he really was. Money, all he had, and enough. Everything else, into the fire. On the table he slapped saddlebags, and stuffed them with everything he needed to keep, except what would go into the pockets of his heavy frieze greatcoat— a handsome coat of rich blue, with brass buttons. Last of all, into the coat pocket he slipped a small pistol, and another into the saddlebags. Then he rang for the landlady, who came presently.

"My letters, madame, call me north tonight on another journey," he said cheerfully. "I must catch the North Mail, so I'll be off. Here's money. If I'm not back in four days, I pray you lay my things away until I can send for them, and rent the rooms afresh. Here are my saddlebags. I'll send a man for them in an hour."

Into hat and greatcoat now, and off, swinging away on a tall cane with gold-tipped handle; a cane just a trifle too heavy for honesty. A glance at his watch, a nod, and he knew he had time and to spare for his business, before going to sup with the king. The thought made him chuckle. He was not supposed to know that the Count von Weissenstein was also the King of England. On the other hand, the Count von Weissenstein was very far from dreaming that Colonel Fitzgerald was actually Will o' the Wisp!

"Which," murmured Desmond, "balances the ball very neatly, begad!"

Here was the coffee house he sought, not far from his ultimate destination in Hanover Square. He entered, glanced around, and found a quiet seat. A few officers, gentry, one or two noblemen. The evening was as yet far from starting.

Having ordered what he wished to eat and drink, he obtained newspapers and spread them out. One was still damp from the press. He glanced over it, and his eye was abruptly caught and held by a paragraph:

> We are informed on excellent authority that the notorious Monseer Feufollet, or Mr. Will o' the Wisp, the arch spy of the French Court, is at the present time pursuing his nefarious schemes in London itself. It is to be hoped that all loyal subjects of his Gracious Majesty will be on the alert to secure the Thousand Pounds offered for the apprehension of this audacious and slippery enemy to the Realm, whose machinations, like those of the infamous Dr. Franklin, are a menace to the peace and security of the world.

Desmond chuckled; then he looked up, as a gentleman approached and took the seat opposite him, with a quiet greeting. A small dark man of fifty, soberly dressed; this was the man in charge of all French intelligence work in London, but from his speech and appearance a thorough Englishman.

"Oh, good day to you, Mr. Hastings; on the dot as usual, eh? What about Marcel?"

The other nodded quietly. "He got away safely and is hidden."

"Get him out of England, then; he'll be a marked man," said Desmond. "I'm off tonight. Have you any letters for Paris?"

"Yes." The other produced a sealed letter, then hesitated, his dark eyes regarding Desmond uneasily. "Will it be safe with you? I understand all roads and the Channel ports are watched, and every ship, diligence and coach is being searched."

Desmond's blue eyes twinkled.

"My dear fellow, if I have any luck at all I'll be traveling under the safe-conduct of His Majesty in person. Give me the letter."

The other obeyed, with a helpless shrug.

"*Mon Dieu!* You work miracles; you are superb! I'm half tempted to believe you must be M. Feufollet himself, my colonel."

"I only wish I were!" And Desmond laughed. Not even his own assistants knew the identity of the celebrated Will o' the Wisp, who appeared now here, now there, with only the news of some amazing coup to mark his passage.

"Have you any orders for me?" the other asked.

"Yes. Send and get my saddlebags, at the lodgings of Colonel Fitzgerald. Have them with a horse saddled and ready, at the Royal Arms in Holborn Street, at eight o'clock. I may not show up before nine, but again I may. And the name of Fitzgerald is no longer safe, at least in London. Have the horse ready for Mr. Smithson."

Mr. Hastings nodded.

"Very well. I wish you were remaining in England; we've accomplished more in the time you've been here than in all the previous years! By the way, about Lady Warr—I've a bit of fresh information. She was received by Lord North this afternoon and was with him for an hour. When she left, she carried a small leather portfolio."

"Good!" exclaimed Desmond. "Your work is splendid; I shall congratulate M. de Vergennes on so able an agent. Ah, here's my supper."

His meal arrived, and he attacked it instantly. The other man rose, bowed, and sauntered away, and presently was gone.

Desmond finished his meal, paid his score, and set out, allowing himself ample time to reach the house of Lord Stormont.

AHEAD OF him, both in Hanover Square and at Dover, lay work of the most ticklish and perilous description. Like many another Irish exile in the service of France, Brian Desmond was impulsive to a fault, but he was not reckless.

He knew that Lady Jane Warr, whose beauty and wealth and talents were devoted to the underground service of England, was temporarily stopping with Lord Stormont. She, and she alone, knew Monsieur Feufollet by sight, though not by name. And with her, as Desmond was too well aware, was bracketed the deadly Constant, no doubt watching over her safety. He had tripped on this snag once today; and tonight he must run the risk of tripping again—but not blindly this time.

Muffled to the eyes, cane swinging, he strode along the ill-lit and shivering streets toward his destination. Suddenly his pace slowed; a thin, terrified voice reached him. He was passing a court, giving upon wretched hovels and old buildings. Again came the thin scream, and he halted.

"No, no! Don't be a fool, Brian Desmond," he told himself, with a subdued oath. "This night you're juggling with the fate of nations—don't risk it. Your own neck is too damned close to the noose—don't risk it! Some poverty-stricken drunk is beating his wife, no doubt—on your way, you fool, on your way!"

Too late. Again came the screaming, this time prolonged. So wild and agonized and frantic was the sound, that it chilled his blood. No woman's voice, either; rather, it seemed that of a child.

An impulsive oath burst from Desmond. He turned and entered the filthy courtyard, and had no difficulty in finding the vile hovel whence the screams issued. Other doors had opened and two or three persons came out, laughing coarsely and jeering. But at sight of a fine gentleman under the lantern in the passage, their voices lifted in swift alarm.

Desmond took no heed of these wretches. He went straight

to the door he sought, and without ceremony flung it open. He found himself on the threshold of a frightful scene.

Two tallow dips burned on a table, at which sat a man of the vilest description, and an old hag in filthy tatters. Both were far gone in liquor, as their looks and the Hollands before them testified. Huddled in a corner were four tiny urchins, blackened and ragged. A fifth was in the grip of the hag, who had stripped him naked and was in the act of beating him unmercifully with a heavy stick. Grimy with soot, his little body was red and quivering with the blows.

At Desmond's sudden appearance, every person froze, staring at him. In a flash he knew he was in one of those dens that housed the chimney-sweeps of London—tiny boys of six or eight years, absolute slaves of their owners, who slipped naked down chimneys to clean out the soot, and who lived lives of horror and misery beyond any description. He knew, too, that by his entry he had stepped outside the law.

"Blow me, if it ain't a bloody toff!" cried the half-drunken man. "He'll be wanting a sweep, my dear. Here's Jem. Hi, you little devil! Come out and show the gemman—touch him up wi' the stick, missus. Quick!"

With a guffaw, he seized the nearest urchin and stripped the rags from him. The old hag laid on the stick. The boy screamed out.

Next instant Desmond was on them, his blood boiling, every other consideration cast to the winds.

This time it was the man who screamed, as the heavy cane swung and lashed him across the face. It lashed him again and again, mercilessly, swiftly, until he folded his head in his hands and pitched forward on the floor, whimpering. Shrieking like a fiend, the old hag hurled herself at Desmond. He wrenched the stick out of her hands and shoved her into her chair again.

"You spawn of hell!" he cried out fiercely. "If you weren't cast in the shape of a woman, I'd give you the thrashing you deserve. You devil in human shape, to be torturing these poor little tykes!

I'd like to wring your scrawny neck. By Heaven, if I had you in Paris this night—"

He checked himself. The hag broke into wild screeches.

"Run for the watch! Police! I'll have the law on 'un for this...."

Other voices, eager, fierce, growling, came from outside. Desmond glanced around. At door and windows were gathered the dwellers of these hovels, clamoring at him, yelling at him, threatening him. A stone flew, missed him and smashed the old hag in the face so that she screeched again and fell back in her chair.

Mad folly; yet he felt better. With a swing of his cane, he sent the figures about the doorway scattering, and strode out.

"What was it 'un said about Paris?" veiled one. "A French spy, bullies! At him!"

Desmond quickened his pace, amid a storm of yells and oaths and vile obscenity. A stone struck him. He went on, cursing his wild impulse. He had done the poor little devils no good, for they were bound by the law; yet a fiercely thrilling joy possessed him that he had struck a blow for them.

He came to the street passage and the lantern. There was a rush. Savage faces, oaths, a glitter of knives—they came like wolves for his back. He swung around suddenly. The cane beat at them, slashed across those snarling faces, broke them and sent them darting away with screams and yells. They did not come again.

Desmond slipped out into the street again and strode rapidly along, heart-heavy for his own folly and for the little urchins whom he could not help. Even so, he had no regrets. There was a new spring to his walk, an uplift in his heart, a gay tune upon his lips; a generous man was Brian Desmond; ever tempted to warm chivalry. To one who serves his country, however, chivalry is a dangerous thing....

His blood cooled as he strode along. His wonted alertness returned. Twice he thought that he glimpsed a slinking figure well in his rear. Had one of those wretches followed him? "A

French spy, bullies!" somebody had yelled. Anything was possible. Most of the spies and informers of London were drawn
from such dens and hovels.

Warily, Desmond circled; in at one door of a tavern, out
another. He waited under a dark portico. His gaze probed the
obscurity. Satisfied at last that he had shaken off any possible
shadow, not daring to risk being late for his appointment, he
strode briskly into Hanover Square at last.

He reconnoitered Lord Stormont's railed and gardened
mansion, and found all clear. No loitering figures there or anywhere. Reassurance flooded into him. This time, at least, there
was no ominous *tap-tap-tap* of a wooden leg to shadow his
mind. With a laugh, he mocked the memory of the sound with
the tap of his own cane.

So, humming a gay tune, Brian Desmond went to sup with
a king.

CHAPTER II

IN THE KING'S NAME!

TWO MEN sat comfortably before a blazing coal fire.
The room was heavily curtained and somber. A table
glittered with silver and glass and dishes, tempted with food,
and wine. Lord Stormont, who owned this house, was grave
and thin in the face, elderly and a bit portly—by no means a
man of quick judgment or shrewd wits, but honest withal.

His visitor was nervous in his gestures, much more portly in
build, very soberly attired, but with a curious face that ran all
to nose. His one lighter touch was the glitter of a jeweled Ha-
noverian order on his breast, and he was by no means fastidious
or even clean in his linen, nails or wig. His voice was harsh and
yet pleasant.

"Damme, Stormont, I have a gift of seeing things clearly,"

he observed, nibbling at a sweetmeat and frowning earnestly. "Sometimes I think North and the rest of 'em are stark staring mad; the whole world's mad! It takes a sane man to see both sides of a thing, and if a man's too demned sane, the world is apt to call him mad!"

"Only too true, Your Majesty," assented Stormont thoughtfully.

"Tush! No titles, confound it—how often must I tell you?" snapped the king, and Stormont bowed. "Yes; the world's mad. There's not an atom of sense in this absurd war, Stormont, and I'm going to stop it. I say again that the sanest person I've heard of in a long time is this rascally American, this Doctor Franklin. I regret that I never met him while he was in England. Yet I understand that he thinks well of me. Eh, Stormont?"

"Very well indeed, Your Highness," said Stormont. "He has spoken of you to me in the highest terms of admiration—as though had you yourself been administering the affairs of the colonies, they had never come to revolt."

"Right, and a true word too," the king said approvingly. "Well, to business. This fellow Fitzgerald—can he handle the affair? Do you know him well?"

"I met him several times in Paris," Stormont rejoined. "An Irishman by birth, of no little address. Rather clever, I should say. He had been in the Austrian army and was out of the service—had come into money, I fancy. When I met him here in London, he seemed the very man to serve you."

The king pursed up his thick lips, and picked his teeth with his little finger.

"H'm! I don't fancy these Irishmen. Too demned independent, as a rule. You don't think he suspects anything, eh? About me?"

"Impossible, sir," and Stormont smiled. "I was quite guarded in my talk with him. He was most friendly and cordial, placing himself entirely at my service. The highest type of gentleman, I should say. There can be, of course, no mention of reward."

"Of course, of course." The king produced a very handsome gold snuffbox set with diamonds and inlaid with his own portrait. He took a pinch of snuff, and let the box lie, at his elbow. "Well, why doesn't the demned fellow show up? It's the hour—"

A footman threw open a door at the end of the room.

"Colonel Fitzgerald, Your Lordship."

DESMOND ENTERED. Stormont advanced to meet him most cordially, and introduced him to Count von Weissenstein. The portly monarch so far recollected himself as to rise and return Desmond's bow, then launched at once into direct questions as to the ancestry, occupation and history of the supposed Colonel Fitzgerald. Laughingly, Desmond supplied the information desired, and Stormont undertook to switch the subject before it became too personal in content or the king forgot his pose.

"My dear Weissenstein," he said, "I mentioned to Colonel Fitzgerald that you were most anxious to send a message to Paris, and he was good enough to offer his services—"

"Yes, yes," broke in the king petulantly. "I know all that. Fitzgerald, have a bite to eat! A glass of wine with you, sir. Admirable Madeira, admirable! How does it happen you're not serving your country when it's at war?"

Desmond's gay laugh was very good to hear.

"Ah, Weissenstein, you don't understand politics! My country is Ireland, and I'm an exile. More correctly, my father was exiled and his estates confiscated, so I was born in France and fated to serve fortune. Begad, it's not treated me badly so far!"

"Then you're an Austrian subject, eh?"

"Quite so. A charming place, Vienna. You know it?"

"No, damme! I have to sit in one spot. However," and the king brightened, "I'm taking a run over to Brussels in June, the middle of June. I'm most anxious, sir, to meet and talk with this American in Paris, Doctor Franklin. D'ye suppose, in the interests of peace, I could induce him to meet me in Brussels?"

Stormont intervened smoothly. "Count von Weissenstein is a personal friend of His Majesty the King, Fitzgerald, and I may say that His Majesty is most anxious to compose the war in America."

"Egad, I know he is!" said the king with energy. "And this absurd French war as well. Look'ee, Fitzgerald. I've composed a letter to this Franklin. As a neutral, you're free to come and go. D'ye suppose you could take him the letter and arrange a meeting?"

Desmond sipped his wine, his blue eyes dancing.

"Faith, why not?" he replied. "I've nothing to hold me here. Begad, I'll leave this very night! It's an idea. Paris, by all means!" He kindled to the idea. "Paris in May! No city in the world like it. Stormont, I owe you thanks for putting the notion in my head. If I can be of the least service to you gentlemen, pray command me. The letter? By all means. Where is it?"

The king fumbled at his pockets and tugged out a sealed letter. Then he hesitated.

"This must be secret, Fitzgerald—of the utmost secrecy. And what guarantee have I that you'll carry through, eh?"

"My word of honor, sir."

"Damme if you don't carry conviction! Here's the letter. Let me have an answer from this man Franklin, in his own hand. Wine, Stormont—where's that demned decanter? Ah, thank you. A health to you, Fitzgerald; success to you. Starting tonight, you say?"

"Faith, I'll be gone within the hour!" exclaimed Desmond, then sobered. "Hello! But I forgot. It's difficult to get across the Channel, they say—search and questions and so on. Do you gentlemen suppose that you could get me some document which would allow me to command a vessel, and avoid cooling my heels in Dover for a week or two?"

"It might be managed, yes," Stormont began cautiously. "But not tonight. I'd have to see Lord North tomorrow—"

"Demnition take North! He's a plaguey old woman," broke

in the king. "What, man! Here's Fitzgerald doing us a service, and we prate of Lord North? Preposterous. I'll write him out a safe-conduct myself—"

"And have His Majesty sign it?" broke in Stormont anxiously. The king recollected himself, and grunted.

"Exactly. Right, Stormont, right. My word on it, Colonel Fitzgerald—an order from the king, eh? In half an hour's time, I promise you. Where shall we send it?"

Desmond laughed. "I'll pack and be off. Why, suppose you send it to the Royal Arms in Holborn—to Mr. Smithson. In his care, that is. My horse is there, in his name. An excellent fellow, Smithson. I knew him well in Vienna. He's a distant relative of the Duke of Grafton."

"Never heard of him," said the king without interest. Then he brightened, "By the way! I can't permit you to take this trouble and annoyance on my behalf, without some faint appreciation of your goodness. It's an honor, sir, to have the pleasure of your acquaintance. May I insist that you accept this slight token of my regard, merely as a memento of me?" So saying, he picked up the snuffbox and put it into Desmond's hand. "A present from His Majesty, sir, and bearing his portrait. It will give me great happiness if you'll accept it."

Desmond, affecting not to note the resemblance of the portrait to the man before him, bowed and expressed his thanks, and took his leave promptly. Stormont, accompanying him to the door, promised that the safe-conduct would reach him in half an hour's time, and Desmond quite understood that it would be written the moment he had left.

"Then for the love of heaven make it emphatic!" he said laughingly. "I may have to commandeer a ship to get across the Channel, for I understand that all sailings are strictly regulated. *Au revoir*, my lord. You may count upon me absolutely in this affair, as in anything you desire of me."

He donned hat, muffler and greatcoat and was let out by the bowing footman.

ONCE IN the street, he hesitated briefly, gay exultation
rioting within him but not dulling his wits. It was only a trifle
after seven; the interview had taken much less time than he
had bargained on. His horse would not be ready before eight.
All delays were dangerous; he wanted to be out of London at
the earliest moment.

"Best kill time at the Royal Arms, however," he reflected.
"Everything hangs now on the safe-conduct coming. If this
thick-witted lord doesn't prevent his simpleton of a king from
sending it—faith, I'll have the game in my hands! And wouldn't
I like to know what's in this letter to Doctor Franklin! But I
gave my word of honor, and that settles it. After all, simpleton
or not, the fellow's a king and I think he means well."

Lady Jane Warr? Constant? He had seen nothing of either
one, nothing to cause him the least alarm. Luck was with him,
certainly. He chuckled in delighted appreciation. That paper,
under the royal hand, would give him power to checkmate Lady
Warr this night and strike such blow for France as would leave
the English ministry aghast. The castles of England tricked and
beaten by using their own king as pawn—ha! It was the sort
of game Monsieur Feufollet loved.

"If it comes—if it comes!" murmured Desmond, aflame to
the possibilities. "If it doesn't come, what then? Time enough
to think about that. And I made no promises about the use of
that safe-conduct, either. I'm in honor free to play the very devil
with it, just so long as I carry out the mission to this American
envoy faithfully. Which I'll do. Well, the poor king's not to be
blamed. Stormont's the fool, to let himself be so tricked and
cozened."

So far as Constant was concerned—well, there the safe-
conduct was useless. Constant had today set a name to the spy
he had so long trailed, and knew him for Brian Desmond—
though he had not seen Desmond's face. By now, too, Constant
would suspect much about Colonel Fitzgerald, might even
suspect the two were one. More, he might well suppose that
here was the person of mystery, the unknown but dreaded Will

o' the Wisp, Monsieur Feufollet! And this meant the reward of
a thousand pounds to be earned.

A fortune, to Constant. On the trail of rewards, of money,
this man stopped at no deviltry. He would trail Monsieur Feufollet across Europe to get a bullet into his back or a knife under
his ribs. Desmond knew enough about the man to be actually
afraid of him. Let Constant once grip the idea that the mysterious Will o' the Wisp was the same with Colonel Brian
Desmond, who was well known in Paris—well, that would be
bad. It would mean death-grips.

These thoughts running through his brain, Desmond drew
near the Royal Arms. The cold drizzle of rain continued; so had
the tap of his cane on the pavement. It put uneasiness into his
head. He found himself thinking again of the *tap-tap-tap* of a
wooden leg, and swore angrily at his own fancies. Again he
imagined a slinking figure behind him, though none was there
when he turned to see. With another muffled oath, he turned
in at the tavern entrance.

Avoiding the ordinary or main room, he beckoned the pro-
prietor and swung into the more secluded room for gentry,
where a few citizens of the better class and a number of officers
were sitting, talking and drinking. He ordered a bottle of wine,
a pipe and a paper twist of tobacco, and handed the innkeeper
a coin.

"Keep the change, for prompt service. A letter should arrive
for me by special messenger, also a horse. The moment either
comes, have me informed. Smithson's the name."

With a bow and a scrape, the other promised.

Desmond's order arrived. He broke out tobacco from the
twist, filled the long clay "churchwarden" and lit it at the candle.
The wine proved to be execrable, and he left it alone.

He sat smoking, waiting, watching those around him. Two
officers of some rank came in, accompanied by a civilian, a man
of distinguished appearance and dress. They took a table behind

that of Desmond, ordered pipes, and fell to talking. Desmond caught their voices.

"But damme, the thing's incredible, Sir Henry!" one of the officers exclaimed. "You saw it yourself!"

"And heard it," the civilian rejoined. "I tell you, the man knew not one of us—yet he called us each by name, and answered our unspoken questions. A girl was there who was in some sort of sleep or trance. At his command she spoke with voices from the dead—no, don't laugh! A grisly thing, upon my word. Further, my own servant was close to death from a flux, and this man put one drop of liquid into the man's mouth, prayed over him, and today he is well as ever."

"Come, come, Sir Harry! Where's this mountebank? Who is he?"

"Where he is, I don't know; in Brussels or Paris, I've heard. His name? The Count de Cagliostro, an Italian title. I've not told you the strangest thing, however. This man, by his own words, though not by any specific claim, has discovered the secret of endless life. I've heard him describe in detail things that happened a hundred, two hundred, years ago, as an eyewitness. He was an intimate friend of King Charles the Second, God bless him! And his lackey, he said, had been with him for three hundred years—"

The two officers exploded in a burst of laughter and raillery. Desmond cocked a whimsical eye at the three; evidently, it was a question of some magician who imposed upon credulous souls like this gentleman. Beyond subconsciously noting the name of Cagliostro, he paid little attention.

Suddenly he sat up. The host was bringing a man to him, a cloaked man whom he recognized instantly as the footman of Lord Stormont. With a bow, the footman extended him a folded paper.

"I was bidden to deliver this into your own hand, Colonel Fitzgerald."

Desmond nodded, gave him a coin, and dismissed him.

Evidently, Stormont was making certain that the letter went into the right hands.

With a fast-beating pulse, Desmond unfolded the paper. Here was the crux of everything; all his plans hung upon this missive. And, with a stab of joy, he perceived that the game was his. The writing was brief:

> To All Officers of Our Realm:
> The bearer, Colonel Fitzgerald, travels by Our order, and it is Our wish and command that he be given whatever furtherance he may desire.
> George Rex.

His heart leaped as he folded it again.

Gad, what a stroke of luck! Luck? Aye—though he had planned it, had schemed it and after his former meeting with Lord Stormont had been certain of it, here was luck none the less. His breath quickened at thought of what power this simple paper put into his hands. Why, with this to help him, he had the farther game won and Jane Warr utterly—

His thoughts seemed to freeze. His rapt gaze leaped to the alert. A cold hand seemed to touch his neck. In upon his brain beat a sound, and this time he had not imagined it—the *tap-tap-tap* of a wooden leg. It halted at his table.

He looked up to see Constant standing before him, looking at him.

IT WAS not the greasy figure of the afternoon, but a Constant well and bravely clad in brown garments of good cut, hat perched on wigged head. Yet one hand stayed ominously under his coat. The face, hard and brown and alert, bore the mark of that blow between the eyes. A squarely massive jaw was threatening, the heavy-lidded eyes of pale gray, brilliant as shining stone, were sinister and inflexible as the eyes of a corpse.

"May I have a word with you, monsieur?" asked Constant in French.

Desmond stared blankly at him and broke into a laugh.

"Faith, I don't understand Italian, my good fellow—"

"I ask whether I may speak with you, sir," said Constant, now in English. "I think you're Colonel Fitzgerald? At least, you have his face, with certain changes, if not his uniform."

"Sit down," said Desmond, with a shrug. "I fear you're out of your head, my man."

Constant drew out the chair and seated himself, hand never moving from the breast of his coat, pale eyes never moving from the face of Desmond.

"I don't make mistakes," he said quietly, with a calm more terrible than any fury. "You came here from Lord Stormont's house."

Desmond smiled. "And if I did?"

"As Fitzgerald, you wore a British uniform. You are a French spy; your name is Brian Desmond." The pale eyes gave birth to a sudden flash. "A clever ruse, a clever blow.... Don't try it again now, Monsieur Feufollet, or my pistol will answer for you."

Desmond's brows lifted in quizzical amusement.

"Not satisfied with fastening a different name upon me, now you leap to a French name!" he said pleasantly.

"Precisely." Constant spoke without emotion. "You are Monsieur Feufollet; your face has been described to me; it answers."

Described to him? Desmond felt a trickle of sweat on his cheek. Then Lady Warr must have described him to this scoundrel.

"On the contrary," he said coolly, "I am Colonel Fitzgerald. I can prove it under the hand of His Majesty. I've heard that some impudent fellow passed himself off under my name—"

A slow, composed smile touched the lips of Constant, and was gone.

"It don't work," he said. "Fitzgerald? Aye. And an hour ago in Fitzgerald's lodging I found the uniform you wore this afternoon. Fast, are you? I'm a bit faster. None of your talk about papers, either. I've got men watching the doors and men in the courtyard, and you're going out with me under arrest with a noose waiting for you. Ready?"

"No. I've my pipe to finish," said Desmond. "Go with you? Of course I will, since you seem to have some authority. I'll be glad to straighten out this intolerable mixup. But I'm damned if you'll rush me off."

He was playing desperately for time, for some opening, and there was none. Those deadly eyes transfixed him with death. Now the eyes shifted slightly to his cane, and back to him again.

"That's the stick you used to beat people with, eh? Chimney-sweeps! Aye, that's what stumbled you, my fine Frenchman. Put a hand to that stick, and I'll have a bullet in you before you can touch it."

Desmond started to speak, then looked up. The host was approaching, and now scraped to him and flung out a thumb toward the courtyard entrance.

"The horse is ready and waiting, Your Worship."

"Well, suppose we go, then. One moment, until I speak to my friends yonder...." Desmond nodded.

And before Constant could guess his intent, he was out of his chair and striding to the table by the wall, snatching the royal order from his pocket as he did so. He looked down at the two officers, and laid the paper before them.

"Gentlemen, your pardon. I am on pressing and urgent duty for His Majesty, as this order shows; you may recognize the signature. This fellow at the next table, some sort of informer or police agent, has the effrontery to insist that I'm a French spy. If he delays me, it will jeopardize my mission. I ask your assistance, as officers."

"Gad, His Majesty's signature! And all in his own hand," exclaimed Sir Harry.

Desmond heard the tap of the wooden leg. Constant was coming.

"Aye, sir?" One of the officers rose. "At your service, gladly. How?"

"Will you engage this pestilent fellow, keep him engaged, so that I can get out?"

Constant broke in upon them. His pistol was out.

"Here, here, no tricks!" he cried, and his voice rang deeply sonorous with alarm. "Under arrest, Fitzgerald—"

DESMOND WAS already heading away. The officer on his feet caught hold of Constant; the second came out of his chair to lend eager help. Constant shouted vibrantly. The pistol banged out. Desmond caught at his hat as the bullet rocked it. Then he was at the door, darting out into the courtyard.

The horse was there, ready, a hostler at the reins. Desmond slipped forward and swung up.

Too late! Two men were rushing at him, pistols raised, shouting. He whipped the little pistol from his pocket, sent the horse at the nearer man, shot the other between the eyes as a burst of smoke vomited up at him.

Uproar, confusion, wild shouts, and the big horse shouldering for the street. He made it. More men here; faces in wild alarm, another pistol-crash. Then they were well behind him, a wild gay laugh on Desmond's lips, heels lifting the horse into a gallop.

"In the king's name!" He echoed the shouts behind him, sent a group of soldiers scattering, and rode on. Around a corner, and another, into a side street, slowing down now to sober pace. The invaluable paper was tucked away securely.

"My soul to the devil if England's not too hot a place to hold Colonel Fitzgerald now!" he murmured cheerfully. "By tomorrow this safe-conduct won't be worth the paper it's written on—but tomorrow's another day. Now for the Dover road; and I'd give a thousand guineas if my bullet had taken Constant instead of that poor devil who stopped it! He was a breath too slow on the trigger."

What a devil that man Constant was! The thought rode with him as he threaded his way through the streets.

Had the man been merely serving his country and playing

the game with a good heart, Desmond would have welcomed him as a worthy opponent. But Constant played for blood-money. He collected a hundred pounds for every spy bagged, and preferred to do the bagging with trap or pistol, or with dagger in the back. There was Boisbriant, at Southampton, shot in the door of his own room by an unseen assassin; there was Deslys, found dead in a Plymouth street with his throat cut; and there were others. Only three weeks ago, Desmond had been walking home of a night with Frontain, the bluff Norman, when a blast of bullets out of a doorway ripped the soul from poor Frontain and sent Desmond doubling back for his life. That was the way Constant usually struck.

"If his assassins had hit me instead of Frontain, that night, he'd have bagged a thousand pounds, eh?" reflected Desmond. "Well, the rogue's after me now; he's hit the scent with a vengeance. He knows me by sight, knows that I'm Monsieur Feu-follet—what the devil! I've slipped badly this trip. And to think it was she who described me to him! Well, why not? It was her business, her right to do so. She knows me for an enemy—and before tomorrow noon she'll know me for a worse enemy, begad!"

A cheering reflection....

More cheering still was the thought of how he had neatly bilked them all, back there in the London streets. Twice he had slipped through Constant's hands, and left a mark on the devil's face for good measure. Slipped through, with no loss—for what matter if Constant did suspect him? Europe was wide, and his work in England done, or would be done in a few more hours.

Tricked them all, fooled proud Stormont, turned the poor stupid king to serve his own ends—h'm! A coup worthy of Will o' the Wisp, indeed. And ahead lay the *Merlin* lugger, sailing in the morning or before. No, not before. She would take no chance of being snapped up by some French frigate cruising the channel.

Suddenly Desmond was aware of a strange sensation—something sticky on his left thigh. He twisted about, to exchange his empty pistol for the loaded one in his saddlebags, and grimaced. A twinge of pain shot through him, then a sharper and deeper stab. In sharp alarm, he drew rein.

He put his hand under his clothes. Blood, yes—if he could not see it, he could feel it and smell it. Not all of those pistol balls had missed their mark.

CHAPTER III

ORDERED BACK

DOVER CASTLE, in the darkness before the dawn, and the sharp challenge of sentries. "Who goes?"

"Colonel Fitzgerald, on His Majesty's service. I want speech with the governor, on the instant. Have ye a surgeon in the garrison?"

"Aye, sir, but at this hour—"

"Damn the hour! His Majesty's service, d'ye understand? Send and waken the governor. Send for the surgeon and bring him to attend me. And don't keep me standing here all night, blast you!"

So Desmond rode into the courtyard and slipped from his saddle, two soldiers catching him as he fell, and supporting him. Stiff with riding, hurt bound with makeshift bandage, racked with pain, he was helped into a room and a fire lighted. After a little the governor appeared, nightcap on head and coat flung hastily about his night-gear. Desmond, sagging in his chair, straightened a little and drew out the king's order.

The governor read it and saluted.

"You're hurt, Colonel Fitzgerald.

"Aye," said Desmond grimly. "I've taken the liberty of sending for your surgeon, sir; I was attacked by footpads on the road from London. However, the hurt's no great matter. I'm on an important errand and must go on. May I ask your assistance?"

"Egad, sir! You hold the warrant of His Majesty. I'm yours to command and your obedient servant."

"It's good of you. I'll report your zeal to His Majesty, at our next meeting." And a shadowy smile touched Desmond's gray features. "The lugger *Merlin* is in the harbor, I think?"

"She is, sir, under government authority to sail at daybreak."

"Then, I pray you, send for her master and command my own authority to him, and bring him to me, for my errand here lies with him."

"At once, Colonel Fitzgerald. Ah! Here's the surgeon now."

The surgeon bustled in with his tools. Water was brought. Desmond was stripped and examined.

"Pistol ball, is it?" said the surgeon. "No great danger, but a close thing. The ball's lodged under a rib. I fear it must come out."

"You're damned right it must come out." And Desmond laughed. "To work and take it out, man! I've no time to waste and must be about my business."

The surgeon grunted. "You've lost blood in plenty. You can't stir about for days—"

The governor, who had exchanged his nightcap for the wig an orderly brought, touched the surgeon on the shoulder.

"On His Majesty's service, sir."

"So that's the way of it, eh?" The surgeon shrugged and opened his bag. "Two of you men, hold his arms; another, grip him about the thighs tightly. Lord help you, sir, here's for it! I'll do the best I can, be sure of that. So God save King George, and we're at it."

He went to work in the rough and ready fashion of his day, while three soldiers held the patient and the candles flickered. At length he yanked up the bullet and held it in his blood-smeared hand before the sweating face of Desmond.

"There y'are, sir, and a good job if I do say it. With daylight instead of candles, I'd ha' done less cutting. Now I'll wash the wound, douse some cold water on it, and clap on a stopper. If you don't lie abed for three days to ward off the fever your spleen may generate, you might be worse off than you are now."

"Faith, if I lay abed three days I'd have worse fever than any the hurt could know," gasped Desmond, with a faint laugh. "Get the bandage on and make it tight, man, tight! Ere daylight I must be on the water."

"In which case it may be a longer journey than ye look for," muttered the surgeon. "I will say, 'twas well borne, with never a groan.

"I mind, three or four years back, the most wondrous iron fellow I ever worked on," he gossiped, as he made ready the bandages. "A Bow Street runner, or some such article, with his knee smashed by the kick of a horse; I mind, it was a bad business. Had to come off, and no one to hold him fast. He lit his pipe and told me to saw away and held the leg out for me with his own two hands. By Heaven, he did! And never budged or let out a whimper until 'twas over and done. Then he fainted dead away, and had bit the stem off his pipe and near choked on it. I mind his name—Ben Constant. I'll never forget that case...."

Constant, eh? Desmond stared at the man, wondering at the ways of chance. So that was how Constant had lost his leg. Devil take him!

AT LAST it was finished. Tightly bandaged, clothed again, and with a draft of mulled ale putting new life in him, Desmond reclined in a chair before the fire. A corporal entered and saluted. The lugger's master had just arrived.

He was brought in, a rough, hearty seaman who touched his forelock to the governor. The latter took matters in charge.

"This, Master Bowyer, is Colonel Fitzgerald, who bears authority under His Majesty's own hand, God bless him! Colonel

Fitzgerald is on His Majesty's service, and has sent for you. He was wounded by footpads on the way hither from London."

"Your Worship caught me just in time," said the shipman bluffly. "I had just ordered the anchor up when the message came."

"Eh?" Desmond's head lifted. "Then your passenger must have arrived. A lady in a coach?"

"Aye, sir. With Admiralty authority ordering me to Ostend."

"Good. Now listen carefully." Desmond's blue eyes glinted, a flush sparkled in his cheek. "I go with you to Ostend also, but my errand's a secret one. Your other passengers must not know I'm aboard."

"Passengers, Your Worship: there's two. The lady and her servant. They went straight to the cabins, being mortal weary. I can berth you sound and not a soul the wiser, sir." Master Bowyer turned to the governor. "Have I your authority to take him, Your Worship?"

"Egad, man! You have the authority of His Majesty himself to obey the orders of Colonel Fitzgerald," the governor said importantly.

The seaman touched his forelock again.

"Right, Your Worship; I just wanted all clear and shipshape. Can ye walk down to the town, sir? The lugger's boat is ashore and waiting for us."

Desmond stood up and winced.

"Walk? Devil take it, I doubt if I can! But I can ride my horse down, if I may have the loan of a man to fetch the animal back."

The governor was more than agreeable, and in five minutes more Desmond was in the saddle and on his way from the castle.

When they reached the wharf stairs, the first paleness of dawn was in the sky. Desmond was helped into the boat, his saddlebags were put in, and the rowers gave way. Amid the shipping, the long lean shape of the lugger, dark canvas flapping, grew ahead of them.

Over the rail at last, staggering wearily, and sinking back against the bulwarks. When the master offered to take him below, Desmond shook his head.

"No; the salt air will do me good. I'll see you clear of the harbor first. I can trust your crew not to tell the other passengers that I'm aboard?"

"Zounds, Your Worship! You can trust these lads to hell and back," said the shipman cheerfully. "Ahoy, lads! Up with the hook and let her fill. Tail on, tail on!"

He went to the helm himself, leaning over the long tiller, and Desmond remained at the rail close by.

Even now, desperate anxiety was tearing at him, warning him, driving him to make all secure. Every moment of this time ashore, he had been in dread. He must have been barely ahead of Jane Warr's coach, on the road. Long ere now, no doubt the roads would be hot with couriers. Every port would be blocked and watched, to keep Colonel Fitzgerald from getting out of the kingdom. There was still chance enough of a slip; he could not relax and seek the bed he craved with all his soul, until Dover lay behind.

Dawn grew in the sky. The anchor was in and catted; the lugger slowly sped through the outer shipping, as the sails filled. Her pace quickened and she heeled slightly, rippling through the water. Out beyond the shipping now.

Suddenly a man forward cried out. From the castle above came a splitting red flash. The dull report of a gun rolled down across the water, and an oath of irritation broke from Master Bowyer.

"Damnation! That's orders to return at once, Your Worship."

Desmond stirred. He left the rail and came to the shipman and stood beside him.

"Don't do it, master. You have your orders from me."

The other turned a startled, troubled face to him.

"But zounds, sir! I be bound to obey and turn back—look'ee! There's another gun!"

"You're bound to obey the orders I give you, under the hand of His Majesty the King." Desmond took the pistol from his pocket. "Refuse, and I'll put a bullet into you. D'ye understand?"

"Aye, aye. True enough; the governor himself said to take your orders, that's true for you, sir." The other hesitated and eyed the pistol. "But—"

"Like enough, it's some mistake," said Desmond, his voice ringing hard. "Is it worth your life to chance it? Remember, you have my orders, from the king himself."

"And will you give me a writing to that point, sir? That I held the course by your orders?"

"And a pistol at your head. Aye, right gladly. And ten golden sovereigns to boot, if we reach Ostend."

The shipman laughed. "Then all's clear and the devil take governor and castle! Haul in on the sheets, lads—closer, closer! Yarily, there...."

The lugger leaned farther over, the water hissing along her lee rail. The cliffs and the land merged behind them in the grayness. Desmond put away his pistol, and laughed. A weight had fallen from him; the tension was broken.

"And now I'll go below and turn in, master," said he wearily. "When should we reach Ostend?"

The seaman eyed wind and water. "You've the fastest craft in the channel ports, and a brisk stout wind. With luck, by sundown tonight."

"Good. Give me a place to sleep and see that I'm not disturbed until four o'clock. Then waken me and fetch me food and drink, and water for shaving. Aye?"

"On the nail, Your Worship. Now take my arm...."

The after cabins were low and stuffy. Master Bowyer explained that the lady had been given the fine large cabin—but Desmond scarce heard what was said, so far gone was he. One glance to find his saddlebags safely stowed, and he lowered himself into the berth. The seaman drew off his boots and spread a blanket over him.

Desmond was already asleep. The creaking and groaning of timbers, the lurching toss of the lugger, the scrape and pound of feet along the deck overhead—nothing could keep him from exhausted slumber, or banish that slumber. Yet, once or twice as the day wore on, he tossed uneasily or broke into fitful challenging mutters—for through his dream-memories wandered another sound, like the recurrent thump of a wooden leg....

CHAPTER IV

BARGAIN FOR LIFE

"EIGHT BELLS, Your Worship!" Desmond wakened to the hearty voice and the bluff features of Master Bowyer above him. "Here's warm water, and food if ye can stomach it. By your sound sleep, you're no channel victim."

"Never seasick in my life, glory be!" Desmond sat up, stretched, and grunted at the sharp twinge of pain. He was devilish stiff and sore. "And the lady? Is she ill?"

"Not she; and a fine blithe lady she be, sir. On deck this minute and loving it. We should see the point of Ostend in another two hours."

"On deck, eh? Then, master, in twenty minutes ask the lady to step down to her cabin. No mention of me, though. Tell her anything that comes into your head."

The seaman assented and went out. Desmond went to his saddlebags, secured razor and soap, and set about scraping his face. Boots on, he arranged his hair and his garments, examined himself with approval in the cracked mirror on the wall, and attacked the food and mug of ale on the tray. All was done very swiftly.

On his feet again, Desmond took the pistol from his greatcoat pocket, examined it, then shook his head and thrust it back.

"More shame to you, my lad, if you carried a pistol in dealing with a lady," he said, his eyes alight. "Especially this sweet lady! No, no; it's bad enough to be doing what ye must do for the honor of France. Do it like a gentleman, and not like that carrion crow of a Constant."

A moment later he was out in the passage, at the door of the large cabin. This was locked. With a chuckle, he produced a bit of bent metal, and in thirty seconds had picked the lock and was inside. Closing the door, he locked it again in the same way.

"Will o' the Wisp's touch, eh? And lucky it was none of your French locks that need a double turn and the devil's own hand at the work."

He surveyed the place rapidly. A comfortable cabin of some size, stern ports, two berths. On one of these was laid a portmanteau, open. Beside it were several letters. Despite the motion of the lugger, Jane Warr had obviously done a bit of writing. A quill lay on the table by the stern ports, nothing else. On the other berth were tossed a cloak and a toilet case.

Desmond's eye swept the place, then he went to this second berth. He moved the cloak, put hand to pillow, to blanket, and finally turned back the mattress. There he saw a small leather portfolio, and with a chuckle tossed it to the table.

He glanced out at the sunny, sparkling sea—then he turned. A step was at the door, a key was scraping in the lock. He dropped quickly into the chair before the table, his back to the light.

The door opened. Lady Warr entered, then halted. A gasp broke from her.

"Who are you? How did you get in here?"

Desmond rose, bowed slightly, and his gay voice lilted on the cabin.

"All doors are open to a will o' the wisp, my dear Jane! Surely you're not surprised to see me? Allow me to set a chair—here we are. No silk and stuffed satin such as fits you, my dear, but a sturdy, broad affair that won't tip with a lurch of the ship—"

"You! It can't be—it's impossible—"

She stood staring at him, her breath coming quickly, a touch of fear and incredulity in her face.

It was a lovely face, alight with youth, eager with command and purpose and firmed with character; a face that could now be very young and joyous and tender, now older and graver with decision. A fur-trimmed hat, a fur pelisse that gave glimpse of slender lines and furred habit beneath.

Color came into her face. She hesitated, advancing slowly, searching him with her dark and unflinching gaze.

"You! Monsieur Feufollet—should I be glad or sorry? Delighted to see you, or afraid of your wizardry?" With a smile she extended her hand. Desmond bowed above it, and then looked her in the eyes, very gravely.

"My dear, will you believe one thing, on the honor of a gentleman?"

"What's the word worth?" she retorted frankly. "I know you for an enemy. I know you for Monsieur Feufollet, for Will o' the Wisp, whom they call a devil in human form. I know you for a charming, debonair, lovable Irishman by your accent, whom I should hate with all my heart—and that's all. Your name—"

"I can't tell you that, to my sorrow," said Desmond. "Enemies? Yes. That's what hurts me. It grieves me that I must be an enemy—and I want you to believe me, my dear, that whatever I do is done for duty, for the cause I serve. Enemies can make truce; they can respect one another, as I respect you with all my heart." His eyes danced, his gay whimsical smile flashed out. "Faith, aren't we commanded to love our enemies? We are, and you're a deuced unusual woman—"

"And I should believe you a deuced blackguard—but I can't," she said with a sudden burst of laughter. "Yes, Monsieur Feufollet, I confess it—you do ring true. Strange as it may seem, incredible as it really is, I do accept your words—"

Suddenly her voice died, as she glimpsed the portfolio on the table.

"Oh, I might have known it!" she cried with swift inconsistency. Fury transformed her on the instant; her cheeks flushed, a lightning flash of wild anger leaped in her eyes, her voice rang upon the cabin like a trumpet peal.

"How dare you—how dare you! With such pratings of honor, when you're nothing but the lowest sort of spy! You've dared too far this time. You're in my power here, d'you understand? I'll call down the crew and have you given your proper deserts— hand me back that portfolio. Give it to me, do you hear—give it to me!"

S H E F L U N G herself at the table. Desmond's hand caught up the portfolio before she could reach it. At this instant, an unexpected wild lurch of the lugger threw them both off balance. She was hurled directly at him; her involuntary cry filled the cabin. Desmond, with the portfolio held behind him, was smashed backward and full against the bulwark, with her weight squarely upon him.

The spasm of agony that shot through him was terrific; it paralyzed him. He could not move or speak. The recoil of the lurch sent him forward, carried him into the table, as Jane Warr swiftly recoiled and broke free of him. His chest struck against it. A flood of new anguish tortured him. By sheer good luck, he fell sideways and dropped into his chair, his fingers still clenching the portfolio.

She, all unaware of his intolerable pain, stamped her feet in hot anger.

"Oh, I hate you, I hate you! I think you must be indeed a devil, to be so base a spy and yet have the tongue of a gentleman. You rogue! I'll have you hanged for this before another hour is past."

Across Desmond's brain flashed the premonition of disaster. He was frightfully hurt, could feel it. She fell silent, staring at him, seeing now his gray lined face, the drawn anguish of his eyes. He made a little gesture, and put the portfolio on the table.

"Sit—sit down, I pray you," he murmured.

Still staring, wondering, suspecting some trick, she drew herself into the chair opposite. Desmond's head lifted, and the ghost of his old smile touched his eyes and warmed them; but his lips remained thinly twisted. After an instant he spoke.

"Wait. You don't understand. I'm no spy. I haven't touched your letters, haven't opened this portfolio. Wait. Give me—give me breath...."

He paused. Every motion was fresh pain, but he managed to tweak the royal order from his pocket. Her dark eyes widened upon him.

"It's no trick; what's happened? You're suffering. What did I do?" she exclaimed quickly.

"Nothing. I stopped a bullet last night."

"Oh! Then it was you—" She checked herself sharply. Her gaze went to the unopened portfolio, then to the letters on the berth, and came back to him. Desmond nodded.

"Aye. You heard about a spy being nearly caught in London, eh? Who told you? Well, let it go. First, I'm no spy. I'm an agent of France, as you are of England."

"Yes, yes; I know that," she said. "Where are you hurt?"

"Stick to business. You're going to be the gainer by it, begad!" Desmond managed a faint, thin smile. He must bargain now. He still had the game in his hands; he must lose something, but he might still win the main stake. He thrust out the royal order. "Read this, my dear. In your power? Devil a bit. It's you who are in my power this minute, just as the master of this ship obeys me and not you. Read it, I tell you!"

The sunset light struck in upon his thinly carven face, brought out its deathly pallor, the edged lines of pain; but his voice compelled her with its urgency. She took the paper, glanced at the writing, lifted eyes of startled incredulity.

"This is genuine! But you—how did you get this?"

"Faith, I cozened it out of the king last night." Desmond chuckled; the wraith of his old gay laugh rang faintly. "At Lord Stormont's house, within a few yards of your own lovely presence, no doubt. Yes, genuine. Tear it up if you like; no matter. Master Bowyer obeys it, and obeys me. At my word, he'll truss you up and take you back to England after landing me. I'll give the word, if I must. It's a fight for life, and more. D'ye understand that? I'll ruin your errand and your whole work if ye make me. Though I'd give my right arm for you, though I'd die for you, though I love you with all my heart and soul—I'll send you back to England a prisoner, the laughingstock of the diplomats, a useless tool to the Ministry henceforth, if I must. Do you comprehend that, my dear, my dear lass?"

His blue eyes were glittering, icy, powerful; his voice rang vibrantly.

She laid down the folded paper, with a gesture of assent.

"You stop at nothing, do you? Yes, I believe you would."

"If you make me; but you'll not. I'll—good God! What's that?"

He started suddenly, sat there with a stab in his brain, listening. A sound had come from the deck above; he could not believe it, but it came again. A sound that set his teeth into his underlip, that sent his pulses hammering—the slow *tap-tap-tap* of a wooden leg. He relaxed suddenly in his chair.

"Constant!"

"MY COMPANION, yes," she said, her brows drawing down, her eyes probing him. "It was he who told me of last night's spy-hunt in London. He's with me as far as Ostend, then has business of his own."

Desmond laughed harshly; he well knew what business. Constant, giving up Will o' the Wisp for lost, so far as England was concerned, was going to catch him at the other end.

"Constant... you described me to him, you helped him lay the snare for me."

"I did," she said quietly. "Why not? We're enemies; you've

beaten me before this, you may even beat me now by trickery and audacity and effrontery past belief. But I'll fight you with every weapon I have, do you understand?" Her voice softened, but held its edge. "Whatever I may think of you personally, I'll fight you as an agent of France, if I must see you shot before my eyes! And Constant is the man to catch you."

"By the Lord, you spoke a true word there! He's the man to catch me—now. Though he couldn't do it yesterday."

Desmond's voice was bitter. He followed the quick, dilating glance of her eyes, looked down, saw the spreading seepage of crimson across his shirt-front. The bandage had slipped, then; the wound had opened. Devil take it! Still, he was not done. He summoned up energy and will for the effort. His eyes warmed, his face changed and softened, and the winning charm of his smile flashed out for an instant.

"Oh, what a woman you are, Jane Warr! Here, now—everything's changed. I'm going to gamble my life on your true heart, on the honor of an enemy. First, realize this: I've got you nipped. I may be hurt, but the crew obey me. I've got you and Constant both by the heels. Bear it in mind. Now turn to something else. You don't know what sort of man this rogue is, or you'd not be working with him. Let me tell you—and every word that I speak is the truth, on the faith of a gentleman."

He leaned forward earnestly and told her of Boisbriant, of Deslys, of poor Frontain and half a dozen others; and as she listened, she whitened under his words.

"I—I never dreamed of such things!" she murmured.

"Of course. Now, my dear, I'm hurt, eh? Nonsense! A bit of blood, a bit of pain—Monsieur Feufollet does not stop for that. I have your papers, all of 'em. I can put a bullet into this devil, I can send you back in humiliation to England; and then what?" He leaned back, his cheeks going gray again. "I can do it. I will if I must; but on my soul I think it'll kill me. And I want to live, my dear. I've no one to meet me at Ostend, I've no way to reach our agents in Brussels, and I've devilish little life or energy left to do anything. So I'll make a bargain with you."

Her forehead was wrinkled as she watched him, anxiety and tenderness and pity struggling with resolve in her face.

"Well?" she said quietly.

Again, from overhead, Desmond caught the slow *tap-tap-tap* that maddened him.

"I know your errand, my dear. Here in this portfolio are instructions from the Ministry to the ambassadors in neutral countries; here are a dozen things, in fact, that I want and planned to get. I'll give 'em all up but one. Write me out, on your honor, the terms of the secret commercial treaty England is making with Vienna—"

"I will not!" Her cheeks flamed suddenly, her eyes flashed. "Do you think I'm such a traitor? Do you think—"

His lifted hand, his smile, halted her.

"I think you're wise, you're clever, you're utterly adorable, Jane Warr! You've not heard all my conditions. First, I want you to separate from Constant, let him go ashore, and you follow later—getting me ashore with you. Keep him in ignorance of my presence. Leave me at the first tavern you come to, and go on. That, and the terms of the treaty. And what do you gain by it?"

Only by a tremendous effort did he hold himself to the task now. Her face was swimming before him.

"Wait!" she broke in, softly. "Before we say more, let me look at your hurt, let me bandage it. I'm skilled in that business. My father was a surgeon and taught me. He was the late king's own surgeon...."

Desmond forced a quick smile, and wagged his finger in negation.

"No, no, my dear! We're still enemies, remember; no truce yet. What'll you gain by the bargain? Everything. First, Constant's life; for if you refuse, I'll walk up on deck and shoot the devil if it's my last step on this earth—"

"I don't care about his life," she intervened passionately.

"But England does—eh? Next, you'll save me the heart's grief of humiliating you and sending you back a prisoner. You'll save all your other papers from the eyes of the enemy; for if you refuse, they go slap to Paris. Isn't that worth bargaining for?"

SHE WAS silent for a long moment. Despite the sunset light streaming through the stern ports, the room was growing dark and chill to Desmond; but he still smiled on, and she did not know that the very life seemed ebbing out of him.

"Yes," she said in a low voice. "Yes. I suppose it is. You may be right."

"My soul to the devil if I'm wrong!" he said confidently. But his head was sagging a little, and his gay voice was less strong. "And something else. I knew you were in Paris last month. I've more than a suspicion that you're headed there now. Very well. You help an enemy, and the enemy will help you. I'll get you a safe-conduct, a passport, to travel in France, on your engagement to do no spying. Oh, I know you'll work there, work like my own, and that's understood. But no spying yourself, mind. You're England's agent, and I'll fight you as you fight me, and you'll be safe from any accusation of being a spy. It's for your own sake; I couldn't bear to see your lovely head in a noose. It should help you tremendously, of course; but remember, I'll be fighting you!"

This was a desperate, clinching offer. Time was running short—his own time.

"You'll really do that?" came her voice, as from far away.

"My word on it. I only ask that you'll tell the French representative in Brussels where you've left me; he'll look after me. The name is Colonel Brian Desmond, my dear. It's my own name, and at your service.... Well, speak up! Is it yes or no? Do I put myself in your hands, or go up on deck and shoot that devil—and leave you—"

She was silent again. He could hardly see her face at all, now. From the deck above he caught that ominous *tap-tap-tap*, like a knell presaging his end. If she refused, he was doomed, utterly smashed and doomed, and he knew it with bitter certainty. But she did not know it.

Suddenly he heard her quick-drawn breath of decision.

"Very well. The answer is yes, Brian Desmond. Here's my hand on it."

His hand fumbled across the table to meet her grasp. A swift word escaped her.

"Why, your fingers are like ice!"

Desmond, relaxing, sighed a little.

"Only the fingers, my dear Jane. If you knew how warm— how warm the heart…."

His blithe voice dwindled out. He slowly slumped down in the chair, and his head sagged forward on his breast.

Jane Warr stared at him, as realization grew upon her. Tricked! He could have done nothing, nothing at all. She had been duped by a man at the very limit of his endurance, fighting to extort her word of honor. And he had extorted it.

She glanced at the portfolio under his hand; resentment and temptation lay in her eyes. Then she flushed, left her chair quickly and rounded the table, falling on her knees beside his chair. Almost incredulously, she looked into his stilled face, and her gaze softened.

"I begin to understand why they credit you with miracles, Monsieur Feufollet!" she murmured. Leaning forward, she touched her lips to the pallid cheek. "Dear splendid enemy!"

Then her hand went to seek the wound beneath that blood-wet shirt….

On the deck above, a man with one wooden leg stood leaning against the rail, looking out at the Holland coast. His eyes were very pale gray, and terrible in their savage hunger. As the lugger lurched along, he swung around and gazed off at the Channel, where the white sail-fleck of a distant frigate broke the sunset-reddened horizon to the north.

Then he turned farther. His eye caught something white,

fluttering and falling from the stern window of the lugger into the wake, and whirling off on the water. A bit of cloth. Another followed it, not so white now. Still others, reddened bits of bandage.

Astonishment and speculation came into his face. He frowned. Then he left the rail, balancing himself to the swing of the vessel, and went to the companionway, and stumped down the ladder. In the little passage below, he went to the door of the largest cabin and stood there, listening.

Suddenly he lifted his head, and his gray eyes flashed.

CHAPTER V

JANE WARR'S WORD

CARRYING AN empty pitcher, Jane Warr came out of the cabin, came face to face with Constant, and halted.

"You want to see me?" she prompted. He touched his hat humbly.

"No, miss." His pale eyes searched her. "There is somebody else aboard?"

"Certainly there is." She thrust the pitcher at him. "Please go and fetch me some water. And I don't care for any curiosity, Constant."

"No, miss." A queer look flashed across his heavy face, a look of surprise, of hurt incredulity. She read his expression, and flushed a little. He stumped away with the pitcher to his own cabin.

As she stood waiting, Master Bowyer came down the ladder, touched his forelock, and went to Desmond's door. The girl spoke quickly.

"You want to see him? Here, in my cabin. He's hurt."

"Yes, miss. It's about a paper he promised to write...."

"Go on in," she said impatiently, and held the door open.

The seaman obeyed, and after a moment Constant returned with the filled pitcher. She took it from him, and looked him in the eyes. "It would be just as well to forget this matter, Constant."

He nodded in silence, but his look brought the red cheeks again. Then, as she turned to the cabin door, he spoke.

"Beg pardon, miss. Something fell out of the stern window."

She swung around and met his gaze. "I know it," she said calmly. And, without making the mistake of any explanation, she went into her cabin and shut the door.

Desmond wakened briefly to the urgent voice of Master Bowyer, who was anxiously demanding his promised acquittal. He nodded to Jane Warr.

"Will you write it, please? I'll sign it."

She complied. He scrawled the name of Colonel Fitzgerald on the paper, and vaguely heard her arranging something about getting him ashore, with the seaman. Then he drifted off again, and everything was lost.

He wakened fitfully to lights, to jolting that hurt him cruelly, to a night sky, to fitful fever-fancies and burning fantasies of engulfing flame. Now high, now low. With the rushing accretion of fever he was in a perfect torment of chaos, of wild visions, of fantastic situations. When it waned and died, he usually slept—but not always. At such times his brain was comparatively clear.

At such a moment he came awake, to find himself lying in bed, in a sunny room, with Jane Warr's hand cool on his forehead. He stared up, perplexed and startled by the drawn anxiety of her face. His thoughts wandered.

"Cheer up, my dear," he muttered. "I'll have that safe-conduct sent to you. To the English ambassador. Where am I?"

"Oh, don't think of it; nothing matters," she burst out, and leaned forward, stroking his hot forehead again. "You're in Brussels, my dear. You're safe."

"Brussels! Impossible. You're an enemy; I must fight you and

*Desmond's
point
flecked in.*

love you and wreck all your plans. Damn that Constant! He's for Paris, I know it. Waiting for me there. Hello! Is that you, Lady Jane Warr?" Desmond laughed faintly. "I'll see you in Paris, my dear."

There were voices, footsteps. The girl stood up, and passed beyond his fitful vision. She was speaking very softly, but by some trick of the senses he caught every word.

"I must put him in your hands. There's no other hope. If you can give me this proof, it is all that I shall require, and I'll recommend that Sir Edward Hope send you on to Paris at once. But this proof of your abilities I must have. Therefore, if you want to serve us in Paris at the price arranged, keep this man from dying."

"I can do only what I can, Lady Warr," said a softly modulated voice, and a man swam into the ken of Desmond's wandering vision. "He is conscious?"

"Somewhat. His wits are dull with fever."

"More likely to be sharpened, I think."

True, in a way. Almost subconsciously, Desmond was striving terribly to keep track of what was said, trying to fix in his mind what passed. Even in his helpless state, he was still Monsieur Feufollet. This visitor was dangerous, was important, was vital; he could feel it. Jane Warr spoke again, in French.

"Shall I leave, M. de Cagliostro?"

"Remain," said the man's voice, with its soft Italian accent.

CAGLIOSTRO! DESMOND'S brain beat and fluttered at its barriers, fought back dizzily to that scene in the Royal Arms, where the officers were laughing at the stories about this man. Against this, the words of Jane Warr lured his thoughts. Sir Edward Hope—he was the English envoy here in Brussels, of course. This mountebank was going to Paris as an English agent....

It all faded out and away, as the man bent above him, examined his hurt, touched his head and wrist. An odd sort of man.

Not old at all, slightly fleshy, handsomely dressed. The face was the vital thing—a smooth, indeterminate face, thick-lipped, nose turned up, eyes impudent and darting. Nothing alive in this face except the eyes, dark and luminous. They were so singular, so filled with odd things that eluded any capture, as to fascinate Desmond completely. Count de Cagliostro, that was the name. In one hand he held a handsome cane; in its head was set a watch surrounded by diamonds that glinted all colors in the sunlight.

"It is not impossible, Lady Warr," said this man, straightening up. "I remember that the nephew of Pope Innocent XIII had an injury of very similar nature; it was in the plague year

of 1723. His Holiness was extremely gratified when I cured the
young man—"

"Fifty years ago? Nonsense; you weren't born then," broke in
the girl impatiently. "I don't want pretensions, if you please, but
results. Can you cure this man?"

Cagliostro bowed, with grave dignity.

"In three days the wound will be healing. In a week he will
be about his business. If I mistake not, you will deeply regret
his cure; I advise you to let him die. Should he live, we may
both regret it, in fact. When I touched this man's head, a terrible warning voice wakened in my brain, like the clashing of
swords and the crying of dead men upon a vast stairway of
stone reaching to heaven—"

Again the girl cut in coldly. "I have put Colonel Desmond's
cure in your hands. Will you have the goodness to cure him,
and then join me in Paris?"

Cagliostro looked at her fixedly for a moment, then inclined
his head in assent.

Desmond drifted off. Somehow, those strange words remained in his memory: "the crying of dead men upon a vast
stairway of stone reaching to heaven." Oddly enough, he knew
just such a stairway, where France came down to the sea. He
was trying to place it in his mind, when he was aware of Cagliostro lifting his head and carefully putting on his tongue a
drop from a tiny vial of golden liquid. It burned like fire.

"In the name of God!" said the soft but powerful voice. "Only
by prayer—"

That was all Desmond could remember of the singular
scene....

He wakened again to sunlight of another day, and looked
from the window beside his bed, out upon the Rue Royale, and
the park across the way. He could see soldiers deploying and
drilling there—Austrian uniforms. His brain was clear as a bell.
Brussels, capital of the Austrian Netherlands, of course. He

recognized the spot itself. He even knew he lay in an upper room of the Ville de Paris, his favorite tavern in Brussels.

Turning his head, he glanced about the room. By another window, reading, sat a woman, exquisitely dressed and of the greatest beauty. A dark woman with sad lovely eyes, who was reading a newspaper. Desmond spoke, and was astonished by the strength of his own voice. In fact, he felt perfectly well.

"Madame, you may be an angel, but will you have the kindness to summon that other angel, Lady Warr?"

The woman rose, smiling, and approached him. Never, thought Desmond, had he looked into any woman's eyes that were at once so tragic and so lovely. She spoke with a marked Italian accent.

"She has gone away, will not come back, and you are recovering."

Desmond felt his bandaged chest, and winced slightly.

"Faith, it's no dream, then! How long have I been here?"

"Four days, monsieur. Liquid food only; it is all arranged. Tomorrow you may get up. In three days you may leave the room, the tavern, do what you wish, go where you will. Now you will excuse me."

She left the room. Desmond looked at the table. His saddlebags lay there, his own clothing and property was in sight. After a little, there came a clumping of feet and the innkeeper appeared, a man whom he knew from of old.

"Ah, Colonel Desmond! You are recovered. Praise be to God!"

"I have my doubts about that last," muttered Desmond, then smiled. "Here, man! Hand me those saddlebags from the table."

The host complied. Desmond found everything safe—his own papers, the letter from George III, the report for Vergennes. He relaxed.

"The woman who was just here. Where is she? Who is she?"

"A carriage was waiting. She went away, saying she would not be back, and sent me to receive your orders, monsieur. The charges are paid. The food for the next three days—"

"I asked you her name, confound it!"

The other threw up his hands. "Ah, ah! You don't know that, when all Brussels is ringing with it? Marvelous, that gentleman! Do you know, he predicted in advance the three first prizes in the lottery, and won them all? A fortune! And he himself was here—"

"What the devil was that woman's name?" demanded Desmond angrily.

"Why, monsieur, I was telling you! She was the Countess de Cagliostro in person! And she said to tell you that the Marquis de l'Isle has been notified of your presence and will be here within the hour to see you. Shall I admit him?"

"Yes," said Desmond. The marquis was the French representative here.

H E L A Y marveling at it, yet somehow not amazed. Behind everything was Jane Warr; he had trusted to her, and she had not failed him. Every detail exact, according to their agreement. So she had gone! Too bad. What the devil—she had promised him the draft of the English commercial treaty with Austria! And it was not here.

The Marquis de l'Isle appeared presently—a faded, blasé nobleman of the old school, wigged and powdered and scented. He greeted Desmond with a touch of weary insolence, and extended a sealed letter.

"This was left for you with me, *M. le Colonel*. Pray consider me at your service. You are ill, I hear."

"My thanks." Desmond tore at the sealed paper. Then his eyes blazed. "Ha! Glory be, rush this to Paris by special courier to M. de Vergennes! And I've another letter to go with it. Of the utmost importance!"

She had not failed. Here was the promised copy of the treaty.

The marquis, who had orders to respect every wish of Desmond as a command from Versailles itself, displayed no astonishment at anything, and very little interest in anything. Desmond knew him well, and presently had him talking.

"Cagliostro? Oh, of course; I've met the fellow." And the marquis affected a yawn. "He's had the rabble by the ears here, I understand, with his miraculous cures and his prophecies and so forth. *Diable!* A regular mountebank. He predicted that Voltaire would be dead within the month, but Voltaire is in Paris and more popular than the king, they say. What's the world coming to, I wonder?"

"Realities, perhaps," Desmond said grimly. "I must ask your help in another matter, my dear marquis. The most damnable of all English spies is at present loose on the Continent, and I think bound for Paris. He has a wooden leg. I wish you'd send out word to have all the roads in France, every diligence and post, watched for such a man. Also, I want a safe-conduct made out in the name of Lady Jane Warr, and sent to her in care of the English envoy here. At once."

"Before sunset," said the marquis. And Desmond knew he would obey his orders to the letter. The marquis picked up the snuffbox from the table, helped himself to a pinch of dust, and his eyes lit up. "Hello! An admirable thing, this—a perfect *bijou,* Desmond! Looks rather like the King of England."

"He gave it to me the other day."

The marquis seemed not in the least surprised. "By the way," he said wearily, "an unfortunate thing occurred only last evening. Vautier left a letter for you with me. An hour later he was picked up in the street, dead. He had been stabbed in the back."

Vautier was Desmond's chief assistant, and one of the ablest men in the service.

"I told you—that damned Constant!" exclaimed Desmond sharply. "The letter?"

The marquis handed it over, languidly. This man would have been maddening, had he not been interesting. Desmond rather admired his bored efficiency.

Tearing at the sealed missive, Desmond stared at the writing with a pulsating hammer quickening in his brain as he comprehended its import. He caught his breath and read it over again to make sure. He could scarcely believe what he read.

The message was brief and pointed, the sort of message he always got from Vautier and now would never get again:

> Salomon of Cologne, Rothstein of Dresden, meeting Sir E. Hope at St. Jean inn near Groote Markt in Louvain, evening of May 23rd. Business: loan of five billions in exchange for full advance information on commercial treaty between England and Vienna.

Desmond whistled. Vautier did get the damnedest information in odd ways! But this—why, this was something stupendous! Five billions? Vautier must have meant francs, of course. Salomon and Rothstein were legendary names, heading two great German banking houses whose tentacles extended everywhere.

Here, in the flash of an eye, showed the heart of a widespread intrigue.

England and Holland were in alliance, with vast commercial interests, and were now arranging a treaty with Vienna, whose influence controlled the commerce of eastern Europe. The English envoy was going to the obscure little town of Louvain. There, with no prying eyes, in the utmost secrecy, he would meet those two bankers who were coming from across the German borders to the same spot. Advance information of the proposed treaty bartered for a huge loan, which England needed sorely; it might turn the whole tide of history.

Desmond silently tore up the message. He demanded back the epistle from Jane Warr, with the treaty terms, and thrust it away. For a moment he was plunged into thought. Then he lifted dancing, exultant eyes that fairly stabbed at the other man.

"What do you suppose the Count de Vergennes would do for an immediate loan of five billions?"

The marquis dusted his lace ruffles, critically.

"Sell his soul, mortgage Notre Dame, pawn the crown jewels, or betray his best friend. Why mention fantastic impossibilities, my dear Desmond? You know that the treasury is worse than empty and the credit of France plunging toward zero."

"Very well. I'm unable to write. Will you have the goodness to send Vergennes a note, by the courier who bears that special report from London?"

"Pray consider me at your service, of course."

"Thank you. Tell him that I've been ill, that I'm recovered, and that I'm bringing him the terms of the forthcoming treaty between London and Vienna."

"Certainly."

"What day of the month is this?"

"The seventeenth of May. Since that fellow Cagliostro predicted the death of Voltaire before June, I keep track of the days."

Desmond lay back on his pillows, thinking fast. He needed help now and needed it bitterly. And the very man for his need should be here in Brussels. Luck, perhaps—the luck of Monsieur Feufollet. He laughed softly.

"I leave here, then; the night of the 20th. Excellent. No doubt there are English spies in Brussels, as the murder of Vautier proves."

"By the dozen."

"And Constant to head them—ah! He didn't go to Paris. He's lending his valuable services to Sir Edward Hope, of course; this is a vitally important matter. My dear marquis, where is that fellow St. Vrain?"

"St. Vrain?" The other frowned delicately. "I seem to recall the name. H'm! You helped him escape from the galleys last year. The king refused to pardon him; you asked me to place him somewhere. Why, the fellow is a scullion in my kitchens, upon my word!"

"Will you have the kindness to send him to me in the morning?"

"With all my heart," said the marquis devoutly, and took his departure elegantly. An odd fellow certainly, but excellent in his post here at the court of Prince Charles of Lorraine, who governed for Austria.

CHAPTER VI

A RASCAL'S AID

WITH MORNING, Desmond wakened entirely himself. He left his bed, shaved, submitted to the liquid diet given him, and found his hurt healing nicely. His feeling of gratitude toward Cagliostro was not unmixed with a slight fear. Stone stairs ascending to heaven, eh? Something queer about that, but he did not recall it distinctly.

What he did know was that he was on the track of the biggest coup of his life, and it fairly blazed on his horizon. If he could secure that loan for France, it would mean everything; France was milked dry, had borrowed to the limit, was threatened with utter disaster.

Somewhere in Brittany an army was assembling for the invasion of England; but all movement there had been checked. Why, Desmond was not aware. He was now aware, however, that Jane Warr had neatly duped him. That portfolio of hers must have contained much information about this loan—and she had bought it from him cheaply enough. Or so she thought. He chuckled to himself. Gone to Paris? Aye, and while she went to Paris, Monsieur Feufollet would strike home a blow. He had the treaty terms, and if he could only play his cards— bloody cards, he feared they must be….

A knock. St. Vrain entered and bowed in silence.

An odd rascal, this. Desmond had actually helped him escape from the galleys and from France, to make use of him. Once a nobleman, now a galleys refugee—the years had hit him hard.

Evil was stamped in his lean, marred features; he snarled at all the world.

"Good morning, St. Vrain," said Desmond quietly. "Do you remember what I promised you when I left here last fall?"

"Yes, monsieur," said the other. "That if I served you, you would lift me back to myself."

"I'm redeeming the promise now."

"Which means, you need me again."

"Precisely. You committed crimes against society; well, I make you a free offer. Help me for a week. At the end of that time, we shall either be dead or bound for Paris."

St. Vrain transfixed him with a sinister eye.

"And, at Paris—"

"You'll be restored to your estates and your rank of vicomte."

A flash of joy lit up the hard scarred features.

"Agreed, Colonel Desmond! You wish me to serve you?"

"No. I wish you to befriend me."

The two men gripped hands.

"In three days," went on Desmond, "we go to Louvain, secretly. Until then, keep your eyes open for a man with a wooden leg,"

"Eh? But there are hundreds of such, veterans of the wars!"

"This is an Englishman with pale gray eyes like the glint of death. Whatever your disguise, you cannot escape those eyes if he knows you—nor can those eyes escape you. Can you still use a sword?"

St. Vrain, who had once been the finest swordsman in France, laughed thinly.

"I have practiced every day."

"Enough. Take quarters here with me."

So came to rest this man who had been soldier, nobleman, criminal, galley-slave, scullion—and who now hoped to turn back the cycle of destiny. Desmond, who alone had inspired him with this hope, could trust him absolutely.

TWO DAYS dragged idly. Desmond fretted over one thing
and one alone—the murder of Vautier, which burned him savagely. He found himself almost healed of his hurt. Only the
scab remained, promising to pass with amazing rapidity into a
scar.

On the third day, St. Vrain went out late in the morning,
bound for the lower town to inquire about the diligence for
Louvain. The hours passed, and he did not return. Mindful of
Vautier's fate, convinced that Constant was somewhere here,
Desmond gradually became prey to an agony of uncertainty.
Despite the orders of Cagliostro, to which he lent an almost
superstitious obedience, he was on the point of dressing and
going out to look for St. Vrain, when he heard the latter's quick,
firm tread. St. Vrain came into the room and closed the door.

"Hello!" broke out Desmond. "Anything wrong?"

"That depends on your definition of the word." With his
twisted, sardonic smile, St. Vrain drew up a chair. From his
pocket he took a tiny vial, then a rouleau of gold pieces, flinging them on the table so that they clinked and rolled about.
Desmond saw that they were English sovereigns.

"First," said St. Vrain, producing tobacco and a short clay
pipe, "remember that I'm tolerably well known here as a servant
in the house of M. le Marquis—a scullion. Well, when I left
here I was followed. I went to the lower town, to the post tavern,
and made inquiries about the diligence."

"For Louvain?" queried Desmond alertly. St. Vrain grunted
and lit his pipe.

"No; for Paris. However, I got the information about the
Louvain coach without asking about it. Good. A man approached me and fell into talk. He was an Englishman."

Desmond started. "Constant!"

"No. This was a fellow with a broken nose, a down-at-heels
gentleman, I fancy. He spoke excellent French. We went and
had a drink together. An Austrian police agent was there, pre-
tending to read a newspaper, but really watching us—a friend

of my man, you comprehend? I was asked if I wanted to make my fortune. Naturally, I did."

St. Vrain rolled that dark and terrible gaze of his about the room, and chuckled.

"This Englishman knew that I had been taken from the kitchens of M. le Marquis, presumably to act as valet and attendant for one Colonel Desmond, who lay ill at this inn. I did not disturb the presumption."

Desmond waited, tensed and fearing the worst; nor was his fear misplaced.

"So, my friend, I was given half my pay in advance—one hundred golden guineas. I get as much more at midnight tonight, but this time in Austrian crowns. It seems these devils of Austrians have put a high price on your head. One of them meets me downstairs tonight, and when the work is done—my fortune! That is, in theory. In actual fact, they'd most likely clap me into jail and finish me."

"And how to earn this stream of gold?" asked Desmond.

St. Vrain pointed to the vial.

"Merely put this into your broth tonight. They know everything! Even to your diet. And as I came in just now I passed two Austrian police spies. You're caught."

Desmond took up the vial, looked at the white powder in it, and laid it down again. Poison. And he was caught, was he? They preferred to poison him rather than take any other action. Constant was behind this.

"No one-legged man anywhere?" he asked doubtfully.

St. Vrain shook his head.

"None, I assure you. I kept my eyes open. Only this rascal of the broken nose."

"One of Constant's men, then. Well?"

"The Louvain diligence departs at eight tonight, reaches Louvain at ten-thirty. Slow, to cover twenty miles. There's only the one tavern, the inn of St. Jean."

Desmond nodded and relaxed.

"Good. At seven-thirty it'll be dark. I've little enough to pack."

He was weak, however, as he found on testing his strength. St. Vrain took the little vial and pocketed it.

"I have a fancy that my broken-nosed Englishman will be haunting this place tonight," he said slowly. "He knows you get your evening meal about nine. I think that I'll be drinking in the tavern room around seven, just on the chance. That fellow wears a sword, and you could use a sword, *mon ami.*"

Desmond met that sinister gaze, and shivered slightly—but he made no comment. So they would use poison, would they! Or was the white powder just a drug?

In the sunset he looked out across the park and the smoke-hazed roofs of the lower town. It was high time for Will o' the Wisp to flit, and to flit fast. Here in Brussels great things were stirring, intrigue seethed, destiny was uncoiling like a sluggish reptile. Austria would not war upon France, but commerce was another matter. Her projected treaty with England would affect Flanders and the German states and Italy. If those Jewish bankers knew the terms in advance, they could clean up vast sums. And all this, from a secret meeting in a dreary little wreck of an ancient university town twenty miles away.

And Jane Warr gone to Paris. Desmond sighed and glanced down at the street below, in the gathering dusk.

He leaned forward suddenly. A carriage was coming, a handsome private carriage with high-stepping horses, two people sitting in it. Desmond knew the man, recognized instantly the proud, intolerant, patrician features of Sir Edward Hope, the English envoy. But the woman beside him....

His heart raced. He leaned forward, incredulous. Just a glimpse—but he could have sworn it was Jane Warr. He couldn't be sure. Her hat concealed her face as the carriage drew below him. Then it was gone from his range of vision.

Jane Warr still here, and not a word from her?

"No, that's ungenerous," murmured Desmond, still staring. "She kept her bargain; she could do no more, could not communicate with me even if she would. I'm an enemy. And yet— and yet...."

The Austrian police had him spotted. At least one English agent was working with them. He had trusted Jane Warr with his actual name. She alone knew where he was. The ugly suspicion tore at him. He put it away angrily, hotly. Perhaps this woman with Sir Edward was another. Jane herself had told Cagliostro she was going to Paris.

Then Desmond, as he sat, had his answer. His eye caught a figure's irregular motion, across the way on the park promenade. A figure stumping along in the dusk, walking with the aid of a huge stick—a figure with one wooden leg. Though he could hear nothing at this distance, Desmond knew that steady, indomitable, irregular stride; through his brain beat the *tap-tap-tap* so familiar and terrible.

Not Jane Warr, thank heaven! Not Jane Warr, but this devil Constant....

THE DAYLIGHT was gone, the darkness gathered, and Desmond still sat there alone with his thoughts, for St. Vrain had been a long time gone. So Constant had nipped him again. Decidedly, that man had the devil's own help!

Brains, rather; give him his due. Not likely that Constant was revealing his own identity to the Austrian police—rather, he was working through one of his own assistants. Vautier, stabbed in the back, basely murdered—now drugs or poison. No, Jane knew nothing of it, suspected nothing; she had been horrified on learning the truth about Constant.

A step, a hand at the door; St. Vrain came into the darkened room.

"What, no lights? So much the better, perhaps," he said. "It's close to seven-thirty, Desmond, and here's the Englishman's sword for you. Not a bad blade, either."

"What?" exclaimed Desmond, starting up. The other's laugh

rang in the obscurity, with a hard, sinister note that chilled the spine.

"Oh, there's a crowd of citizens downstairs, drinking and gabbling! My Englishman was in a corner, and I joined him. Told him you were asleep, that I'd put the stuff in your broth later. He said, by the way, that it was only a drug to put you into a deep slumber. I hope to Satan he lied!"

A drug, eh? Good. Desmond relaxed with a breath of relief.

"Why do you hope that?" he demanded. "And how did you get the sword?"

"Oh, one learns things in the galleys." And that terrible laugh sounded again. "I emptied the powder into his wine, and he drained it. Eh! That's poetic justice for you! And across the room were two Austrian police spies. He's snoring over his corner table now. If he lied about the powder...."

"Give me the sword," said Desmond. "A rapier, eh? Excellent. Now tear the blankets into strips; we must get off. Knot the strips together; make a double rope that'll reach down from the balcony to the street."

St. Vrain grunted. "A single rope would do. It's not far."

"Obey orders, my good angel!"

The other complied. Few people were passing in the street.

Ten minutes later, St. Vrain lowered Desmond at an opportune moment, then followed with agility down the knotted blanket-strips.

Desmond caught one end, pulled the makeshift rope clear, and chuckled blithely as he coiled it about his arm.

"We'll throw this away, farther on. Forward, comrade! To the diligence and its crowd of beer-swollen Flemings, and safety!"

So, once more, Monsieur Feufollet had simply vanished without leaving a trace. And Brian Desmond was on his way to a bloody path toward fortune. It is inevitable that when one serves destiny, death must be in close attendance.

CHAPTER VII

A SPY IS TRAPPED

A DRAB PLACE and rotting away, was Louvain. Within the ancient ramparts were tilled fields where once houses had stood. The university, the buildings from ancient days, were like gray shells. The little town was busy and placid, out of the world and lost. Even the St. Jean tavern seemed asleep except when the diligence or the post came through.

Apparently strangers to each other, St. Vrain and Desmond occupied un-adjacent rooms on the upper floor. Desmond had only a vague plan of action, for everything depended on circumstances. He was well ahead of the meeting-time, at least, and by keeping to his room of days, going forth only at night, and eating heartily, he meant to build up his strength.

"Use your gold," he told St. Vrain, who knew their errand here only in a general way. "We have three days. Buy two of the best horses you can find, with saddles, and on the evening of the twenty-third see that they're ready and waiting to go at a moment's notice."

St. Vrain eyed him cynically. "You expect the worst?"

"No. I expect the best, but I prepare against the worst. And get yourself a rapier. If I mistake not, we'll nip that fiend Constant before we leave."

"Don't forget it requires a silver bullet to kill the devil." And St. Vrain laughed. "Keep those brass pistols of yours loaded, my friend. Advice for advice!"

So came the day, gray with a high moaning wind and storm-scud in the sky, deepening into a gale as the hours drew on. The diligence from the east, by which the two bankers would most probably arrive, got in of late afternoon. Desmond guessed that Sir Edward would come in his own carriage from Brussels.

In this he was right. St. Vrain came into his room shortly after two o'clock.

"Arrived," he said curtly, and the look in his blazing eyes brought Desmond erect.

"Who, then?"

"Sir Edward Hope. And with him—your man of the wooden leg." St. Vrain's eyes held a dancing devil of exultancy. "What's more, they have taken the room adjoining mine."

Constant here! Desmond's pulses leaped.

"You seem highly delighted by it."

"I am," and St. Vrain uttered his harsh, terrible laugh. "I have learned that my Englishman of the broken nose lied, after all. That white powder was not a drug; it was poison, and my English-man is dead."

"Oh!" Desmond frowned. "Damn it! I wish I'd stopped you. My soul to the devil if I can stomach such work—"

St. Vrain gestured airily. "Bah! That's what he gets for lying. But you haven't asked me how I learned this pleasant informa-tion."

Desmond glanced up quickly. "Eh? How, then?"

"Come to my room and I'll show you. It's quite safe now; the one-legged devil has gone down to the tavern below."

Desmond caught up his sword-belt and followed along the corridor.

His own room was at the far end. The inn was built about a hollow square—the big courtyard. Along one wall, stairs mounted to the rooms above, open stairs overlooking the court-yard. St. Vrain's room was almost at the head of these stairs.

Glancing down, as they passed, Desmond could see a figure standing by the inn door, in talk with the host. It was Constant. At sight of the man, he gripped his hands. Ah, Vautier, Vautier! There would be payment now for your murder!

Constant had his back turned. A moment later Desmond was in St. Vrain's room and the door was closed.

As Desmond was about to speak, St. Vrain made an imperative gesture of silence. Then he motioned to a chair. Puzzled, Desmond seated himself, a bit awkwardly, having a loaded pistol in either pocket of his coat. St. Vrain, with his thinly sinister grimace of a smile, brought up another chair, set it down quietly, and slid into it.

"Worse rogues than we have occupied this chamber," he murmured, his lips almost at Desmond's ear. "Now wait."

With a whimsical lift of his brows, Desmond obeyed. Directly below these rooms were the stables of the inn; a faint stamp of hooves could be heard. Then another sound, one that brought an angry glitter to Desmond's eyes—the *tap-tap-tap* of that wooden leg on the stairs and in the passage. It halted. There was a knock at the adjoining door, and then Desmond started suddenly.

"Come in, come in," said the voice of Sir Edward Hope, as though he had been in their very presence. "Any news?"

"None, sir," answered Constant. "The diligence won't be in for an hour or more."

"Very well. Go and amuse yourself until it comes; I wish to sleep. Tell these people of the inn not to disturb me until I summon them. Damme, I want no hostlers and chambermaids bustling in and out."

Desmond stared at the black oaken paneling in front of him. Following the exultant finger of St. Vrain, he discerned that a strip of the wood had been ripped away, leaving a thin gap which obviously opened into the adjoining room. Enough to allow anyone to hear and see what passed in this next room.

"Very good, Milord," said Constant's voice. "Shall I arrange about the other carriage and the change of horses, and food—"

"Yes, yes, confound it!" broke in the imperious, impatient tones of Sir Edward. "Sink me, you rogue, you have orders already; why bother me about them now? Go and see to everything. We may have to remain here the night."

"Beg pardon, Milord," said Constant humbly, yet inflexibly.

"I think it is understood that I am at liberty to depart for Paris, the moment this matter is concluded?"

"Certainly. To the devil, if you so desire!"

Constant departed; the sound of his wooden leg lessened and was gone.

Desmond's chin sank on his breast for a moment; he was weighing every chance. "The other carriage"—what could that mean? Perhaps Sir Edward's carriage had broken a spring or something else, on the way from Brussels. No great matter. Why delay? Why not act now, this instant, and catch the two of them one by one instead of together?

He came out of his chair, plucked a pistol from his pocket, and thrust it into the hand of St. Vrain. With a brusque gesture, he stepped softly to the door, opened it, and went out. No sign of Constant in the courtyard. All was clear.

WITH ST. VRAIN at his elbow, he went to the door of the adjoining room. Having heard the bolt shot, he did not waste time trying the door, but knocked sharply.

"Damnation! What is it? Who is it?" came the angry voice, in French.

Desmond counterfeited the calm, emotional accents of Constant.

"Beg pardon, Milord. A message from Herren Salomon and Rothstein."

From within, a startled exclamation and a thud of feet; Sir Edward had evidently removed his boots. The bolt was shot back and the door opened.

Desmond shoved hard at it and walked into the room, his pistol out and lifted. St. Vrain followed closely.

Sir Edward stepped back with a burst of indignant oaths that died out under the lift of the pistols. St. Vrain closed and bolted the door.

"Shout for help, and I'll kill you," said Desmond, and saw that the words went home. This arrogant, handsome, efficient gentleman, who was in his late thirties, would not lose his head by any means. Putting up his own pistol, Desmond turned to St. Vrain.

"If Sir Edward lifts his voice, shoot him," he said.

St. Vrain said nothing, but his sinister face spoke for him.

"Why, damme! You know me! Is this robbery?" exclaimed the Englishman.

"Capture, shall we say?" Desmond uttered a gayly lilting laugh, and bowed. "What, Sir Edward, you don't remember me? I had the honor of your acquaintance at the ball given in the palace by Archduke Charles, in January."

The envoy regarded him for an instant.

"Oh! I remember, of course. Colonel Desmond, the damned Irish traitor."

"You flatter me," said Desmond affably. This angry man knew nothing of his identity with the famed Will o' the Wisp, obviously. Constant had kept that matter strictly to himself, for his own purposes.

"Well, sir?" snapped Sir Edward. "What's the meaning of this cursed impertinence?" Then his face changed. "Why, damme, you spoke of Salomon and—" He checked himself.

"And Rothstein, yes." Desmond bowed again. His blue eyes twinkled. "By the way, may I inquire who the lady was that I saw driving with you in the Rue Royale yesterday?"

"You insolent low rascal!" exclaimed the other, flushing hotly. "None of your cursed business. Get out of this room, d'ye hear?"

"Steady," said Desmond. "You're a prisoner; best remember it, unless you want to be tied up and gagged."

With these words, with the change of tone, the unfortunate man perceived something of the truth. The pistol, the menacing gaze of St. Vrain, the assured air of Desmond, the mention of the two bankers—all these things broke in upon his brain. He changed countenance, lost all his angry bluster, and became very pale.

"Careful!" warned Desmond. "A shout would do you no good,

for you gave Constant very implicit orders about disturbing you. And you'd be dead before it could be heard."

"Damme! You must be the devil in person!" gasped Sir Edward. Desmond shrugged.

"If you like. May I introduce the Vicomte de St. Vrain? I'll ask you to accompany him. Suppose you escort Sir Edward to my room, St. Vrain. He'll be safer there—"

"One moment, if you please!"

Sir Edward spoke calmly, startled comprehension sending his eyes from one to the other of his captors.

"Yes?" Desmond's brows went up inquiringly. "Oh, you'd like your boots? By all means."

The Englishman ignored the words. "Do you actually intend to rob me?"

"No," said Desmond. "We are merely replacing England with France in this little interview with the two bankers."

"But you are gentlemen," said the other, desperately.

"Certainly. Gentlemen of France."

Like a flash, the hand of Sir Edward whipped across Desmond's lips. Then he stood, white-faced, resolute, unflinching, as St. Vrain took a step forward and raised his half-lowered pistol. Desmond checked him swiftly.

"No, no! We are not assassins. Sir Edward, there can be only one answer to that blow. As you're well aware."

"At your service, sir," and the Englishman bowed.

DESMOND INSPECTED him briefly, admiringly; the desperate action was after his own heart. True, he had not the least business fighting this man, for it would jeopardize his whole mission. His thought leaped into words.

"Faith, if I were a rascally spy like your Constant, I'd kill you and be done! But I don't serve France in that fashion, praise be. Do you choose pistols or swords?"

Sir Edward smiled coldly. "Swords, by your leave. Must I fight both of you?"

"You'll not have the chance, me lad," said Desmond. Then St. Vrain intervened angrily.

"Why risk everything? Let me fight him; I'll kill him in two minutes."

Desmond sighed. "My dear fellow, as a damned low insolent Irishman, I'm condemned to work in my own fashion—that is to say, according to the dictates of honor. If Sir Edward has the luck to kill me, clear out and ride for your life. Perhaps you'll help him find his sword?"

The Englishman, who had flushed a little at those words, spoke stiffly.

"I apologize for my heated expressions, Colonel Desmond. My sword is with my luggage, yonder—a rapier like your own, I perceive. I think we'd better open the windows?"

Desmond nodded and stepped to the casement windows, which were closed against the afternoon light. He flung them wide. A slight action enough, and necessary to give light into the room—yet the least action may, much later, have astonishing consequences....

St. Vrain remained by the door, gloomy and scowling. Sir Edward slipped on his boots and picked up his rapier. Desmond threw off his coat, bared his own blade, and nodded.

"I think we may dispense with formalities?"

"As gentlemen, naturally," added Sir Edward. "On guard, sir!"

The blades crossed, clinked, rasped.

Now and again, for a fleeting instant, they hung motionless in air; then a flash, a thrust and riposte, a swift flicker of steel in the sunlight, a lunge of bodies—and they were together again, as though welded.

Desmond was smiling a little, his eyes alert and dancing. But as the moments passed, into the set, fixed countenance of Sir Edward crept a light of dismay, almost of despair. He moved back and back until he could retreat no farther. The point of Desmond's blade played around him, and sweat started on his forehead; he was no longer attacking, but defending.

An exclamation broke from the intent St. Vrain.

Almost too fast for the eye to see, Desmond's point flecked in and out, and hung motionless again. The Englishman's eyes flew wide open. His fingers loosened on the rapier, which clattered on the floor. They caught at the air, at his breast, at his throat. He swayed and toppled forward.

Desmond caught him as he fell.

"Quick, St. Vrain! Right. To the bed with him. Not mortal, I hope."

Together they laid the gasping figure on the bed, and St. Vrain explored, to straighten up with a disgusted word.

"Bah! He's no more than pinked. You could have killed him a dozen times over; why hold your hand?"

"Killing comes soon enough. Can you bandage the hurt?"

"An education in the galleys, my dear Desmond, comprehends everything. Leave him to me. I'll use his own linen for the bandage. By the way—you want him tied up?"

Desmond, picking up his rapier and donning his coat again, hesitated. Yet it was necessary, if his scheme were to go through.

"Yes, and gag him to boot. Not cruelly, however. He played fair."

He turned to explore the belongings of the hapless envoy, and promptly settled down at the table with the documents to hand. After a moment, he broke off for brief word.

"St. Vrain! Your title and estates are safely in the bag."

"With luck," muttered the other.

Desmond found the envoy's writing case, opened it, and sharpened a quill. He had work here, and fell to scribbling as he went over the papers. Delight grew upon him. Under his hand was everything that he might require, not only for the present work but later, for the eye of the minister at Versailles. Here was what England offered, what England would demand—and what England would accept. Confidential memoranda from the ministry in London, instructions, conditions. Even assurances of the loan, in blank, to be signed by the two bankers from Germany.

The victory was not only certain, it was absolute.

As Desmond scanned the instructions, he chuckled. Sir Edward had been ordered to send word to London by special courier "instantly the negotiations might be approved." They would wait long for that special courier!

"Has it occurred to you as singular," spoke up St. Vrain, who had in the meantime finished his work of bandaging and truss-ing the envoy, "that this Englishman should arrive here by his own carriage, yet with only one man accompanying him? And that man neither lackey nor groom, but our friend Constant?"

Desmond glanced up. The fact had already struck his atten-tion, but he dismissed it with a shrug.

"What of it? The meeting was to be so secret that Sir Edward probably would not dare to trust his own servants. He could, however, trust Constant."

Taking up a paper he had just written, he sanded the ink and gave it to St. Vrain.

"Here's a passport for you, as being in my employ. It'll take you safely past the frontier and on to Paris if necessary. When I've finished with those financiers who'll arrive at any moment now, I'll give you their signatures; that paper will be the most important of all. Here, take these as well," and he sorted out one or two of the most important from the pile of documents before him. "You'll have the cream of the business, the informa-tion that must reach Vergennes at all costs. I'll take the others myself."

"What the devil!" The bitter eyes of St. Vrain searched him. "What d'ye mean? Don't we travel together?"

"We do not." Desmond spoke crisply, curtly. "You go by Brussels and Mons; I'll go by way of Charleroi. We meet at St. Quentin, across the frontier in France. At the Lion d'Or, an excellent inn. I'm quite well known there."

"Why?" shot out the other. "Why separate?"

"Because all peril follows me, not you. Too much has been learned about me; even when that devil Constant is dead, things will be risky. The frontier will be watched. I'll have to slip through somehow. You have everything of prime importance to France; get through to Vergennes in case I fail. I'm giving you the more direct way, but I'll have few towns to pass through, so I may get there ahead of you. No argument, please."

St. Vrain met his look, and assented.

Desmond carefully stowed away his own loot. This made twice that he had more or less carried off an identical coup—and he had better luck now than last time. Twice he had struck his talons in with an eagle-swoop on his prey. After this, they would take more precautions against Monsieur Feufollet! He laughed softly.

His laughter died away. His eyes darted up. From outside he caught a sound that had haunted his dreams—a sound that he believed he was now hearing for the last and most welcome time. He made a brusque gesture.

"Behind the door. Pistol ready."

Swiftly, St. Vrain moved. More swiftly, Desmond darted to the bed, drew the coverlet over the helpless figure of Sir Edward, and was back at his chair. At his elbow lay his pistol. A flash of terrible exultation shot across his face. He would cheerfully have given his right arm for this moment—and it had come to him unsought.

The *tap-tap-tap* ceased. A heavy knock came at the door.

"Eh? What is it?" Desmond imitated the harsh accents of Sir Edward.

"Milord! It's Constant. They're here."

"Damnation! Ye rogue, how dare ye disturb me—"

"They've come, Milord. You bade we waken you."

"Oh, right, right! One moment."

Desmond stamped on the floor, and motioned. St. Vrain shot back the bolt, then was gone behind the door as it swung open. Constant started forward into the room.

"Beg pardon, Sir Edward," he began, touching his hat. "They didn't come by the diligence but by private carriage. They've ordered rooms... rooms...."

His voice died out as St. Vrain swung the door shut and held a pistol against his side. Desmond looked up. At recognition of his face, the countenance of Constant went white as death itself.

The spy was trapped.

CHAPTER VIII

THE SHOT THAT MISSED

CONSTANT STOOD speechless. His pale, deadly eyes widened on Desmond. His heavy jaw swung open for an instant; his face was a ghastly caricature of itself. He was dressed in sober brown, as Desmond had last seen him. The curls of a long, freshly powdered wig hung about his shoulders.

"So you don't make mistakes, Constant?" said Desmond calmly. "You've made one now—and it will be your last. St. Vrain, shoot him at the first move. Constant, lift your arms— that's right. Now draw his teeth, *mon ami.*"

Still the man was utterly unable to speak a word.

He raised his arms, and St. Vrain went through his pockets. Papers, money, a watch, a knife—two knives. Odd-looking knives, heavy-bladed, balanced, keen as a razor.

"Come over here," said Desmond, pointing at the wall opposite his table. "Stand there and compose yourself. Watch him closely, St. Vrain; he's quick as a rat. Let me have that stuff of his."

The pale eyes flickered frantically about the room, came to rest on the gaze of St. Vrain, and slipped away from it. That gaze held more menace than his own. Constant moved, a sound like a low groan coming from his lips. The sunlight flooded in pitilessly through the open windows. Constant, as though stricken dumb, went to the spot Desmond had indicated, standing against the black oak wall, helpless. St. Vrain put the things from his pockets on the table before Desmond, then stepped away, pistol trained on the hulking figure of the man with the wooden leg.

Desmond glanced through the papers, then looked up, his face even colder than before.

"Anything to say, Constant?"

The man stared at him, wet his lips, and spoke.

"Why, sir—what d'ye mean? You've naught against me for doing of my duty?"

"Of course not." Desmond's voice was as icy cold as his gaze. A trickle of sweat stole down the cheek of Constant. More deadly and inflexible than his own pale eyes were the blue eyes of Desmond, and the silence that now fell. He glanced at the bed, and saw the figure hidden there, and caught his breath.

"You—you've killed him!"

"As I am about to kill you," Desmond said.

Constant regarded him for a moment, squared his shoulders and spoke with a voice that for a brief space was once more composed and steadied.

"I didn't expect to see you here, sir. I thought you were in London."

"In your own language, Constant, it don't work," Desmond said coldly. "No lies; they don't become a man about to be shot."

"Then you mean it!" Constant said, almost under his breath. His composure fled. He broke out in sharp, swift words. "You wouldn't do that, sir! Why, Colonel Desmond, you're a gentleman—you couldn't shoot me! And for what?"

"Execution, not shooting." Desmond picked up one of the knives, fingered it curiously, and laid it by with a slight shiver. "This knife, no doubt, murdered Vautier."

"Vautier? I never heard of him!" exclaimed Constant vigorously.

"A lie. Here are two documents you took from his body, bearing his name."

"So help me, Colonel Desmond, I never heard of him!" persisted Constant, but the sweat was streaming down his face now. "I was carrying those papers for Sir Edward!"

St. Vrain intervened, in French. He understood English perfectly, but seldom spoke it, disliking his own accent.

"Let me speak," he said. His black, saturnine gaze gripped the man against the wall. "This rascal talked with his master in this room. My Englishman of the broken nose was dead. This fellow had given him the poison for you, monsieur."

"You lie!" shrilled out Constant. "There was no mention of any poison!"

"At least, you said he had bungled his orders; that's enough. You gave him his orders. And here's another thing." St. Vrain gestured with his pistol at the table. "Those knives. You know what they are, monsieur? Another fact I learned in the galleys. They're throwing knives, balanced for such work. A throw from a dark doorway—"

"No, no!" cried Constant. "I tell you, they're not mine—"

"Enough of this." Desmond's voice was edged, and stilled Constant instantly. "You murdered Vautier, Constant, and here's the proof if I wanted it. But I don't demand any proof; consider this point well."

Constant quivered. "What do you mean, sir?"

"That all talk is useless. You murdered Boisbriant in Southampton, Deslys in Plymouth, and others. You murdered Frontain in London. You didn't kill them, understand. You murdered them for the rewards offered, as you've murdered others. You don't serve your country. You're an assassin who strikes from behind, for money. I know this; your lies are useless."

He picked up the pistol as he spoke, and cocked it.

"YOU WILL allow me the pleasure, perhaps?" asked St.

Vrain, his thin nostrils flaring eagerly. "You took the master; give me the servant!"

"No." Desmond spoke the word curtly. "I will ask no one to do what I refuse to do myself. This is an execution, an act of justice. If the shot draws any attention, you slip out and take care of the inn people with some plausible story."

Constant drew a deep breath, fastening Desmond with a look of incredulity, of deepening realization.

"Do you—do you really mean to kill me?" he broke out.

"I do," said Desmond quietly. "If you wish to say a prayer, say it."

"Why, sir, I'd like to commend my—my soul to God, I would that," Constant replied, breathing hard. Then his face lit up. "Wait! I'll tell you something. I'll make a bargain with you—"

"No bargain," snapped Desmond. "Death. Ready?"

"No, no! For God's sake, wait!" cried the man frantically. "You don't understand! It's about the French army gathering in Brittany, and what's going on there. I can tell you everything—why that army will never invade England, who's doing the work, what the plan is —"

Contempt flashed in Desmond's icy look.

"Betray your own people to save your dirty life, would you? No!"

"It—it means a lot to France, sir!" The spy blinked, with the sweat that ran into his eyes. "It won't do you any good to kill me; I haven't told anyone that you're Monsieur Feufollet; I swear I'll not tell a soul, sir! And if you don't let me go, think what it'll mean to France! That army won't move—"

Desmond smiled, and it was not a nice smile. It silenced the frantically arguing man, who read in it his doom.

"So you haven't told anyone, eh?" said Desmond. "That would be an excellent reason for killing you, Constant, if I were a man of your sort. But it doesn't matter a jot. You're sentenced to death for murder."

"Will you—will you listen to any excuses, sir?"

"Certainly," said Desmond, with open derision. "They’d be interesting."

Constant dropped the hat he had been holding. He tugged a big handkerchief from his pocket, mopped his streaming face, and then deliberately took off his wig and let it fall on the floor beside the hat. He wiped his bare shining head, and straightened up a trifle, his pale eyes fastened on his judge.

"Very well. I did kill that spy Vautier," he said composedly.

An odd sort of dignity settled upon him as he stood there. With his bald pate, he looked like some incredible, monstrous creature, half man, half vulture, and his eyes shone with a sinister coldness.

"So you confess the murder."

"No, sir—not murder," expostulated Constant. His agitation had vanished; now his voice deepened and took on added sonority. "I’m not a fine gentleman like yourself, Colonel Desmond— just a poor man with one leg. It’s my business to hunt down spies. We’re at war, and if I can catch spies and get a bit of money for doing it, then I can live; and I’ve got a right to do it. If I do find a spy, what can a poor cripple like me do? Kill him in any way I can, that’s all. A sound man has the advantage of me, and a knife evens up for it. That’s all I have to say. If you’re minded to shoot me down like a dog, and me with only one leg and helpless, why, I can’t prevent it; but that’ll be murder."

With this, he settled into an absolute composure, the resignation of despair. He carefully tucked away his handkerchief, folded his hands, and gazed at Desmond with a calm, untroubled face.

"Your excuse, as you call it, isn’t valid," Desmond said coldly. "You’re condemned to die for the murder of Vautier which you’ve just confessed."

"Not murder, sir—"

Desmond’s pistol lifted.

"If you want to say a prayer, say it. At the Amen, you die."

"All right, sir." A flash of emotion came into the pale, fixed eyes. "So she tricked me, like I thought! If I'd stuck to it, aboard the lugger, I'd have pinched you. And me thinking she had some fine gentleman lover in her cabin—it took me aback, it did—"

"No more talk," snapped Desmond with finality. "Say your prayer or die with it unsaid, you blackguard."

Constant caught his breath. "Just a Paternoster; that's the prayer the Good Lord Himself gave us, and it's all I need. And I don't bear any grudge, Colonel Desmond."

Awkwardly, the man started to kneel. The sunset light, streaming in through the open casement, glittered on his bare pate reddishly. He shifted his weight, put out a hand to a chair to steady himself, and—

The chair slipped. It went hurtling back against St. Vrain. With a tremendous thrust from his wooden leg, Constant sent himself through the open window, headlong! Desmond fired. The explosion drowned the oaths of St. Vrain, but the bullet missed.

With a leap, Desmond gained the window. Below, and behind the stables of the inn, was an enormous pile of manure, after the custom of French hostelries and farms. Desmond saw the figure of Constant go rolling. St. Vrain came to his side, just as Constant went scrambling beneath some sheds at the rear corner of the inn.

St. Vrain rushed to the door and was gone, in pursuit.

CHAPTER IX

THE ROAD TO PARIS

DESMOND TURNED back to the table and laid down the pistol, in such bitterness of spirit that he could find no words. His own fault, absolutely. He had been so neatly duped, so absorbed in the man's apparent readiness for death,

so resolved to kill this murderer on the spot, that he had been
flung off guard.

And now Constant was gone—gone, with all he knew. It
was typical of the man's clever mind that he must have known
of that manure pile before he leaped, must have counted on it.

"St. Vrain won't get him, either," muttered Desmond deject-
edly. "Crippled he may be, but he's too smart for all of us! If I
hadn't wasted time, begad, he'd be dead this very minute! And
that's a lesson for me. I'd best be wasting no more time this
night! Get my business done and over, and be off."

Whether St. Vrain had satisfied the inn people, or whether
the shot had not drawn any attention, he neither knew nor
cared. His own folly had lost him Constant. Now he must make
certain of the larger game.

He left the room, stepping out into the passage and locking
the door after him. He caught sight of a chambermaid, and
beckoned her.

"The two gentlemen who have just arrived—where are they?"

She was Flemish and spoke no French. However, his gestures
made her comprehend; she pointed to a door farther down the
corridor, toward his own room. He went directly to the door
of the new arrivals. He knocked, and a guttural voice told him
to enter.

He stepped in, and bowed. Here were two men—one gray-
haired, one younger. A glance told him they were the ones he
sought.

"Herren Salomon and Rothstein?" he said in German. "I am
Colonel Brian Desmond of the French army. You came here
to meet Sir Edward Hope; he will not meet you. Instead, you
are both in great danger. Allow me to present my credentials,
under the signature of His Majesty Louis VI and the Count
de Vergennes. I regret to say that the Austrian court has intervened to prevent your arrangement with London. In fact, you
are to be arrested here before midnight; you must get fresh

horses and start at once back for the frontier, as troops are now leaving Brussels to catch you.

"However, your journey need not be wasted. Where England fails you, France steps forward. I have here a draft of the proposed treaty, initialed by the English Ministry—"

Startled, suspicious, bewildered, they eyed him in silence.

When Brian Desmond set himself to win over any man, he had a golden tongue, and a charm of manner that was beyond resisting. He was now in the most furious earnest, and exerted it against a silence that was ominous.

More than his words, counted the papers that he slapped down. His commission as an agent of France, countersigned by the minister and sealed by the king in person with the three Lilies of France, counted for most of all. The documents Sir Edward had so obligingly furnished, the blank assurance of the loan—now filled in for France—backed up his words. Still the two bankers sat stroking their beards and staring at him, probing him with glittering eyes that drove deeply.

Playing against time, Desmond flung down his last card. He came to his feet and smiled cheerfully at the two men. His documents had quelled their suspicion, his words had reduced their bewildered alarm to keen thought; now he deftly included himself in their threatened status and attacked their silence.

"Gentlemen, I must be frank with you. To gain this interview I have risked much; I must be off for the frontier in ten minutes, or I may be caught myself. I ask only your signatures, which need no bond for France, and the treaty draft is yours. The terms may be settled through your Paris correspondents, with the Count de Vergennes. Take five minutes to talk it over, while I make my own preparations for departure."

With this, he strode out of the room.

In the corridor, he encountered St. Vrain, raging up and down in search of him. As he thought, Constant had slipped out and off, ducking into the narrow streets of the Groote Markt or hiding in some shop.

"He's scotched if not killed, at least," grunted St. Vrain. "I had only one glimpse of him, limping badly; must have hurt himself or his bad leg in the fall."

"Forget him," said Desmond sharply. "Our own necks hang loose now; we must reach the frontier before he finds help or aid against us. The horses—"

"Saddled and waiting with a groom, down there. Pistols in holsters, loaded." The harsh, mirthless laugh barked out. "And loaded with silver bullets. I told you nothing else would do for that devil's brother! I had a goldsmith make them yesterday and paid high. Unluckily, I didn't see to the loading of your pistols. Plague take this separation! I don't like it. A lonely man has little luck."

Desmond grunted.

"Wrong; he has the best luck. However, it may be necessary. I haven't won this game yet. If I do win it, then remember— meet at the Lion d'Or. Give me one day after you get there, for ordinary road delays. If I don't come, get on to Monsieur de Vergennes at all speed. Use my name to reach him."

"Your name, eh?" St. Vrain gave him a curious glance. "You know, I didn't realize until that scoundrel talked, who you must be, Desmond. I've heard fantastic tales of this Monsieur Feufollet. I never dreamed he existed in the flesh. And to find you are he!"

"Silence is golden."

"Mine is steel, not gold, my friend."

A GOOD reply, thought Desmond. Thanks to Lady Jane Warr, thanks to Constant, the secret would soon be a secret no longer. His usefulness was drawing to an end, he could perceive. Well, he was not sorry.

Dusk was gathering fast. Servants were flitting about the place with lights. Two grooms or lackeys belonging to the Jewish bankers came along the passage with lights and went into the room of their masters. After a moment they came hurriedly out again, making all haste to the stairs and down into the courtyard. Desmond's pulses quickened. His story was believed, then! He gripped the arm of St. Vrain.

"Get down to the horses. I'll be right along."

He strode to the door of the room and knocked. A bolt rasped back. Salomon, the elder of the two bankers, admitted him. Rothstein beckoned him forward to the table where candles were now burning, and for the first time broke his silence. He spoke perfect French.

"Colonel Desmond, this is not a matter into which one can rush blindly. Suppose we give you our words, instead of our signatures, that we'll take up the affair of the loan with Monsieur de Vergennes, through our Paris correspondents; will you then turn over to us the treaty draft?"

Desmond's light, gay laugh rang upon the room.

"Come, come, monsieur! Place all my cards in your hands, give you full power to deny that this interview ever took place, trust you with information that'll pile up a huge fortune—and for nothing except your spoken word? Is that business?"

"You haven't answered my question," Rothstein said coldly. "Yes or no?"

"Yes, of course." Desmond threw down the initialed treaty draft taken from Hope's papers. "Here you are."

Rothstein clutched the document, and glanced at it with exultation in his keen dark face. From Salomon broke a thin cackle of amusement.

"Ah! I told you this man was honest, Rothstein."

The other broke into a slight smile, and thrust a paper at Desmond. It was the assurance of the loan; it bore the signatures of both men. Rothstein's voice bit out at him.

"You would accept less; you shall have more. That's the way we do business, Colonel Desmond. The negotiations will go forward through our Paris agents, at once. You haven't mentioned the usual matter of a commission for yourself?"

Desmond's blue eyes looked sharply down at him.

"You serve money, I serve France. Thank you, gentlemen. I advise you to leave here at the first possible moment. Adieu!"

He strode out of the room, and down the corridor. At its end, he remembered the hapless Sir Edward, and paused to unlock the Englishman's door, then went on to the stairs.

The courtyard below was in confused uproar, for the diligence was just arrived. Lights flitted about, hostlers dashed here and there, the carriage of the two bankers was being made ready. Near the entrance waited St. Vrain, with a groom holding two saddled horses.

Desmond threaded his way through the uproar. Meeting the inquiring look of St. Vrain, he handed over the folded assurance.

"With your life. God keep you!"

"And you, *mon ami*," said the other. Then he was swinging up into the saddle. Desmond spoke to the groom, as St. Vrain went spurring out of the courtyard.

"Hold the other horse for me one moment more—do you speak French?"

The Fleming did not, and with a subdued oath, Desmond sought out the innkeeper amid the confusion. He thrust a coin into the man's hand.

"Here. After those two German gentlemen have departed, the English milord wishes to speak with you. Not until then."

The innkeeper assented.

Free at last, Desmond hastened to his horse, tossed the groom a coin, and settled himself in the saddle. His veins singing with exultation, he spurred out and into the darkening streets. Done! Even if he had missed Constant, what of it? Here was a great game won for France, a game that would impact on the destiny of nations. And now for Paris, Paris and Jane Warr!

HE CLATTERED through the streets, slowly until the cobblestones should be left behind and the gates passed. Here were ruinous old houses; on ahead glimmered lights about the gate of the ancient ramparts, where a guard of stolid burghers waited. There was no Austrian garrison in this decaying town.

Paris lay to the south and west. He had given St. Vrain the most direct course, and for St. Vrain safe enough. He himself must avoid Brussels and the larger towns lying that way, since the Austrian police were clearly enough on his trail, thanks to Constant. So Jane Warr had tricked that devil, aboard the lugger! A lover, eh? True enough, in one sense, but that rat Constant had thought something else. And Jane Warr had let him think so.

"The darling!" murmured Desmond, warm at the thought of her. "Bless her sweet soul, she's true steel, that woman! Glory be, when I find her at Paris there'll be time for an honest word between us—hello! I should have given St. Vrain that letter for Doctor Franklin, with the others. Well, no matter, except to me. Devil take it, if that meeting should take place and peace really result from it, then I can go find Jane Warr and not a soul to prevent us! No more of this work, in such case—"

The gates loomed ahead, and his drifting thoughts were cut short. His papers, in his own name, were clear; he got them ready, drawing rein. Two country wagons were coming in and he was forced to wait until they were by.

The wagons were past. He forged ahead and halted under the lanterns of the burgher guard, whose officer glanced at his passport and returned it.

"A pleasant journey to you!"

With a gay rejoinder, Desmond lifted his reins and passed on.

Trees and fields and starlight; but under the great trees lining the road—they were to be cut down by the Prussians nine years later—was a gloomy obscurity and darkness. Just ahead, a lantern was bobbing, off at the roadside under the tall trees.

From the gates, behind, came a single shrill, high whistle.

Desmond suddenly woke up, leaped to the alert. He fancied a movement in the darkness to one side, a movement of shadowy things. The lantern ceased its bobbing. Echoes of that strange whistle lingered in his brain, spurring him to alarm even as he spurred his horse. As the beast leaped forward, Desmond reached down to one of the holsters and pulled the pistol free.

His thoughts darted back to the words he had heard through the wainscot—something about another carriage. What the devil! He had thought it odd at the time that Sir Edward would come with only Constant for servant, guard, and groom. All in an instant, a riot of possibilities, perils, conjectures seized upon him.

And in the midst, too late, he saw the thin black line against the light road, like a rope stretched there. He drew rein frantically. The horse whistled and plunged forward, and went down.

With only so much warning, Desmond had his feet free of the stirrups as the crash came. He was thrown clear, went sliding through the dust, rolled over and came to one knee. His pistol was gone with the shock. A man was rushing at him, with eager voice. Not rising, Desmond whipped out his sword and thrust. The man screamed, twisted on the blade, and Desmond wrenched it loose. Springing to one side, he whirled to meet another rush from the rear, tripped this assailant and sent him sprawling, and flung himself toward the trees and the blackness that promised escape.

Abruptly, he checked himself. Something moved before him, and a lantern suddenly flashed out from under the cloak of a dark figure. With an oath of dismay, Desmond shortened blade and thrust savagely.

There was a low cry. The lantern fell and smashed—but not before that flickering light touched full upon the face of Jane Warr.

Desmond stood for one instant absolutely paralyzed, incapable of movement. Then a *pad-pad* of feet from behind, and they were upon him. He went down under a swirl of figures, with the vision of the girl's white face still before his eyes.

CHAPTER X

IN THE ENEMY'S HANDS

THE FIGURES scurrying under the stars resolved themselves into clarity as another lantern was brought and passed around.

A gleam fell upon the shape of Constant, who lay under the trees, propped on one elbow. His voice lashed out.

"You've got him? You've got him?"

Desmond was dragged to his feet, his wrists pinioned. His head cleared. He caught sight of Jane Warr, and his voice burst forth.

"Jane! You're not hurt? Thanks be! I didn't know you—"

"Hold your tongue or I'll have you gagged," she said coldly. "Make sure of him, men. Anyone hurt?"

"Jem's done for, Your Ladyship," said one of the figures, growling. "Skewered like a quarter o' beef, he was—right through the heart. And owed me four and six, he did."

"Move him out of the road," said the girl, and turned to Constant. "Sir Edward's dead?"

"Murdered, miss," Constant blurted. "I'll take this spy back to Brussels as soon as I can walk. Where's the other one?"

A man came up, running. He who had given the signal from the gate.

"There was only the one," he panted out.

"I'll take him in Sir Edward's carriage," said Constant.

"You'll do what you're told," lifted Jane Warr's voice. "Two of you men help Constant back to the inn. Have Sir Edward's body put into his carriage and drive it back to Brussels. Better pick up Jem, here, on the way. Sir Edward's secretary can arrange all details with the authorities."

"And me?" growled Constant. "Where'll I go, miss?"

"To the devil, whom I think you must serve," said the girl

acidly. "Wherever you go, keep out of my way in future, I warn you."

"And that's what I get for catching him!" Constant cried angrily. "There's a thousand pound on his head, and the Austrians here have offered twice as much! You tricked me once to save him, and you won't do it again! If I hadn't hurt myself, I'd show you what for, here and now. And he's murdered Sir Edward Hope with his own hand—"

The men around echoed low growling oaths. Jane Warr held up the lantern with one hand. With the other, she lifted a pistol and cocked it. The oval of her face was set, resolute, drawn in harsh lines. She seemed no longer a girl, but a woman.

"You men were told to take orders from me. Take them," she commanded. "Jacobs and Logan, tie this man's wrists and ankles securely, and put him in my carriage; we go at once. You others, move as I've ordered you."

"You've not heard the last of this, miss." And Constant's voice, as two of the men helped him to rise, held a snarl.

Desmond was roughly led away, to where a carriage stood under the dark trees. Jane Warr, carrying the lantern, followed, passed him, and stepped into the carriage. She hung the lantern on a hook from the ceiling, then got out and stood looking on as the two men tied Desmond's wrists and ankles.

"I should have let him take you," she said, her voice shaking with passionate anger. "To think that you murdered Sir Edward in cold blood!"

Desmond laughed a little. "To think that you'd believe such a tale!"

She started. "What? It's not true?"

"Oh, you've lost the game, right enough," smiled Desmond. "But Sir Edward is only trussed up under a coverlet, with a trifling hurt that's well bandaged. By this time the innkeeper has seen to him. However, the two birds from Germany have flown home. May I ask what you intend to do with me?"

Jane Warr lifted the cocked pistol.

"Search him," she said to the men. "Give me everything from his pockets, put him inside, and drive on. You have your orders."

"What about his horse, miss?" said one of the two. "The animal's yonder."

"And the rope," said Desmond, with a chuckle. "Don't forget the rope, Jane. Faith, somebody else might bounce over it this night."

"Bring the horse, ride it, Jacobs," she said to one of the two. "First, search him."

SHE GOT into the coach and settled herself on the pillows. Everything from Desmond's pockets was given her, then Desmond himself was bundled in opposite her. One of the men closed the door and mounted to the box, the other went to get Desmond's horse. The carriage started forward, lurched into the road, and went rolling away.

For a little, Desmond watched Jane Warr, as she scanned his papers. She caught her breath, read on, gave him one angry glance.

"You took these from Sir Edward!"

"He lost them," Desmond corrected her cheerfully. "Jane, tell me something I'm most devilish curious to know. Sir Edward's not the man to plan this work with any finesse; why did he have you here, and this carriage? You're not the special courier he was to send to London. What's your part in all this?"

"The plan was mine—all of it, from the start," she said. "I wanted to see it go through, then I was going on to Paris. That's all. It meant—it meant everything. And now you've wrecked it."

"Your plan!"

"Mine," she said bitterly. As the lantern swung, he caught the glint of tears in her eyes.

"Jane, I'm damned sorry," he said softly. "I didn't suspect it. I did think I saw you driving with Sir Edward yesterday—"

"Have done with your talk," she broke out angrily. "Oh, I hate you, I hate you! We're enemies, do you understand? Enemies! You've spoiled everything for me, for England, for all I had hoped—"

Her words were checked. She swiftly sorted out the papers in her lap, and came upon one that was sealed. She eyed it, then held it up.

"What's this?"

"A private letter I promised to deliver," said Desmond. "From the King of England. You can see the address for yourself, in his own hand. Break the seal if you don't believe me, my dear. By the way, Jane! I'm devilish glad my sword missed you."

Ignoring the words, she broke the seal of the letter and read it.

"Weissenstein! Why, yes—I believe the king does use that name sometimes." She lifted her eyes to his face. "And I doubted your word—I'm sorry. Here; take it, and your own passports and private papers. I don't want them. The rest I'll keep."

She thrust them into one of his pockets. A lurch of the carriage flung her against him. She drew back quickly, angrily.

"Faith, you've made a fair haul at that," said Desmond. "Also, you've nabbed Will o' the Wisp this night, which no one has done before. Jane, dear, the heart stood still in me when I saw your face, back there! I thought I'd killed you. After that, devil a bit of fight was left in me. So that scoundrel Constant got away, reached you, and laid the trap for me, eh?"

She eyed him coldly, but with a flush in her cheeks.

"Yes, Constant was sure you'd come this way, and not go by Brussels," she said quietly. "Not that there was much time to think. He only reached us fifteen minutes ahead of you. He said you had tried to murder him, as you had murdered Sir Edward."

"I did my best to kill the rascal, begad!" Desmond said amiably. "Another thing, Jane. You kept your word to me like a gentleman, and I love you for it—for that and a thousand more reasons."

"This is no time for such talk!" she exclaimed hotly. "When you've just wrecked the thing I've been hoping for and planning—oh! And yet I hate to do it."

"Do what?" he prompted quizzically.

"Turn you over to the Austrian police at Wouvre. I'm meeting two of their agents there; it's only twenty miles south. But I must do it."

"And why the devil would you be meeting two of them there?" he demanded.

Her gaze widened a little on him. "Don't you realize it's the end of you?"

"Oh, devil take me! I'm only interested in you, my dear. Ah! You're bound for Paris, of course! You're meeting them, they're lending you help in France—what! But Austria's not at war with us, Jane!" His blue eyes were alight and shining. "What's it all about? Tell me, like a good soul! True, Vienna would cheerfully see Monsieur Feufollet strung up or shot, but that's different; a war under the surface, as it were, without benefit of declarations, and with law and justice in the discard. Well, well? Why the Austrians?"

She shrugged slightly. "A mere exchange of information, my dear Feufollet. I'm only too afraid you're right. Once in their hands, you'd meet with no justice or law. And I must tell them that you're Monsieur Feufollet, too. There's only one way I can get out of it, Brian Desmond. Please help me."

Thunderstruck, Desmond lost his cheerful air.

"What d'ye mean? You're not sorry for me?"

"For you, bitterly sorry," she said softly, her eyes warming. "But not for Feufollet. It's duty, I tell you; I must do it, unless— well, I'll take your word of honor, Colonel Desmond. I'll set you free and give you your horse, and keep silence, if you'll promise me to give up this work of yours, give it up entirely and absolutely, never be Will o' the Wisp again, from the moment we part."

DESMOND STARED at her. In this moment his brain was racing; no illusions blinded him. This woman was none to love lightly or be lightly loved. She was striving to spare him, as he would have striven had positions been reversed; but she would not spare herself. If it must be, she would hand him over.

"Don't you see?" As the coach swayed and rattled, she leaned forward earnestly, intent upon him. "Just as I must keep you tied here, Brian Desmond, so I must hand you over to the Austrians. Not that I want to, mind! I don't—oh, I most des-perately don't!" And for an instant her voice broke, so that Desmond's pulses hammered with the realization of all her words and eyes implied. Then she steadied, calmed herself, fastened upon him those dark and lovely eyes, now bitterly resolute.

"You understand? Give me your word," she said. "I don't work for myself; it's England that must have you out of the way."

"To the devil with England," and Desmond chuckled.

"No, no! You must agree, you must—for my sake!"

"That's different, my dear," he replied slowly, gravely. "That's different. I've been hoping that I might come to you and say those same words, and all my heart in them. To you, Jane Warr; but not to England. And it's to England I must talk now, as you must talk to Monsieur Feufollet, with a break in the soul and no help for it. We're neither of us poor weak folk to compromise with the devil and betray honor."

The color drained out of her face in the flickering light. She looked older, wearier, more sadly resolute, as she met his eyes.

"It's a pity," she said, "that two such people as we are, must be enemies."

"True it is. Listen, Jane Warr! I'll ask some other offer from you; what you ask is too steep a price."

"What could you give," she asked, frowning, "that would not be a betrayal?"

"Right," he said reflectively. "Thanks be, I'm no Constant to barter everything I know to save my neck."

"Oh! Did he do that?" she cried.

Desmond smiled. "No. He wanted to, like the devil! But I refused. And he got away before I could kill him."

She drew a deep breath. "Well—Monsieur Feufollet! I'm offering you life and freedom. Will you accept or not?"

"As I said before, my dear—to the devil with England!"

"Then I must do it. I have no choice," she murmured, her eyes desperate, her white face strained and drawn.

Desmond laughed a little, to hide his own hurt. "You'll have a fine time proving that Colonel Desmond is Monsieur Feufollet!"

"They can do that, once they have you fast, and under suspicion. And no mercy or justice, as you yourself said. Oh, Brian Desmond! Is there no other way?"

There was, and Desmond knew it well. One mention of St. Vrain, with what St. Vrain bore—he could save himself in a flash, by throwing overboard what he had done for France this day. He shrugged lightly.

"No other way, begad!" he answered cheerfully. "Make up your mind to it, my dear, and more power to you. And have no fears; I'll trick those Austrians. I wish you'd put out this confounded lantern, though; it drips oil on me."

"Of course. Are you comfortable?"

"God bless you! Trussed up like a Christmas goose, and am I comfortable?" Desmond broke into a laugh. "What a glorious enemy you are, Jane Warr! Well, I'd like my snuffbox back, for one thing, and a pillow under my head. The one was a present from King George, the other is sadly needed to save my brains from bumping out; so you can aid my vanity and my skull at the same time."

She regarded him with a sad smile, stuffed the jeweled snuffbox and his other personal effects into his coat pocket, and stood up. Unhooking the lantern, she sat down heavily to a bounce of the carriage, and extinguished the light.

In the obscurity she leaned forward, lifted Desmond's head, and put a pillow beneath it. He could feel her there, close to him, touching him. He raised his face a little and his lips found hers. Her hand, behind his neck, tightened convulsively, holding him more closely against her....

The driver chose this moment to halt the carriage with a grind of brakes, and came scrambling from his seat.

Instantly Jane was back in her own place. When the door opened, she leaned forward, and in her heart-hurried voice Desmond could sense the hammering of his own pulse.

"Well?" she demanded peremptorily. "Well? What is it?"

"It's a crossroads, Your Ladyship. I don't know which road."

"Follow the signpost, of course! To Wouvre," she said impatiently.

"But I can't read, Your Ladyship. And Jacobs ain't come up. He's on the horse, and we're ahead of him. Shall we wait?"

She hesitated. The starlight was soft, brilliant. The moon was just peeping through the trees but as yet lingered on the horizon.

"No, we'll not wait," she decided. "I'll come and look at the signpost."

She got out and went with him, leaving the carriage door aswing.

Instantly Desmond was in motion. Had his wrists been tied

behind him it would have been impossible, but they were crossed in front.

He writhed off the pillow, came down between the seats, and his feet were through the opening. He desperately edged himself along. He was through to the knees, then to the hips. A final urge and he went toppling through, cut his cheek on the carriage step as he fell, and landed face down in the dust. This was lucky. A push with his elbows and he was over, rolling into the darkness under the carriage, between the wheels.

There he lay quiet. His one chance was that she might not notice his absence until after the carriage started. The moonlight was not yet in the road.

Steps. She got in, and the door slammed. The driver mounted to his box; with a creak and a rasp, the carriage rolled away. Desmond looked up at the stars and chuckled. Would she come back to search for him? Would she accept his escape as a relief from her dilemma? Would she even discover that he was gone, for a little? All a gamble....

He rolled over and over, gained the grass and weeds at the roadside, and then got his teeth at the cords about his wrists. They were tight and well tied; no fooling with these Englishmen.

Even through his excitement, his effort, burned the memory of her hand at his neck, her lips on his.

His teeth explored, tore at the cords; they loosened a little. As he lay, the *clop-clop* of a horse came to him along the ground. That would be Jacobs, coming along on his own horse.

Suddenly his heart leaped at a thought. He redoubled his efforts, head bent forward, lips bleeding, teeth at work. The cords gave again, loosened. His arms came free. His ankles were still tied fast, and the horseman was close.

"Jacobs!" His voice lifted hoarsely. What the devil was the name of that fellow driving the carriage? Ah! Logan, of course.

"Who is it?" The rider drew rein. "Who's calling me?"

"It's me, Logan." Desmond tried to imitate that man's tones, pantingly. "Give me a hand, man—here I be, tied up. Here, beside the road."

With an exclamation of astonishment, Jacobs dismounted. He came to where Desmond lay, and bent over the prostrate figure, a wondering question on his lips.

Then Desmond had him by the throat with iron fingers.

CHAPTER XI

DOCTOR FRANKLIN

PARIS TALKED and laughed and glittered and starved, these days, quite as usual. War? It was very far away. There was no animosity in it, no hatred of England, no war spirit. The court went its gay course. The polished, affable, iron man who ruled from the ministry could always provide more millions, somehow. Versailles disported itself merrily.

The king, pompous and well-intentioned and inane, went about his little affairs. The queen and her frivolous ladies and more frivolous nobles listened of nights to music under the stars, on the lovely terraces of the fairy palace. An old gentleman was trundled out in his coach from Passy, to an interview with the minister who really ruled France.

In the apartments of the Count de Vergennes, all was business. Secretaries were at work, messengers came and went, endless red tape was winding. The old gentleman, in his sober garb and sparse white hair and spectacles, was ushered in with great honor, and the resplendent Vergennes received him warmly. They talked together in a room lordly and quiet and beautiful, where cupids disported themselves on the ceiling and satin covered the walls.

"Always it is more money!" said Vergennes, with a grimace. "Upon my word, you are insatiable! Have you no pity on a poor devil who must scrape millions from nowhere?"

"But you always scrape them," said Benjamin Franklin, with his charming smile.

Vergennes gave him a serious look.

"My dear friend, I have supplied your colonies a billion and a quarter of francs; and now you ask more. Well, you shall be satisfied—but I warn you, things are not very pleasant for me. Within the next two months I must find a hundred millions in cold hard cash, and I haven't the faintest notion where to look."

"I'm only asking five millions this time," Franklin said placidly.

"You shall have them. What do you offer in exchange? Promises?"

"Naturally. And a bit of information." And the old gentleman beamed. It was impossible to tell whether he was in jest or earnest. "I heard this morning that Voltaire is very ill, perhaps dying."

"Voltaire!" repeated the minister, with a disdainful gesture. "An enemy of society."

"On the contrary, a man of ideas—which may be the same thing," said Franklin. "The point is, however, that it was predicted that Voltaire would die before June; and tomorrow is the first of June."

Vergennes fastened a keen look upon him. "Predicted?"

"Exactly. By a man who is now in Paris, they say—a most extraordinary person, who claims to be deathless, to have the philosopher's stone. He turns lead into gold, tiny pearls into enormous gems. You perceive, my dear Vergennes? Your problem is solved. Send for this man and let him provide you with gold."

Franklin smiled as he spoke. Vergennes broke into a laugh.

"Upon my word, I might do worse. But seriously, you surely don't have any faith in such nonsense? Predictions, philosopher's stone, magic?"

"Not an iota," Franklin said. "I have great interest in it, however. I'm of the firm conviction that common sense can dispel all such mystery. I'd like to investigate such a man from a scientific aspect. The odd thing is that he cannot be altogether a charlatan. A child living not far from me, in the Avenue Mozart, was restored to perfect health by him, only two days ago. She was almost at the point of death with a flux of the lungs. Yesterday I myself saw her, well and happy."

"Who's this miracle monger?" Vergennes asked slowly.

Franklin looked at him for a moment, and the hard old blue eyes softened.

"Ah, my friend! You're thinking of your daughter. Tell me. How is she?"

"There is no hope," Vergennes replied quietly. "The physicians had a meeting last evening. They do not understand her ailment; it is a decline, a slow loss of vitality, a thinning of the blood. She will ultimately die, that is all."

"My heart is sore for you, my friend," Franklin said. "I beseech you, don't let my words turn you to this charlatan on her behalf—"

"I'd employ the devil himself, if God fails!" broke out Vergennes with sudden heat. "Can I see my child die and not exhaust every means? Who is the man?"

"An Italian, I understand. The Marquis di Pellegrini, who claims to be head of the Rosicrucian order and initiate of all the mysteries of Egypt." Franklin rose, with a shrug. "They say he manufactures gold, whitens diamonds, turns cotton into silk, and brings the dead to life. Accept the advice of an old man, and have nothing to do with him."

Franklin took his departure.

VERGENNES SAT plunged in thoughts of gloom. The first man in France, envied, respected and obeyed on all sides, of practically supreme power, he was by no means happy. Death was in his own house, a slow and lingering death. And death, of another sort but equally certain, was striking at his reins of power.

For France, he could see nothing ahead but bankruptcy. He

had furnished the giddy queen uncounted millions; already she was being nicknamed "Madame la Deficit." More money had gone to the rebellious colonies in America. Pledging the credit of France, he had borrowed heavily on all sides, at constantly rising interest rates. The war with England had shoved him out above a bottomless pit.

Now he had to pay the piper. There was no escape.

Suddenly came a knock. A lackey swung open the doors and spoke inquiringly.

"Monsieur, a Colonel Desmond seeks admission."

"Desmond!" Vergennes straightened up in his chair. "Admit him, admit him! And let no one disturb us. Desmond, of all people!"

Desmond walked in and bowed profoundly. Vergennes ignored the bow, gripped him by the hand, all but embraced him.

"Upon my word! I thought you dead in England, until I had word from l'Isle in Brussels of your safety! Come, sit down, make yourself comfortable. There's no man I'd sooner see just now. What news?"

Desmond's eyes twinkled. His black hair was powdered; he wore a court suit of flowered silk, a jeweled rapier, the finest lace imaginable. He was, to all appearance, the gayest of the gay fops who thronged the corridors of Versailles.

"Oh, I've news to burn," he said cheerfully. "But first, I must ask a favor."

"More money?" Vergennes asked with resignation.

"Devil a bit. I want the Vicomte de St. Vrain restored to his estates and title, with a free pardon for all past offenses."

"*Mon Dieu!* My friend, are you out of your mind?" exclaimed Vergennes. "The king has once before flatly refused. This man is a galley slave. His crimes—"

"Bah! God forgives sins; therefore Louis XVI can forgive crimes."

"The argument might appeal to him. I hadn't thought of it."

Vergennes smiled. "I fear it's useless, Desmond. His Majesty is stubborn."

"So am I," said Desmond blithely. He sat down. From beneath his waistcoat he produced a flat silk wallet, crammed with papers, and began to sort them over.

"You sent word from Brussels that you hoped to learn something about England's projected commercial treaty. You were very ill, I hear. What happened?"

"Oh, a magician brought me back to life." And Desmond laughed. "The treaty? Yes, of course. I have it here, or rather, its terms."

"Good Lord! You have it?" gasped Vergennes. "Give it to me, this instant! I must take immediate action—"

Desmond looked up coolly. "My dear Vergennes, I'm no lackey."

"What?" The minister's brows drew down. "Desmond, don't forget yourself. You're in my service. No matter how valuable you are—"

"That's your mistake," said Desmond, and leaned back in his chair. "I serve France, not you. Shall we argue the matter?"

"Damnation! Of course not." The other's face cleared. "Pardon me. I'm torn by a thousand hooks in every direction, my dear fellow."

"You do look a bit worn," Desmond said critically.

"Thanks," was the ironic response. "What was it you said about a magician?"

"Oh, a real one, I assure you! An Italian, I believe; he has a charming wife, whose eyes are like those of an angel in hell, if you can imagine such a thing. By the way," and Desmond spoke with more interest, "Paris is in a ferment. They say Voltaire is dying. And this man, a month ago, predicted he would be dead before June!"

Vergennes started. "Hello! It must be the same man. He's here in Paris; some Italian name—the Marquis di Pellegrini, that's it."

Desmond's brows lifted. The name was different; the man was the same, undoubtedly.

"Well, I'm a bit of a magician myself, as you should know. Tell me frankly, monsieur! What is the one thing you—which is to say, France—most need?"

Vergennes gave him a hard look. "Money. France is desperate. Within two months, I must raise a hundred millions in cash. It's an impossibility."

"So it appears to any but a magician, eh? You're a drowning man. You've piled up an enormous deficit, you've borrowed on all sides until you can borrow no more. Would you care to have a loan of five billions at not over three per cent—in cold cash?"

Vergennes flushed angrily.

"Colonel Desmond, I advise you not to presume too far upon my good nature and your own valuable services. I do not relish insolence, or what is worse, a jest of such description."

"Faith, I don't blame you," Desmond retorted amiably. "I have in my pocket the offer of such a loan, guaranteed by the bankers Salomon of Cologne and Rothstein of Dresden."

THE FACE of Vergennes slowly whitened, as his eyes burned into Desmond. His slim, polished fingers gripped the desk before him.

"*Mon Dieu!* You would not dare jest—no, you are in earnest," he murmured. "Salomon, Rothstein—the two greatest bankers in Germany! Is this true? Is it true? Let me have it; let me see it—"

"No," said Desmond coolly. "If you remember, you once before made me a promise in regard to the Vicomte de St. Vrain. Your promise was of no avail. The king refused. This time I'll take no chances. Thanks to St. Vrain, I'm here with this loan for you. You have secretaries who can write. The king is not far away—in his workshop filing locks and keys, no doubt."

Vergennes sat back in his chair, loosened the lace at his throat, and stared.

"You're the most damnable, imperturbable, cold-blooded and insolent scoundrel on the face of this earth!" he burst out. Then he rose. "I'll be back in half an hour; His Majesty can't refuse, in view of all this. Make yourself at home. You would, anyhow. Is there anything I can have sent you?"

"A light, if you please," said Desmond, getting out a pipe and a twist of tobacco. Vergennes grimaced and went hastily out of the room, calling his secretaries.

Half an hour passed. Footsteps sounded, and voices. Vergennes came back into the room, breathing hard, flustered and agitated.

"*Diable!* It's done. And God help you if you've played any tricks. The document is signed and is now being sealed. Are you content?"

Desmond, who was standing, bowed deeply. The time for impudence had passed.

Another fifteen minutes and their business was finished. Desmond leaned back and looked at the man before him. Transfigured, looking ten years younger, the minister had regained his vigor and assurance.

"Colonel Desmond, what can I do for you?" said Vergennes abruptly. "A title, a pension, a step in rank—France owes you anything you ask."

"Faith, you might make peace with England!" Desmond laughed, then started slightly. "Oh, I forgot! Yes, there's something I do want. An introduction to this American envoy, Doctor Franklin."

"Of course." Vergennes gestured impatiently. "But of greater things—"

"There's nothing greater, thanks," Desmond replied thoughtfully. "My work's close to an end, monsieur. I was valuable to France, only when I remained unknown; but this time my identity has been pierced. I'm known to be Monsieur Feufollet. With your permission I'd like to enjoy a vacation—safely inside France,"

The minister eyed him speculatively.

"H'm! I foresee that this is the prelude to something singular."

Desmond smiled. "I hope to spend a week or more in Paris, but shall hardly have the pleasure of seeing you again, monsieur, unless you have need of me. Then I propose going to Brittany and the west coast. If I mistake not, His Majesty has what are euphemistically known as two royal chateaux, which in common parlance are two royal prisons. One, the Bastille, which is here in Paris. The other, Mont St. Michel, called the Bastille of the Ocean, is an island off the Breton coast. Am I correct in thinking that a *lettre de cachet* may be issued consigning a person to either of these royal prisons?"

"You are," said the minister, now intently absorbed in what Desmond was saying.

"I may be worthy of your confidence to such an extent," went on Desmond gravely, "as to request two *lettres de cachet*, in blank, and also the power of arrest in general. This, with my present commission as your direct agent, should give me a rather enviable position in the provinces."

"It should make you one of the most powerful men in France," said Vergennes dryly. He opened a drawer of his desk, took out a small iron box, and from this box drew two printed forms of the *lettre de cachet*. Picking up a quill, he filled them in with the name of Mont St. Michel and countersigned them; they were already signed by the king. He pushed them toward Desmond. "The powers you request, with the letter to Doctor Franklin, will reach you this evening at your lodgings in the Rue Du Bac. Is this proof of confidence sufficient for me to ask you a very obvious question in return?"

Desmond picked up the printed forms. His eyes were sparkling.

"You mean, the identity of the two persons to be immured in the royal prison? I don't know, frankly; this is merely a precaution. I've received positive information that the army now gathering in the west to invade England, will not cross the Channel. Some very definite scheme is under way by agents of the enemy."

The minister started slightly.

"Oh! Spies, eh?"

"More than mere spies, I believe. Much more. I know nothing definite yet."

"DESMOND, THAT army is the agony of France—I had almost said, the death agony," and Vergennes resumed his look of intense anxiety. "We've poured into it every resource, we've staked everything on it—not only for the invasion of England, mind you! To hold Europe at bay. The countries around us, Austria, Prussia, the German states, are waiting to leap at the throat of France. Our queen is an Austrian, yes; that makes no difference. With this army in her hand, a superb weapon, a very thunderbolt. France is like a man with a whip amid a pack of dogs who hate but fear him."

"I've heard a lot about this army. What has it done?" Desmond asked dryly.

"Nothing. Five months inactive, spoiling, rotting. The navy does nothing. Maurepas, minister of the marine, hesitates and shrinks from action. The Army of Brittany has not moved. We've decided now on a fleet and expedition to England in July. Will it go through or be blocked? I cannot say."

"Strange talk for the minister who rules France," commented Desmond bluntly.

The other threw out his hands in a helpless gesture. Then he began to fumble in his waistcoat pockets, and in other pockets.

"The weather's against us; lack of supplies; an epidemic of sickness and disease; one thing after another. General de Castries, in command, is an admirable soldier. So is his second, the Chevalier de Boufflers. You know them both, I think. Yes, yes, your work lies there, Desmond! Save that army, and you save France. Save the army from what? I don't know. English agents, court intrigue, a dozen things! Some damnable influence is at work there. Go, by all means! Confound it, I must have left my snuffbox where I talked with His Majesty—"

"Do me the honor of accepting mine." Desmond extended his handsome souvenir. "True, it's English snuff, but I value the box as a gift from the gentleman whose portrait it bears."

Vergennes helped himself, delicately, then regarded the box admiringly. As he recognized the portrait of George III, he shot Desmond a startled glance.

"My dear fellow, I'm well aware that you fly high—do you mean to say that you met the king?"

"Yes, I supped with him." Desmond chuckled and came to his feet. "Well, I'm off. Have you any commands?"

"I'd like you to appear at court," said Vergennes. "His Majesty would be pleased to see you again—"

Desmond shook a finger in swift negation.

"No, no! Prominence would ruin me for any useful work in future. As Monsieur Feufollet, I've resigned from the service. But, as Colonel Brian Desmond, I shall apply myself to rooting out this cancerous growth of spies and enemy agents here and in Brittany. The most able is, of course, Lady Warr. I think you know her."

Vergennes nodded. "A charming woman. A dangerous enemy."

"It was she who planned the loan for England—now at the service of France. I gave her a safe-conduct into France," Desmond observed.

"You did? Why?"

"To find her, and through her, the spies at her command. Will you have the goodness to order reports sent me the moment any trace of her turns up?"

"Gladly."

"She may be in Paris by this time; hard to say," Desmond said thoughtfully. "I did not make a rapid trip myself. My papers were too precious for me to take more chances. Those two bankers are no doubt safely at home in Cologne and Dresden by this time, and you should be able to get in touch with their correspondents here at once. By the way, the document in regard to St. Vrain?"

"It should be in the hands of my secretary now, sealed. I'll go with you."

Five minutes later, with St. Vrain's pardon in his pocket, Desmond climbed into his waiting carriage and shook the dust of Versailles from his feet. He disliked with all his heart this artificial place.

As the horses trotted toward Paris, he gazed out at the countryside, at the distant heights of Passy, and untold relief held him in luxurious content. He had just now accomplished a really remarkable thing, quietly and without the fact being realized. He had destroyed the most powerful diplomatic servant of France, the mysterious personage dreaded in half the courts of Europe, the flitting, unseen secret agent who was known only as Monsieur Feufollet.

"And I hope he never has to come back to life anew!" Desmond murmured complacently. "It's too damned risky, begad!"

The coach lurched. He pitched forward and recovered his seat, as it halted with the brakes grinding. Alongside flashed a rider—a courier in the blue and silver of the royal household, who leaned far over as Desmond swung open the window.

"Colonel Desmond? I was sent to bring you back instantly."

"Back? By whom?"

"By the Count de Vergennes, monsieur."

BACK, THEN... back to the long stone-flagged courtyard, back to the anterooms, back to the study of the minister himself. It was empty. The secretary who conducted Desmond in was agitated and stammering excuses. Desmond turned to him.

"Come! What's happened?"

"Heaven knows, monsieur!" exclaimed the pale and anxious

secretary. "Couriers arrived; one was from Paris, one was from the north, I think from Brussels. Perhaps it is his daughter."

Desmond frowned. "His daughter? What the devil has that to do with me?"

"Pardon, monsieur; I forgot you had been away. His daughter is desperately ill, has been in a decline for a long time. Poor Monsieur de Vergennes is like a madman at times. They say she cannot be cured, that there is no hope for her. See, this is the child."

The secretary took from the desk a miniature that lay face down. Desmond regarded it attentively. He noted a singular sweetness in the face; a child of perhaps thirteen, with the peculiar far-away expression that some children have, as though they see things, hear things, beyond the eyes and ears of ordinary mortals.

"Yes, it must have been bad news from her," murmured the secretary. "Will you be seated, monsieur? He must be close by."

Desmond laid down the miniature, unwitting that thus fate was in his hand and out again. His thoughts were not upon children, however sad and lovely. A moment later he swung around at clicking heels, as Vergennes burst into the room— flushed, disordered, wig awry.

"Ah! You are back!" The minister halted and blinked rapidly at Desmond. "Well, I do not blame you. It is not your fault. It happened while you were on the way here. That accursed Englishwoman! A swift courier from Brussels brought the news five minutes after you were here. I called you back. It was she, it was she! Lord Stormont had come to Brussels—Stormont, do you understand? He's been placed in charge of espionage work. He came to Brussels. And that woman—"

The almost incoherent words, the flushed and apoplectic visage of the man, were startling.

"What woman?" Desmond curtly demanded.

"Lady Warr, Lady Warr! I tell you, she has the brains of the devil himself!"

"Well, what has she done? I left her on the highway, bound for France."

"And she went back to Brussels. And what did she do, this woman, this creature who can command the whole resources and power of England and her German king? This, this!" Almost beside himself, Vergennes slapped a paper that was in his hand. "England has the German states under her thumb. They do as she commands—as this woman commands! Here, read it for yourself."

Desmond snatched at the paper, opened it, and read. His face whitened under the impact of the blow.

Salomon and Rothstein, the bankers of Cologne and Dresden, would not make that loan now; their signatures were worthless. They had crossed safely into Germany, and they had died there. They and their servants together—robbed, murdered, put out of the way.

"Clever woman!" exclaimed Vergennes hotly. "Clever she-devil, rather! And once more, France faces bankruptcy. That woman—that woman! And you gave her safe-conduct into France! Well, I shall revoke it. That woman must die, do you understand? We're dealing with assassins—"

"Wait." Desmond's cold, penetrating voice stilled the excited outburst. "She's not that kind. I know her well. I know Sir Edward Hope; he's not that kind. These people are honorable—"

"Bah! Would you say this thing was an accident, then?" shot out Vergennes with bitter sarcasm.

"Not in the least. It was an assassination, of course; but she didn't instigate it. We all have servants, monsieur, who do not share our own notions of honor. England has this man Constant—able, brilliant, unscrupulous, himself an assassin. This is his work."

"And your work is to root this deviltry out of France! Set about it. And mind you, I order that this Lady Jane Warr be removed—killed, imprisoned, what you like. Removed, do you understand?"

Desmond bowed. "Allow me to point out something you overlooked. You still have the signed agreement. You have the treaty terms. There are other bankers. Well, get to work! All these big German houses have agents in Paris. Act!"

"You are right," murmured Vergennes. He passed a hand across his brow. "*Diable!* I am torn in a thousand directions—my daughter—well, well, life is like that! Yes, you're right, Desmond. Go, and send me back word that this accursed woman is dead."

Desmond departed. He had promised nothing, but he had his orders....

B Y A singular and even ironic quirk of destiny, the same hour that witnessed Desmond's interview with the minister of France, witnessed a somewhat similar interview in a room of the British envoy's residence in Brussels.

Sir Edward Hope, more damaged by his surgeon than by Desmond's sword point, lay propped up in bed. Lord Stormont, his aristocratic features set angrily, sat by the window and said nothing. Lady Jane Warr was doing the talking, and plenty of it. By the door, wearing an expression of resignation, stood Constant, his pale gray eyes flitting from one face to another. As Jane Warr paused, he spoke very humbly.

"My lady, I thought I was obeying orders. You ordered me to bring back those two bankers, true; you also said that they must not reach their destination. I had to pick my own way—"

"You picked it for the last time," said the girl, white with anger. "I refuse to be associated with anyone who makes a steady practice of murder and assassination. My Lord Stormont, you've heard all that I have to say regarding this man and what he has done in the past. You know what he has just now done. England may dispense with his services or with mine, this very moment."

"What have you to say, Constant?" asked Lord Stormont coldly.

"Nothing Milord," Constant replied. "I've put afoot great things in France. I've served well. I've brought to light the identity of this Monsieur Feufollet; and so help me, I'll see that man dead whether or not I serve England! If you want to turn me off, I have nothing to say,"

"England," said Stormont, "does not deal in assassination, my man. Obtain your wages and a hundred pounds extra from my secretary, in half an hour. You may go."

Constant touched his forehead, turned, and with one flash of his gray eyes at Jane Warr, stumped out of the room. The door closed.

"Faugh! The air was unclean," said Lord Stormont. His face warmed, his eyes kindled, and he smiled suddenly. "My dear Jane, are you satisfied?"

"A woman may be content, but never satisfied, egad!" put in Sir Edward, with a laugh.

Jane Warr's flashing smile leaped out.

"At least, I'm tremendously relieved," she exclaimed. "Aside from all other considerations, the death of those two men was a frightful error. While they were alive, the whole matter of the loan could have been settled properly, under the right pressure. Now, France can negotiate elsewhere."

"And will do so," said Stormont, with a nod. He frowned again. "Fitzgerald—Desmond—Monsieur Feufollet! That man must be removed. You, Lady Jane, must remove him. Go on to Paris and Brittany—"

"One moment, if you please," she intervened. "You forget. I have put other things in train. If you want Colonel Desmond removed, get someone else to do it. I shall carry out the work in Brittany, yes. More important still is the matter of getting Vergennes into our power, under our control. This, as I've shown you, can be done. Constant has already got everything moving smoothly in Brittany. For this, I am no more than a paymaster and collector of information. The great stroke is—Vergennes!"

"Yes," agreed Stormont. "Once he becomes as putty in the hands of this Cagliostro, or whatever the fellow calls himself, history will change rapidly. Meantime, however, I insist that Monsieur Feufollet be removed. And, my dear Lady Jane, I do not mean killed. I mean put into our hands, clapped away safely. You alone know him. You can do this, and you must. For England."

"I—I cannot," she said in a low voice. The light died out of her eyes. "Don't ask it, I implore you!"

"I don't ask it," Stormont said. "I demand it. Not I, but England, demands it. Why, Jane, the man's a positive menace! You're able to cope with him, you know him personally; you have an advantage no one else possesses. He plays ducks and drakes with all Europe, but you can handle him, and must."

"He's a gentleman, Stormont," she objected.

The other shrugged.

"So am I. Also, I'm an Englishman, my dear. You're the one person who can do this work; do it. Set your personal feelings aside. This is something higher, greater, more vital! The rebellion in the Colonies is of no moment. True, Burgoyne surrendered and gave them a momentary advantage, but within a few months this General Washington and his ragged rebels will be wiped out. The real crisis is here in Europe—and whether England wins or loses, is in your hands. This Will o' the Wisp must be removed at all costs, and you must do it. I think there's no more to be said."

Jane Warr bowed her head. "There's no more to be said," she agreed at last.

CHAPTER XII

THE DARK HOUSE

DESMOND HAD an apartment in the Rue du Bac, on the left bank, convenient to all sections of Paris. Here St. Vrain was domiciled with him. Although taken up with the legal details of repossessing his estates, St. Vrain had no intention whatever of leaving Desmond for the present.

The days passed, with Desmond busily at work and producing no results. At first it was impossible to transact any business, for Paris was in a turmoil from high to low. The death of Voltaire, the funeral of Voltaire with its scandalous details, convulsed the entire city. The popular hero, whose pen if not his actions had made his name a synonym for democracy and liberty, was dead and gone his way; his thin old hand remained deathless.

Desmond had St. Vrain at work, had a dozen more men at work, and was at work himself. The various embassies were under constant watch, as were the coffee houses. The barriers of Paris, which closed every avenue in and out of the city, sent daily reports to him. The police of the metropolis gave him every assistance. Yet Desmond drew blank. No sign of Constant, no indication of Jane Warr, came from anywhere. Jane had not made use of the safe-conduct, therefore. If she were in Paris, it was under another name.

The Marquis di Pellegrini had been located without difficulty. It was curious that Pellegrini had arrived in Paris with some ostentation, had made himself greatly talked about for a few days, then had suddenly changed lodgings and dropped out of sight.

"If you're hunting spies at work in the west, why not go west?" drawled St. Vrain, from whom Desmond now had no secrets. It was late in the morning, and Desmond was dressing with his usual scrupulous care.

"Because Paris is the nerve-center of all activity," replied Desmond. "Pellegrini is stopping at a small tavern across the river, behind the Palais Royale. Apparently he's doing nothing and has no visitors. Never mind, we'll trip them yet!"

"And meantime, the lady and the one-legged man are lost to sight."

"Quite so." Desmond adjusted the lace at his throat. "I doubt whether Constant is here. If he knew about the plan to disorganize the army, he must have a share in it. He'd not be working with Lady Warr; and yet, one never can tell. She distrusts him, while he hates her for rescuing me from his hands. I'm afraid of that man's hatred for her, St. Vrain! Well, how go your own affairs? The estates?"

"Oh, well enough," St. Vrain said carelessly. "I thought we might go there as a base; the chateau is in Brittany, you know, just south of Pontorson, but my lawyer told me yesterday that the place has been leased to the end of the year, and to break the lease would cause no end of trouble and red tape. The money's been turned over to me, so I may as well forget it. Deuced gloomy old hell-hole, anyway."

"Pontorson, you say?" Desmond frowned slightly. "Why, that's close to Mont St. Michel, isn't it?"

St. Vrain nodded. "It's the hamlet from which one gains the Mont, yes. The chateau is a few miles south, on the shore of the bay. Why an Italian would want to occupy the place is more than I can see."

"An Italian?" Desmond swung around. "What Italian?"

St. Vrain grinned. "Oh, not your magician, be sure of that! Some merchant prince, a friend of Baron Deaurevel of Castries' staff, who has sent his own servants and family there. His name is Giuseppe Balsamo."

"Whose servants and family?" queried Desmond dryly. "The baron's?"

"No, no; Balsamo's," and St. Vrain laughed. "Hello—one of your confounded spies."

A knock. A man entered, and saluted Desmond. It was the man who had been watching Pellegrini.

"Nothing to report, monsieur," he said. "He had no visitors yesterday; he left the inn only twice, once to buy handkerchiefs and lace at a shop, once to stroll through the streets for half an hour. He spoke to no one."

"What shop was it?" said Desmond idly. "Do not forget that details may be important."

"A shop in the Rue St. Honoré, close by, where fine Flemish

and Holland laces are sold. A little place, opened last month and doing a good business."

Desmond stood motionless for an instant. Through his mind flashed the memory of Cagliostro, of the lovely, sad-eyed woman who was Cagliostro's wife.

"Tell me," he said quickly. "Something I forgot. Pellegrini has a lady with him? His carriage is kept at the inn?"

"No, monsieur," said the spy. "He has no carriage. He is quite alone. He has not even a lackey."

"Give me the address of that shop…. Good. You may go."

THE MAN departed. Desmond turned, his blue eyes dancing, his face alight. "I'm of to Passy. My audience with Doctor Franklin was arranged for today. My friend, your linen is in a deplorable condition. The Vicomte de St. Vrain has money to spend, and must at once provide himself with the finest lace obtainable."

"Eh?" exclaimed St. Vrain, puzzled. "Why, I bought some Venetian point only yesterday, and my linen's new—"

"Mechlin, St. Vrain!" exclaimed Desmond. "You must have Mechlin lace; it's all the fashion. Why, man, don't you see? That shop, of course! We've hit it. Pellegrini is all alone, inactive. Why? I don't know. But he buys lace. There's the go-between. Put a man to watch that shop. Watch it yourself, for an hour, and check all visitors. Then go in and buy lace, and be fastidious about it. I should be back by then and will meet you there."

St. Vrain grunted. "You may be right. Haul some poor devil of a spy off to prison? I don't like that job."

"Devil take the spy! Lady Warr's in Paris, I'll stake my life on it, arranging all details, getting reports, making ready to work with Cagliostro. She's in touch with him through that shop, and he with her. It's the clearing-house for all English operations here."

"You jump damnably at conclusions," grumbled the other, rising. "All right. Next thing, you'll be wanting me to buy handkerchiefs."

"I haven't seen you show off any."

"Bah! In the galleys, a man learns to blow his nose on his thumb." And with a laugh, St. Vrain was out and gone.

Desmond presently gained the street, where a hired carriage was waiting, and started for Passy, on his errand for the King of England. His thoughts of Jane Warr, of that kiss in the dark, of her hand at his neck, pricked him hard. He had to find her, for his own peace of mind more than for the work to which he had set himself. And now he felt that he was on the track. Inaction here irked him, but it was the wisest course; he could not start for the West until he had picked up some thread to follow.

Cagliostro? That man was no more than an English tool, and not a spy; Desmond thought lightly of him, and not ungratefully. He had not even bothered to make certain that Pellegrini was the same man, this he took for granted. His brain, almost subconsciously, busied itself with Constant, and as the carriage jolted over the cobbles across the river and along the quays toward the heights of Passy, he thought again of that scene in the inn at Louvain, and Constant's offer to betray the English schemes in Brittany. Queer, he reflected, that this man of iron should have been so weak.

Weak? Desmond started slightly. Had he been wrong all this while? Had he leaped too swiftly at conclusions? Constant was acutely shrewd and farsighted; his dogged determination to drag down Monsieur Feufollet had become an obsession, a personal matter of dark hatred. Perhaps, in uttering those words, he had not been at all careless.

Had he, then, in truth, in the bitter moment when he stood against the wall facing death, still looked forward to the future and striven to attract Desmond into the circle of activity of that future? Yet this seemed so far-fetched and unlikely that Desmond dismissed the whole matter with a shrug.

His carriage curved into the drive of the old Hotel de Valentinois. Other carriages were here, people were about in crowds. This was one of the busiest spots in Paris, with American ship captains, office seekers, Parisian merchants and exporters, thronging it. Secretaries, messengers and flunkeys were in action.

Desmond cooled his heels for a time, then was summoned. Alone in the quietly ordered study, he bowed to the old man with sparse white locks, who inspected him with a smile.

"Well, Colonel Desmond? Vergennes speaks most highly of you. I hope you're not one of these soldiers of fortune who seek a fortune and future that America cannot offer?"

Desmond laughed. "I seek nothing, Doctor Franklin, except to deliver a letter that was entrusted to me in London. Here it is."

His mission was accomplished.

Franklin donned his spectacles, read the letter without mention of its broken seal, and lifted his shrewd blue eyes to those of Desmond in some astonishment.

"I cannot understand this at all," he said slowly. "It cannot be a jest; either these words were written in mockery or in tragedy. I never heard of any Count von Weissenstein in London. And the letter says that the bearer is Colonel Fitzgerald, which is not your name."

"It was the name I used in London," said Desmond quietly. "Count von Weissenstein himself gave me that letter. He also presented me with this snuffbox, which bears his portrait."

FRANKLIN TOOK the jeweled snuffbox, glanced at it, and his face changed. For a long moment he sat motionless, then picked up the letter and read it again. He let it fall with a sigh, but it was a sigh of eagerness. Desmond had the fleeting impression of a benignant old gentleman whose cast iron jaw belied his general appearance, and whose eyes could bite harder than the jaw.

"A most amazing thing!" Franklin murmured. "Meet him in Brussels in June—why, bless me, this is June now! There's barely time to get word back to him in London. Yes, of course I must do it. But first I must write him in plain words the position of the Colonies. What a chance, what a chance! To put before King George of England, in words addressed to Weissenstein, exactly our attitude!" He glanced up sharply. "Do you carry any reply to this letter, sir?"

"No; I've done my errand," Desmond answered. "If you'd be so kind, I would like some brief acknowledgment that you've received the letter. This I may send to Lord Stormont, through whom I met Weissenstein; and so far as I'm concerned the matter is then ended. If you'll write Weissenstein in care of Lord Stormont, the meeting can be arranged."

"Yes, of course. Who broke the seal? Does Vergennes know of it?"

"No. It was broken by an English agent who captured some of my papers en route. It was then returned to me."

"I see. H'm! I must consult Vergennes about this. Oh, yes, the receipt, of course! At once, sir. And I offer you my thanks for your great kindness."

Franklin reached for a quill and a sheet of paper. His hand was shaking with excitement, as he scribbled a brief acknowledgment and then handed the sheet of paper to Desmond. Then a sharp exclamation broke from him.

"Oh, one moment, one moment! Bless me, it's the very name, of course it is! Here, sir, this must be for you. It reached us several days ago and we've been unable to understand it. Yours, of course."

Fumbling through a drawer of the desk, he handed Desmond a sealed letter addressed to him in care of Doctor Franklin. Astonished, Desmond looked at it blankly, and with a word of apology tore it open. He found brief but startling information:

My dear: I'm glad you got away safely. You'll be glad to know that C. has been dismissed from the service. There gladness ends. Truce ends. When we meet again, there's no mercy. I am England, you are France. Remember it. I am now
Your Enemy.

His heart leaped. Jane, of course! She knew of his letter to Franklin. So she had sent this note here, by messenger. She must, therefore, be in Paris. He looked up, with so joyous a face that Franklin broke into a slow smile.

"No bad news, evidently, and a lady's writing—h'm! Congratulations, Colonel Desmond, and my renewed thanks."

"And mine to you, sir. Most hearty ones, begad!"

Desmond departed, stepping on air, his eyes alight.

Once in his carriage, he folded the sheet of paper on which Franklin had written. A black smear caught his eye, printing, a huge shell and cross-bones. He looked at it curiously. On the reverse side was one of the usual flaring invitation to "funeral pomp" issued by French funeral parlors. This was to the funeral of Voltaire.

"The old rascal! He didn't pick up this paper by chance, then—sending the King of England an invitation to Voltaire's funeral!" Desmond chuckled. Then he turned to Jane's note and read it again. His smile faded. "Constant dismissed—good! I'm glad Jane's out of his way now. There was virulent hatred of her in his voice, that night. But—"

Gladness ends, aye. They were enemies; he was even now hunting her down, and not for love's sake either. What would he do when he found her? He did not know; he refused to think about it now. The queer, childish frankness of her words fascinated him. They were not written in whimsy, he now realized, but in stark and terrible earnest. This was a warning to expect only one thing from her—enmity. She was here. She was hunting him, as he was hunting her. He could read behind these words. What she deemed her bitter duty, she would do.

"Bah! Things will work out somehow." He dismissed gloomy thoughts as he left his carriage in the Rue St. Honoré. His spirits soared again; he was once more blithe and debonair, careless of what the future might hold, confident.

THE LACE shop was a tiny little place, one of the mercantile establishments crowding into this street of lordly houses and old mansions, the "hotels" of the great families giving place to newcomers.

Desmond walked in. He found St. Vrain inside, talking with the shopman, a thin fellow who claimed to be a Fleming. Greeting his friend, Desmond bought a few handkerchiefs and they passed out to the street together.

"*Diable!* You look different!" St. Vrain exclaimed.

Desmond broke into a laugh. "No wonder. Did you have any luck in there?"

"Admirable luck," replied St. Vrain. "A lackey from the Prussian embassy called and left a package. The fool was clumsy with it. I had a glimpse, just a flash. The name of Warr, and an address in the Rue St. Dominique. I failed to get the number."

"Then I was right about her. Here, read this note!"

St. Vrain complied, and passed it back. "Constant out of the game? Excellent. Your lady is a jewel. I fear that this is a warning to be respected, my friend. Not joy wrote those words, but heartbreak and duty. She's out to get you now."

"That's nothing new," Desmond said gayly. "Once things start breaking, they break all along the line; wait and see. I'll tip off the police and Vergennes about that shop, and goodby to one spy! Or I may reach Lady Warr through that Fleming. Another day or two, and we'll have something definite. Then off for the west, and to work!"

They sauntered on across to the left bank and the Rue du Bac.

Upon approaching his own lodgings, Desmond noted a man loitering in the street, a fellow shabbily clad and of ill-favored visage. The man came up to them and spoke to him in a whine.

"M. le Colonel Desmond? May I have a word in private, monsieur?"

At a gesture from Desmond, St. Vrain went on.

"Well? How do you know me and what do you want?"

The fellow grinned. "A message, monsieur. If you're free

tonight at nine, I'll meet you and take you to someone whom you may want to see."

Desmond frowned, instantly suspicious and wary.

"Speak plainly or begone to the devil. Who sent you?"

"A lady, monsieur." The man lowered his voice, speaking as though reluctantly. "I do not know her name; I heard her called Miladi Jeanne."

A swift thrill swept Desmond and flung his suspicions aside.

"Jeanne? Perhaps you mean Jane?" He gave the word its English pronunciation.

"That's it, monsieur, that's it."

"Where is she? What's her address?"

The other shook his head. "I can't tell you that; strict orders. It's not far from here, though. In the Rue St. Dominique. Yes or no?"

The name of this street was enough, taken in conjunction with what St. Vrain had learned in the lace shop.

Desmond's brain leaped at the explanation. She was not sure he had received that note of warning; she wanted to see him, speak to him in person, settle frankly and honorably this future in which they were to be enemies and nothing else. Good!

"Yes, of course," Desmond rejoined, even as he played with these reflections. This man, obviously, was some gutter rat who did not disdain English money. Perhaps the Rue St. Dominique housed all the English spies in Paris. "You'll come here?"

"I'll be waiting here at nine, monsieur."

Flinging the man a coin, Desmond went on to join St. Vrain, in the entrance to their lodgings.

"Ha, comrade!" he exclaimed joyously. "Good news from that rascal. I'm to see her tonight."

St. Vrain twitched his sardonic lip.

"Indeed? An Englishwoman? You're not playing with fire, but with ice; that's risky," he grumbled, as they ascended the stairs. "I don't know about this. Where is she?"

"He wouldn't say, except that it was in Rue St. Dominique."

"Oh! Then you're probably in luck; that changes things. And we know Constant is out of the picture. Yes, I imagine your luck has altered…. Hello! Look there! Here's your fox back again."

Before the door of Desmond's rooms waited the man who was shadowing Pellegrini.

BEYOND A greeting, no words passed until they were inside and the door closed. Then, breathless and eager, the spy imparted his news.

"Monsieur, no complaints of me this time, I hope! He went out at noon. I followed him to the Hotel des Postes, and inside. I was at his elbow when he inquired about stagecoaches, diligence for the west. There are two, one at daybreak, the other toward noon.

"He turned away and went back to the inn, and to his room. I was drinking inside, twenty minutes later, when he came downstairs and paid his score. He is leaving in the morning. He sent a groom on an errand, and I followed. The groom went to the Hotel des Postes and reserved two places in the diligence of daybreak. Two places as far as the city of Rennes."

"For Pellegrini, eh?" said Desmond with keen interest.

"No, monsieur," and the spy grimaced. "There is no such name on the list of reservations. To make sure, I obtained a copy of the list. Here it is."

He handed over a grimy scrap of paper. Desmond glanced at the list of names. Only one of them meant anything to him, but this one meant such incredible things that he started, lifted amazed eyes to St. Vrain—then checked himself and recovered his composure. Taking out a gold louis, he handed it to the spy.

"You've done well." Excitement shook in his voice. "Tell the others to report here before nine tonight and get their pay. The work's ended, and I'm leaving Paris tomorrow. You, however, be on hand when that diligence leaves at daybreak. Names mean nothing; I want you to note every passenger with care, then come straight here and describe them."

"Understood, monsieur."

The man took his leave.

When the door closed, Desmond swung around and thrust the list at St. Vrain, his blue eyes alight.

"What did I tell you? Now we've got everything. Look at it, man, look at it! D'you see what it means?"

"Hanged if I do." St. Vrain scowled at the list. "No Pellegrini here."

Desmond's voice rang out. "The fourth! The fourth name!"

"What? Oh—the pox take me! Why, it's Balsamo! Joseph Balsamo!"

"Precisely." Desmond laughed exultantly. "You see? The man who's occupying your old chateau! And this man is the Marquis di Pellegrini—or, if you prefer, the Count de Cagliostro. Now everything's coming clear, everything!"

St. Vrain exploded an obscene galleys-oath.

"This is plain enough, at least. What else?"

"Lady Warr is going west the quickest way, by diligence. With this Cagliostro. That's why she sent for me—the only chance for us to meet is tonight. You comprehend? She didn't know whether I had received the note or not."

St. Vrain nodded. Then his fierce, darkly saturnine eyes flashed suddenly.

"Ha, comrade! This looks bad; all kinds of chances, possibilities. Now I think of it, that scruff-wigged lawyer said my chateau had been leased for Balsamo, not by him. Leased for him, by his friend Baron Deaurevel. Giuseppe Balsamo—Joseph Balsamo, the same name! But Deaurevel is a major on the staff of the Army of Brittany. Eh! There's a possibility for you! And here's another," he added with energy. "If you want to find out what goes on in this gloomy old house, I'm your man. I spent my whole damned boyhood there. I know it as no one else does. And it has secrets, that house!"

Desmond regarded him thoughtfully.

"Interesting, yes; we'll talk of it later. Will you send and engage two places in the westbound diligence—the later one? It leaves about noon, I think. And I suppose a vicomte, homeward bound, should have a servant. What about hiring lackeys?"

"Lackeys be damned—depend on ourselves, I say," growled St. Vrain. "You don't know that rough west country. If you want servants, those Breton peasants of mine will do the job. Dark, ignorant, stubborn devils, and like all ignorant people, proud as Lucifer. But glad to serve me. You'll see."

Desmond assented with a nod. He had scant use for ceremony or for servants.

By nine that evening, his hired spies had arrived, reported, and departed with their pay, all save the one man covering Pellegrini. St. Vrain was gone on errands of his own. Desmond donned his rapier, threw a dark cloak about his shoulders, and descended to the street. His guide was waiting there, and saluted him.

They started off together. Desmond, who cared little for such company, suggested that the man give him the address and begone. His guide refused flatly.

"Your pardon, monsieur. I was told to bring you. Nor could you very easily find the place without a person to answer for you; the approach is guarded."

"Oh!" Desmond laughed in comprehension. "In such case, lead on."

The infrequent street lanterns shed but faint light. In Rue St. Dominique it was darker yet; the masses of the gray and gloomy church and convent of this name fell to the rear. So the English spy nest was well guarded, eh? Desmond laughed softly. He cared no whit about spies this night. Jane Warr little dreamed that with the morrow he would be hard on her westward trail!

The share of Cagliostro in all this, the purpose to which she would put that man of mystery, puzzled him more than anything else. For he did know definitely that she was directing Cagliostro's actions in France.

"Here we are, monsieur." The man touched Desmond's arm, speaking apologetically. "If you will permit me to lead the way...."

He turned in at the courtyard of an old and ruinous mansion. A man appeared beneath the entrance light, checked him sharply, then motioned him on. Desmond followed, conscious of the curious stare the guard directed at him.

Turning sharply to the left, he followed his guide up a darkly winding stairs. Some ancient mansion given over to lodgers, thought Desmond; an excellently safe spot from which Jane Warr could operate. Yet, with the safe-conduct he had supplied her, she should not need such precautions, being in no particular danger.

The third floor. These houses had been built in olden days, when nobles lived surrounded by scores of domestics and retainers; some of the hotels of the great families could house a hundred people or more. Here the guide halted, rapping sharply on a door. The door opened a trifle; there was a low-voiced word exchanged. Then Desmond's guide turned.

"My business is done. You are free to enter, monsieur."

Desmond stepped past him as the door swung open. He had a glimpse of a huge, high-ceiled room that revealed remnants of ancient luxury. The man holding open the door was saluting him respectfully. As he passed inside, the door was swung shut and a bolt shot home.

Then, and only then, Desmond felt a cold chill. A sound reached his ears, drifting to him past the light of the candlesconces along the walls, a sound which he thought he had dismissed forever. And as he swung around to the *tap-tap-tap,* he saw the grimly smiling face of Constant.

CHAPTER XIII

THE FLIP OF A CLOAK

D ESMOND TENSED to steel.
Trapped... The unexpected shock of finding Constant here was like a sickening blow that left him for a moment stupefied. This gave way to self-reproach. He had taken so much for granted, he himself had so fed the infernal flames of this trap, as now to waken swift hot anger in his brain—anger at himself. He had been a fool, and no word in the lexicon of Brian Desmond could be less easily forgiven.

"Quiet, monsieur!"

The man at his side presented a cocked pistol, slid his rapier from its sheath, and left him unarmed. Then he moved a pace away, and waited.

The room was thirty feet square, empty of furniture, and disused. Tatters of silk and tapestry hung from the walls. Shutters along one side, giving upon the street, were closed; those on the other, probably opening on the courtyard in the center of the old building, hung crazily ajar. Behind the looming figure of Constant showed a doorway, a wide one, concealed by hangings that were in rags. These moved a little, showing that the doors were open.

Constant, coming into the center of the room, halted. He fastened upon Desmond a look of such malevolence, such indescribable venom, that it lifted the hair upon Desmond's neck. His voice sounded, calm and composed.

"I'm not the pretty you expected to see, eh? Well, sir, she's the next to be settled with, but you come first."

Desmond hitched his cloak around and laughed lightly.

"Come, come, Constant!" he said. "You love money too well to pass the chance of it by. What's your price?"

"It don't work," said Constant grimly. "You're bound for hell here and now. Not for any money! You're done."

"What?" Again Desmond's laugh rang silvery, gay, light-hearted. "You don't think I'd come without a man or two following? No, no, Constant; you're plucked this time, my man. And you're dismissed the service now. So talk terms."

Constant snarled at him.

"Yah! It don't work. Just one thing I want from you, and that I'm going to have, and no more talk about it."

As he spoke, Constant moved slightly. Desmond caught the glint of steel. His brain raced back to those knives left on the table in Sir Edward's room, and what St. Vrain had said about them. Throwing knives....

Thought flashed, even as the quickened brain gave orders. The last snarling word was scarcely dead, the glint of steel was still showing, there in Constant's hand, as Desmond shifted his cloak again, loosened it from his throat, held it by the frogged collar in his hand, and spoke. Constant's hand was rising, was going back for the throw....

"Wait! Will you take five thousand guineas for my life, Constant?" He stepped forward quickly, eagerly, his left hand going to his pocket. "Here's the money—five thousand guineas, Constant!"

The man stood with legs extended, a peg of wood from left knee to floor, balanced. Those words checked him.

"Five thousand—guineas!" he echoed. "Five—no!" He spat out the word like an oath. "Devil take you, stand back there—"

Desmond was close. The cloak flew out from his hand, spread in the air like a black cloud, straight for the face of Constant. And with the jerk of his arm, Desmond ducked sideways. A slither of steel through the cloak; it was over his head, and he was plunging forward. His foot shot out and hooked that wooden leg.

It was fast work—and it had to be. Even before the crash of Constant's cursing fall, even before the explosion of the Frenchman's pistol, Desmond was falling—throwing himself headlong as though diving into water. He heard the whistle of the ball going over him, heard it smack into the wall, in the instant before he touched the floor. Then he was down, going straight at those slightly waving curtains, a gamble to break his neck if wood stood there.

But the doors were open.

HE CRASHED on the floor, saved his face with his arms, went plunging through ragged hangings and doorway. Over now, rolling like a cat and coming erect in a room lit by a dim candle, a squalid room with bed and food and wine smelling the air, and another door close to his hand. With a scream of fury rising behind him, he flung himself at this door and it opened into the blackness of a stairs winding down, a narrow back stairs.

Desmond took the stairs at a leap, stumbled, gained the landing below just as a door opened and men came rushing out. He smashed into them, losing his balance, staggering against one man and clutching to save himself. They lashed out at him with wild blows and oaths of alarm; that pistol-shot had roused all the place into instant action, into frantic uproar.

What happened here was impossible to say, in the confusion. Desmond, breaking clear and poising for the steps below, received a fearful blow in the groin that doubled him up. He was sent rolling head first, pitching forward and tumbling like an inert sack of grain down the stairs.

On the landing below, he brought up against a wall with a crash, perfectly conscious but helpless to move a muscle, the wind knocked out of him, bruised and agonized, a stab of pain in his right leg.

This landing was dark and silent as the grave.

Desmond struggled desperately to break his invisible chains, and could not. Momentarily, his body refused to obey the dictates of his brain. Up above, he could hear the voices of Constant. Then, descending the stairs, came that *tap-tap-tap* of the wooden leg. The thought of being caught here helpless, butchered in the dark, was horrible.

With convulsive effort, Desmond tried to move. He clawed at the wall, drew himself partly erect, and then collapsed. Something wrong with his right leg. As he went down, a low groan of despair escaped his lips. Constant was on the landing above, cursing at the men there for passage.

Something fluttered against his cheek—a hand. He could see nothing, but now someone was stooping over him, pulling at him, helping him. He came erect, but his feet dragged. He repressed a cry of pain as his right foot touched the floor. Then, mercifully, a door swung shut and the noise died away. He had been drawn into the rooms that opened off the landing.

Not a glint of light showed. Desmond leaned against the wall, gasping for breath. On the stairs and landing outside sounded the *clump-clump* of Constant, and then went on down. He had missed him!

A stir of movement close beside him, and a light step. His unseen rescuer touched him, found his hand, and drew at it with a low word.

"Come." A slim, tiny hand, this one clutching his.

Still doubled up with pain, Desmond collected himself, summoned up his will, and forced himself to move, hobbling. He was, he knew, on the first floor, the one above the street. He was still unable to speak, could scarcely drag himself along.

A door was suddenly flung open, and he was drawn into candlelight that blinded him. The slim hands pressed at him and he yielded, dropping into a chair.

He was sick, faint, agonized by that blow and by the pain in his ankle. He could think of nothing but himself as he dropped in the chair. His ankle was swelling; good! He had turned it in the fall. A day or two with a stick, nothing worse. But the deathly faintness, the giddy sickness, held him motionless and without volition. He stared dully at the dingy, filthy room, at the child before him.

A girl, a child, no more. A creature with thin pinched cheeks and great eyes fastened widely upon him. A single ragged garment half covered her, giving glimpse of bony shoulders and budding breasts. Her face was wild, eerie, distorted by fear and wonder. Desmond realized that she was speaking. Dimly, her words came to him.

In the next room, voices were disputing....

"Why, you—you're a gentleman!" she was saying, gawking as though looking at a being from another world.

Desmond tried to smile, but could not. "So it would seem." His breath came whistling. Speech was hard. He had hit and hurt his throat against something in that fall. Blood was in his mouth, trickled down as he spoke.

The girl reached forward, lifted her ragged garment, and wiped the blood from his chin, with a little sound like a groan of pity.

"The police are after you?" she said, as a matter of course. "You're safe enough now. You must stay quiet. Perhaps you can help me, too."

Desmond nodded. "You? How?"

"I don't know. I thought he might help me. The man with the wooden leg. He's the only one who has been kind—that's because he's a stranger. He never kicked me. See?"

She drew the rags aside and showed him a blackened bruise on her thin little thigh. Desmond felt an insane desire to burst into laughter. Constant, eh? The only person who had been kind to this little waif. The idea of Constant representing kindness had a wildly ludicrous touch. But why not? The man was human.

Slowly the dizziness passed, the sense of unreality passed.

"My boot. Try—" Desmond leaned forward to reach his ankle, and almost fell out of the chair. He relaxed feebly. The child went down on her knees, touched his ankle, and he groaned. She worked at the boot and loosened it, to his instant relief.

"Well enough. Leave it so, thanks. Who are you?"

"Me?" she stood up again. "I am Celie."

"Celie—what?"

"That's all. And I'm horribly afraid. Help me, please?"

"From what?"

"I don't know. Something terrible. I heard them talking; they're selling me. It's something—something terrible!"

Her voice was thin with terror. As she turned in the light, another bruise appeared across her face. Her face....

It whipped at Desmond. He was taken back in memory—this thin little face of hers clutched at him somehow. Groping, he stared at her. Some look in her eyes, something definite about her thin face, caught at him strangely.

Ah! That day when he had gone back to Versailles, had entered the office of the minister. The miniature lying on the desk—that was it! This child had the face of Vergennes' daughter. Not the exact features, perhaps, but the strange, eerie look of far away and long ago. So strong, so striking was the resemblance that Desmond fancied this thin little waif powdered and gowned like the rich noble's daughter; yes, in such case she would be the very image of the other!

POOR CHILD! He could do nothing for this little Celie. Such creatures, such children of the gutters, were like the sweeps of London; things to be bartered or even sold at will. They had no hope and no appeal.

On their behalf, only those who were rich and great and above the law, might intervene. He himself could intervene here, somehow. He must do something. This child had saved him. He must act, yes.

A dozen things he must do, all came rushing across his brain. It was too late now to get Constant. The man would know his danger, and would by this time be on his way to some safe hiding.

Desmond tried to gain his feet. He fell back into the chair, hand pressed against his side, brain awhirl. That accursed blow! Nausea gripped him. His legs seemed dead, without feeling or use.

A bleat of fear escaped Celie. A door opened, a voice rang out.

"He'll be here any minute now. The rest is your affair, not mine. I must be off—hello! Name of the devil, would you look at this!"

A man appeared, blinking and staring—a man whom Desmond recognized instantly. It was the thin Fleming, the spy, the fellow who kept the lace shop in the Rue St. Honoré. At the Fleming's startled words another man, a Frenchman, came rushing into the room. With him was a tattered, fierce-eyed woman. She cuffed the child away into a corner and stood gawking at Desmond. A chorus of growling oaths broke from all three.

"You!" Frantically, Desmond lifted a hand at the Fleming, and forced out the wavering words. "You! Get Lady Warr. Must be somewhere—this street. Lady Warr, understand? Tell her that Colonel Desmond is here…."

His brain was wakening from its lethargy. He understood that this thin Fleming, this spy, must live somewhere in the old rabbit-warren. Nothing strange about Constant being here, therefore. Constant would naturally find a refuge where other spies went to earth; no doubt he had lived here when in Paris previously. Even if he were no longer in the English service, this place would be the best and safest for him.

Desmond's words brought startled realization to the Fleming's face. He nodded. As the Frenchman flashed out a knife and an oath, the Fleming turned on him.

"Stop, you!" he cried sharply. "This is my affair; do as I say. Don't touch this man. Don't touch him, I say! I'll be back."

He turned and was gone, swiftly.

The Frenchman, the woman, glared at Desmond. The man held his knife ready, glowering, muttering oaths, finally breaking into speech. The child Celie crouched in one corner, terrified.

"How did you get here?" demanded the man, in a hoarse growl. "Out with it! Are you of the police?"

"No. No danger to you."

Desmond forgot his injuries in the necessity of appeasing this couple. He heard a sharp knocking and saw the woman dart away to answer it. Coming up out of his chair, he felt in his pocket for a coin....

A blinding stab of pain from his ankle. He fell, half across the chair-arm, and then slipped to the floor, in a dead faint.

CHAPTER XIV

DEVIL'S BROTH

VOICES, STEPS, pierced vaguely to Desmond's consciousness. The thin, shrill voice of the child, lifted in frantic terror, almost roused him, but not quite. He drifted. He felt himself being hauled about, and opened his eyes groggily. In the chair again. Another voice now, as he muttered weakly. This voice really roused him.

"What's that? For whom did he send—oh! Warr. Was it Lady Warr? Then clear out of here, quickly! Here's your money. You know what to do. Out with you!"

A voice that burned and lifted with its sonorous energy. Desmond saw a blurred shape before him; it came into focus gradually. The man was examining him, hurting him, so that he flinched. The other stepped back, and Desmond's brain cleared with a rush of incredulity, as he heard the voice afresh.

"Bah! Nothing you won't be over in a day or two, worse luck. But to find you here, here of all places, at this moment—I don't like it by half. It smacks too much of destiny at work. There's danger in you."

Desmond's eyes opened. Yes, the same man, regarding him with those same piercing, compelling eyes. Cagliostro—or a vision? No, the figure was real. Everyone else was gone, but this man remained.

"The devil! You? Cagliostro—Pellegrini—" Just in time, Desmond checked himself.

"So we meet again, Colonel Desmond!" Cagliostro spoke smoothly, suavely, with not a hint of anything except pleasure. "This time you're in no need of my services, so I'll bid you goodnight. No, you're not dreaming, as you think; but I warn you most solemnly not to cross my path again. I have read in the stars, Colonel Desmond, that—"

A knock, reiterant, loud. Cagliostro broke off, uttered a startled exclamation, and went to the candle. He extinguished it, and the room was plunged into darkness save for a faint glow from a light in the adjoining room. Then, perfect silence.

Steps and voices sounded. A man appeared, holding up a lantern; it was the Fleming. Desmond glanced around for Cagliostro, but there was no sign of him. In utter bewilderment, Desmond's gaze searched the room.

Then Jane Warr, cloaked, came quickly to him and was beside his chair. The warm touch of her hand wakened Desmond to reality.

"My dear, my dear, what on earth brought you here?" she exclaimed. "What's happened? You're hurt...."

The overwhelming relief, the joy of her presence, the sudden safety, left Desmond in a blur. Then things cleared for him. She was giving sharp orders. Two or three men with her were hastening to obey. A carriage; a surgeon. His brain came awake with a rush.

"Hold on! Where to, Jane?"

She swung around, came swiftly to him, and caught his hand. In her face he read queer agitation, coldness, resolve.

"I've no choice," she said abruptly, sharply. "You're in my hands now, Colonel Desmond. I warned you. Take advantage of you? Every advantage. We're enemies—"

"Jane!" he burst out in amazement. "One moment love on your lips, the next moment, ice in your eyes! Enemies?"

"Love on my lips? I think you were dreaming, Colonel Desmond," she said in a hard, cold voice. "Nothing of the sort. Now you're caught. You're in my power. No matter what it costs me—I do what I must. I'll get you out of here, yes. You're my prisoner and my enemy."

Her lips were white, but she meant her words. Desmond gathered himself.

"All right," he said, summoning up every energy, every force of will, to meet this sudden menace. "I appealed to you; I did not surrender. I appealed to Jane Warr, to the woman—"

"Jane Warr is not a woman, to you," she flashed out, desperately. "She's an agent of England, as you very well know."

"You lie, dear Jane, you lie!" and Desmond laughed a little. "All right; agreed. Have it your own way. And if you do so, you're lost. I have your address, in this very street. That package which came to you today from the Prussian embassy, to the lace shop— do you comprehend? At midnight, my men are arresting you, every one of you, and all your network of spies and agents. Think quickly, Jane Warr! I'll trade you safety for safety, rescue for rescue, once again! I'll call off my men, begad, if you take me home safe. If you refuse, midnight sees every one of you bagged and jailed. Choose!"

The momentary rush of energy served him well—head up, eyes aflash, he met her startled gaze. She could not know that he lied. His mention of the package from the Prussian embassy gave his words conviction and force. She stared at him for a moment, her eyes dilating, her lips half parted in startled indecision.

"So Constant is still working for you, eh?" Desmond threw in the mocking jibe, which he knew to be untrue. The bolt went home; her eyes were stricken and hurt. "He got me here. I evaded him, to fall into your hands, and you finish me, eh? Fine work, fine work! But you'll be finished, you and Cagliostro, your

Flensing, everything! Yet I'll call off the whole thing if you say the word. Friend or enemy? Choose!"

The words, the outrush of fay energy, all but cost him consciousness. But here, as in the luggar's cabin, he bluffed her, tricked her, mastered her. She had a vision of everything to gain or lose—and she broke.

"Cagliostro!" she muttered. "Then—then it's true! You do know—"

"Everything," said Desmond. "Everything! I'll bargain with you. I'll give you until noon tomorrow. You, Cagliostro, everyone who serves you. Is it worth the price?"

She came to him, stooped, took his hand. A smile grew in her face.

"Yes, my dear," she said quietly. "It's a lovely price; I'm glad of it. I'll take you anywhere you say, have a surgeon ready—it's a bargain. Once more, for a little while, we can be friends."

Desmond felt himself slipping. He gave his address in the Rue du Bac.

"Right, my dear, right," he said. "No more gladness, eh? For this one moment, then. With noon tomorrow, enemies again. No quarter!"

"Next time, you'll not be able to buy off." And she laughed softly. "Next time, my heart breaks; but I do what I must, without flinching. Next time, no quarter! But for now, my dear, we can...."

SHE FADED out. Desmond remembered little of what happened, except the jolting of a coach and her arm around him, supporting him. He realized desperately how thoroughly she had meant to make sure of him, heartbreak or not. And he had beaten her, bluffed her, forced her to let him go.... It all vanished again with the ghost of a laugh.

Next thing he knew, St. Vrain was storming and cursing, while blinding candlelight was on everything around. He wakened to St. Vrain's furious imprecations, as a surgeon worked at him.

"You damned jackanapes, to call yourself a surgeon! Bleed him, will you? Cup him? By Heaven, I'll cut your throat if you try it, you fool! Go to the galleys and you'll learn something about surgery. Give him strength, not weakness, d'ye hear? Bandages, now. His ankle, first of all. Whew! A devil of a crack under the belt. Nothing broken, luckily. Get to work, you ass! Healing, not bleeding!"

All came clear gradually, clear and distinct. The child, Cagliostro, Jane Warr—he remembered everything. Presently, bandaged and coming around in warm comfort, Desmond swallowed the wine St. Vrain held to his lips. It put life into him. He looked around; they were alone. He was lying in bed, his own bed.

"Hello! Where is she?"

"Gone, comrade; here and gone again. *Diable!* What a flame of a woman she is! I don't blame you for being a fool about her. What happened?"

Urgency pricked at Desmond, brought him to one elbow with a rush.

"Listen! No time to waste. You've got to act. Get the police. Find that child."

St. Vrain's jaw fell as he stared "Child? What child?"

Desmond told him, sketchily, what had happened. Then, quickly enough, St. Vrain acted....

A police agent arrived, saluted at sight of Desmond's authority, received his orders and departed hastily. St. Vrain pressed for more details, chiefly in regard to Pellegrini or Cagliostro; he was interested in this man.

"Oh, he's of no great importance," Desmond rejoined. "Perhaps I was dreaming about him—no, he was real enough. But damned if he didn't disappear into thin air! Probably he was devilish silent about it. Well, did she say where to find her?"

"Who, Lady Warr? No. So it was no lovers' meeting, eh?"

Desmond grunted. He explained what had taken place. St. Vrain listened with a dark frown, and shook his head.

"Listen, comrade. That woman serves, as you serve. She's under pressure to make an end of you, one way or another. She's convinced that it's her duty. A woman can be convinced of anything if she's handled right. Now look out for her. She's dangerous. She'll finish you if it breaks her heart!"

"So I've gathered," Desmond said dryly. "Can we get away in the morning?"

"By diligence, yes; by noon, yes. You'll be all right in a couple of days. The ankle was twisted, nothing worse. That blow in the groin is bad, but it'll pass. You'd better get off to sleep and stop talking."

"Right. Waken me if any report comes about that child Celie."

In the darkness, Desmond's brain was still busy with that tormented child. The startling resemblance of her face to that of Vergennes' daughter was haunting. Her terrified words, the sinister glimpse of Cagliostro, the whole suggestion of something afoot, of some intrigue into which he had literally stumbled, intrigued and baffled him. At long last, he dropped off to sleep.

MORNING AND sunlight. A clear head, a clear memory of everything at last. Desmond wakened to find the police agent in the room, and questioned him eagerly.

"No luck, monsieur; the birds had flown. We found that the child belonged to that couple. *Canaille,* all of them—gutterbirds. Even so, it would be difficult to interfere, or to take the child from them. We are searching, and that's all I can report now."

"It's devilish little," said Desmond angrily. Somehow, the memory of the child tormented him. "What about the one-legged man?"

"He's been living there for a week past, monsieur, but little is known about him. He has not been seen since last night. As you directed, I'm having every barrier put on the watch for him; I'll warrant he can't get out of Paris! And I've put twenty men to work, bringing in every man with a wooden leg who can be picked up."

The agent departed. Desmond met the bitter, sardonic gaze of St. Vrain, and shook his head.

"They won't find him. Devil take it, I care more about saving that poor child Celie than I do about nabbing Constant!"

"An angel is always preferable to a devil." And St. Vrain grinned. "Well, what about a shave, and a morning draught, eh? We'll get the noon diligence, right enough. I've taken all the places, so we'll have it to ourselves, inside. Those who must travel, can ride on top."

"I'm in two minds about going at all," Desmond replied. "Confound it, I can't get that child's face out of my mind! I'm staying until we find her, and that's settled."

St. Vrain cursed under his breath, but Desmond was obdurate. "Something terrible—I don't know what, but something terrible!" He could hear her thin frightened voice again, as he dressed and shaved, with the help of St. Vrain.

A knock, and in came the spy who had been set to watch Pellegrini's departure. Desmond had forgotten all about him, but now caught at the man with questions.

"Was Pellegrini at his inn last night, or did he go out? Were you watching?"

"I had another man on the night shift, monsieur. No, he did not leave the inn. A light was burning in his room until nearly midnight."

Desmond stared blankly. A soft chuckle broke from St. Vrain.

"*Diable!* I think you'd better take more heed to that man, comrade. He's a smooth one. Magician, is he? I never saw one of those rascals yet that I couldn't smash like an eggshell, and I've met several."

With a gesture, Desmond ordered the spy to proceed.

"I myself was at the Hotel des Postes this morning, monsieur. This Pellegrini had very little luggage."

"He had taken two places," said Desmond. "His companion was a lady?"

"Oh no, monsieur! A child. A little girl."

"What?" burst out Desmond. "A child? Thunders of heaven! You hear that, St. Vrain? A child—did she have a bruised face? Was she a child of perhaps fifteen?"

"Or less, monsieur. Yes, there was a bruise on her face."

Desmond exploded in hot oaths. "Then he's the one who bought her! That's what he came there for, last night—and I never suspected it! What devil's work is going on there?"

"At least," observed St. Vrain sardonically, "I think we travel today."

"Yes. No overhauling them, of course; but we'll follow." Desmond turned to the spy again. "Now, about the lady—"

"No young woman of any sort, monsieur."

"The other passengers?"

The man checked them on his fingers. "Five, monsieur. An old Norman woman, an *avocat* and his wife bound for Rennes, and his clerk, and a merchant of cheeses who was very drunk."

"Hm! Did Pellegrini talk to anyone? Did the child seem frightened?"

"Frightened? Not at all; she was laughing and talking with him. She was playing with his cane—a very handsome cane, monsieur. It had a watch set in the head, with brilliants around it."

"Cagliostro's cane. That settles his identity, if it needed settling. And he talked with no one?"

"Only with the old Norman woman, monsieur. He helped her into the coach, I remember. She had a large face and heavy jaw; she was very ugly. Gray hair and a starched Norman peasant's cap. She was quite lame, walking with a stick—"

Desmond went white. He caught a low oath from St. Vrain, and nodded. He paid off the spy, and as the door closed, gave St. Vrain a grim look. St. Vrain was frowning darkly.

"So! You realized it, too."

"Aye. Old Norman woman, eh? There went our friend Constant, comrade."

Desmond repressed an oath. "I don't know what, but something terrible…." The words haunted him, the child's terrified eyes haunted him. Yet she had gone laughing and talking freely. Why had this merchant of superstition bought such a child? Why did Constant, no longer in the English service, know Cagliostro and travel with him? Jane Warr knew nothing about it.

St. Vrain, pursuing the same thought, whistled softly.

"An ugly business, comrade. There's some devil's broth coming to the brew, there in the west."

Devil's broth? Desmond thought again of the child, thought of the deep, fathomless eyes of Cagliostro, and shivered as though a cold hand had touched his spine.

"Let's pack," he said abruptly.

CHAPTER XV

AMBUSH

THE ARMY was gathered in Brittany—the one and only army of France.

It was the whole hope of France, the fruit of desperate, frantic effort. The fleets had taken many of her soldiers afar, into the colonies, into America, where this war was being waged. Here in Europe was this one army, upon which her very existence was being staked. Her agony, Vergennes had called it; and now, in his same bitter term, here threatened to be the death-agony of France.

Five months and more of dreary, uneventful camp life, through winter's snow and the rains of spring, stuck away in a back-country corner of France, would disorganize any fan's army. With England almost in sight yet far out of reach, the Army of Brittany was no exception. Ill housed, ill fed, sickness mounting to horrible heights, it drilled and died daily.

About the countryside spread broken men, veterans, rascals. Some officers who were wealthy nobles caroused in extended leave, visited at chateaux up and down the coast; others labored devotedly in the vast camp, among them the entire headquarters staff. This staff had been chosen with the greatest care by Louis XVI himself. Even the old warhorse Boufflers had nearly lost his appointment because the king thought that any man who wrote light verse could not be a good soldier; the king took himself very seriously.

Somehow, the army survived. Fresh levies marched in to replace the dead. New hospitals were established. From Brest to St. Malo, all Brittany was one vast turmoil—none the less, it was a turmoil underlaid by agony. Then at last came cheering news, definite plans, definite orders.

Thirty-odd ships of the line were concentrating at Brest. In July, at latest, the Army of Brittany would invade England. At last! Another month, and then action! The Duc de Chartres was to command the fleet of invasion. No backing out this time! Be the weather what it might, the army was sailing.

Joyous news for headquarters, this. Gloom was dissipated. A gay ball was given, attended by ladies from the surrounding district, and none moved in that brilliant throng more bravely than Baron Deaurevel. He was eager, a young fellow of infinite charm, of incredible dissipation, repeatedly ruined at cards yet somehow writhing clear.

Now, between dances, he cornered one noble here, another there, for a few brief words with each. And always his refrain ended in the same way.

"The opportunity of a lifetime! Next weekend, remember. Boufflers will arrange it for you. He's going himself."

Boufflers, that gay wit and hardened soldier, whose ugly features were the life of the camp as they had been of Parisian salons, listened to Deaurevel in his turn, took a pinch of snuff, and frowned.

"Never heard of the fellow, my dear baron."

"That's natural; you've been away from Paris a long while. For one thing, he predicted to a day the death of Voltaire! I understand he has contributed a million to the war funds. He has rented this chateau up the coast and wants a party of us for next weekend. Boufflers, you'll see marvels such as you never heard of before! I hear that he can summon up the dead; he himself claims to be immortal. And his miraculous cures have set all Paris talking."

"What's his game?" growled Boufflers. "Money?"

"Bah! He predicted the winning numbers of the Brussels lottery, bought the tickets and won. Money's nothing to him. He's an Italian nobleman who loves France."

"As Mazarin loved France, and lined his pockets," Boufflers said skeptically. "Oh, all right; anything for a change! You may count on me. But I warn you, when it comes to any supernatural powers, I want to be shown. And on my own terms."

"Listen, then." Deaurevel spoke low-voiced, eagerly. "I've thought of something to test his boasted powers. Something absolutely impossible. I'll tell you about it later. You know the little daughter of the Count de Vergennes—well, never mind now. Tomorrow."

Despite high hopes and brave hearts, Boufflers had his troubles. He was second in command here, and since his chief, Castries, was sick with fever and the itch, Boufflers had full charge.

It was a charge to make any man stand aghast. France was in a death-grapple with England; but the Army of Brittany was fighting for its life against invisible enemies.

Everything went wrong. Supply convoys disappeared. A powder magazine caught fire and took fifty men to hell. The water supply went bad, mysteriously—poisoned, some said.

*Castries pitched
out of his saddle
as a dozen
figures streamed
from ambush.*

Cavalry mounts died like flies, or simply vanished. And there was worse, much worse, which only headquarters knew.

There was some wild talk of spies at work, but nothing to back it up. Spies in the army? Spies, here in the backwoods of Brittany? The very idea was absurd.

Not at all absurd was the question of women. Paris leave for the men was impossible. As a result the towns were filled with camp followers and bordellos. Men on leave were not restricted in any way, or policed. Robbery and crime flourished, until the whole countryside lay groaning.

Into this situation rode Colonel Brian Desmond, well mounted and equipped.

EXCEPT FOR an ankle that was still a bit weak, he had recovered from his hurts. He was alone. St. Vrain had branched off to reconnoiter his own estates; they were to meet in four days.

Desmond was dismayed and appalled by what he saw on every hand; if this army were the hope of France, it was a sorry hope. He came at last into the great camp whose stench rolled on the air for miles—a camp of primitive sanitation, of well-meant but ignorant efforts.

Skeleton regiments and squadrons were at drill. The camp streets were lined with weary wretches rotting with scurvy. The headquarters camp, a little apart, offered a better spectacle; yet over the whole place the air was heavy with dust and filth and the odor of mortality.

Knowing the Chevalier de Boufflers, Ségur and others of the staff, Desmond found himself at once welcomed and made passing comfortable.

"Still on detached leave, eh?"Boufflers greeted him. "Lucky dog, Desmond! Tell us about Paris, how things are going, what gossip is afoot! Is it true that Voltaire was refused burial by the cure of St. Sulpice?"

"True—and also true that the King is expecting an heir."

This news threw the whole camp into joy, as it was throwing all France into joy.

Desmond said nothing to anyone about his real errand. The one man he wanted to meet was Deaurevel; and he met him that day. In the evening he sat alone with Boufflers over a bottle of wine. He was sharing the quarters of the chevalier, whose former sparkling brilliance had become a haggard weariness.

Already Desmond had heard the rumors of couriers killed mysteriously, of despatches missing, of how it was unsafe for any man to ride the roads alone. A frightful vision rose before him, of this army strangled, betrayed, utterly ruined by unseen hands.

Boufflers spoke of the weather, of discouraging delays, of the sabotage that seemed to prevail on all sides. He sniffed at Desmond's hint about English agents.

"It's possible, yes—but only if some of us were traitors, Desmond. And we're not. Poor Duquesne was shot, killed and rifled by robbers last week; only headquarters knew he carried despatches from Brest. If you lay that to spies, for example, you must presuppose a traitor at headquarters itself."

"Why not?" said Desmond.

"Absurd, man. They whisper that old Beausite, the adjutant, might take English money; and why? Because he has an English wife. Bah!"

"No old soldier would be a traitor," Desmond said slowly. "A man in years couldn't bend his mind to it. A young man could; it wouldn't seem very terrible to him. Especially if he needed money. He might not even realize what he was doing. A woman, in fact, might be the link."

Boufflers gave him an indescribable look of conjecture and questioning.

"Give me facts, not theories, Desmond," he said quietly. "I've an idea or two about you and what you're doing. If you dig up anything, let me know."

Desmond nodded in silence.

Next morning he visited with his old regiment, officers and men, but it was only the wreckage of the corps he had once known. Sick at heart over the whole business, he rode out of camp after lunch, taking the first road to hand, aimlessly. The lack of system, the lack of energy, was appalling. The wastage was incredible. Everybody seemed helpless.

"Conquer England, with such an army?" he thought gloomily, as he rode. "Sooner conquer the moon."

Ringing hoofbeats drummed behind him. He drew rein, to see young Castries, a nephew of the general, overhauling him. The other slowed with laughing greeting.

"I saw you heading away from camp and came along for a ride, my colonel. Besides," added the gay, vivacious lieutenant, "it's unsafe to travel the roads alone. Do you mind?"

"Mind? I'm delighted," exclaimed Desmond. "Come along; anywhere! What's the first town we come to?"

"None, by this road," said Castries with a grimace. "Here and there a hamlet; this way lie forests. Ha! What about a visit to a chateau? All these Breton nobility live on their own lands, instead of residing at Paris. They're savages, but hospitable."

Desmond shrugged. "Lead where you like, my friend."

They rode, talking and laughing together, by green fields and the dark, ominous Breton woods. Not even the hot June sun could dispel the gloom of those bosques and thickets, inhabited by shaggy peasants whose very patois was utterly unintelligible to French ears. It raised doubts in the soul, this countryside; it was secretive and ominous, heavy with dread and suspicion. Few people showed themselves.

"THERE'S A village ahead where, I understand, the inn has really magnificent wine," exclaimed Castries, after an hour of this. "And the Keradec chateau is somewhere in that vicinity. To tell the truth," he added with an eager laugh, "I've been hunting an excuse the past two days to ride out this way."

Desmond gave him a smiling glance. "Oh, a lady?"

"No, a divinity! A distant relative of the family, a Viennese countess, and the most adorable person imaginable," confided the young officer. "I met her three days ago when I was in St. Barbe. She's a discovery, I tell you! And amiable, you comprehend? She, too, suffers from ennui in this savage place; she said so. Well, she'll suffer no longer! By the way, you're just from Paris; did you hear anything there of this man Balsamo?"

Desmond's horse leaped under the involuntary spur-touch. He reined in.

"Who's Balsamo?"

"An Italian marquis. A sorcerer, a magician, they say. I hear that he predicted the death of Voltaire and all the important happenings of late. It's a dead secret, but Boufflers and several others are invited to spend the weekend with him. Ah, there's the village at last! What do you say to sampling the wine, and then riding on to Keradec, if it's not far?"

"With all my heart," Desmond replied indifferently. He was stung by what the volatile youngster had just told him. The weekend, eh? Chevalier de Boufflers and part of the headquarters staff—what the devil!

It was eight days now since he had left Paris. The main thing had been to learn whether Constant had gone to the Chateau de St. Vrain with Cagliostro and the child. This, St. Vrain was certain to discover. A man could not very well hide in this country.

Three days more; that would be Saturday. By Breton roads, it was a longish ride north to their meeting-place. Therefore, thought Desmond, best leave camp on the Friday, so that he might be on hand when St. Vrain showed up on Saturday. Then to consult about this weekend party, and what to do. Much would depend on the information St. Vrain managed to pick up.

They were in the village now. It was a sparsely built little hamlet of straggling cottages, huts, a squat stone church, and an inn which was by no means palatial.

At this country inn, the wine indeed justified the words of Castries; it was superb, no less. As they drank, they questioned the surly innkeeper, who spoke a little French, in regard to Keradec.

"It is three miles north," he said, with a shrug, and then furtively crossed himself. "Accursed, I have heard. A good place to avoid."

"You don't know it," and Castries chuckled. "On the contrary, my friend! Just at present, an infinitely charming place."

"Well, there is no good said of it," grumbled the man. "I've never seen the place myself, but my grandfather used to say queer things happened there. Suit yourself."

He left them. Castries broke into laughter.

"Isn't that typical of these folk, Desmond? Three miles away and he's never been there. His grandfather said it was accursed—oh, this is rich and rare! What d'you say? Shall we lift the curse from the chateau?"

"Faith, when we're this close it'd be a pity not to have a glance at your charmer!" Desmond replied cheerfully. The ardor of young Castries amused him. "What about her family? Met any of them?"

Castries shrugged and rose. "I know nothing about them. The usual Bretons, no doubt—poor, proud, savage. These provincial nobles are touchy, too, punctilious as the devil or Don Quixote himself! Ready?"

Desmond finished his wine; they left.

On again, through thick and tangled woods that hemmed the road closely, on past rapid torrents and forested crags. The wild and rugged beauty of the country, its savage desolation, was a surprise to Desmond. Now and again they could catch a far glimpse of the ocean in the west.

"These chateaux are as dark and angry as the woods or the people," Castries declared. "Uncouth, rude survivals of the old days when noble warred upon noble and no man's life was safe. My faith! Perhaps we were foolish to come so far without escort. There have been too many murders and assassinations of late. If we were not so near our goal...."

Desmond caught a glint amid the bushes, then another.

"Look out, Castries!" he cried, and reined in his horse.

A BURST of explosions drowned his words. The thick green walls spurted white smoke-jets, then waved and broke as a dozen figures streamed out from ambush. Musket-balls whistled. Castries slumped forward and pitched out of his saddle.

Desmond wheeled his horse, reaching for one of the pistols holstered before him—then with a savage oath drew rein. Other men were leaping into the road, blocking it, lifting muskets and covering him. Wild, bearded, shaggy runagates of the woods. No Breton peasants, these, but broken men, plunderers, deserters, some of them still wearing rags of uniforms.

Desmond was speechless, choked with fury, white with helpless wrath. Two of the men had flung themselves on the riddled Castries and were rifling the body, Another stepped out with hand uplifted, and grinned mockingly at Desmond.

"Will it please your gracious highness to dismount?" he called in excellent French. "Or must we waste good powder by shooting you out of the saddle?"

Desmond's eyes gripped the man icily. A lean man with a scar from mouth to ear.

"You damned murderous hound!" he exclaimed hotly, and checked himself. For at that moment a cry of alarm broke from the men. Some darted back into the bushes, others whipped around with muskets leveled. A creak and a rattle of wheels, a rumble, a clatter of horses, and into sight swung a carriage.

"It's all right, Balafré!" sang out one of the men. "It's madame!"

The word might mean any lady, married or not, or even a child.

"So I perceive." And the scarred leader grinned again. "Search that soldier well. Keep your pieces on this civilian," and he gestured toward Desmond. Then, turning, he swept off his shapeless hat and bowed to the woman in the carriage, as the horses were drawn to a halt. Others of the men saluted respectfully.

But she, leaning out, was staring down at Castries, and her face was white, her eyes wide with recognition.

"Monsieur de Castries!" she gasped, and then lifted her gaze to the staring Desmond. "No, no—it cannot be—"

The scarred Balafré was speaking, jauntily, impudently.

"An officer bagged, madame—no dispatches, apparently. We've not yet searched this civilian. A hot-tempered rogue, by his looks." He broke off, frowning uneasily, and a little silence fell.

The woman was still gazing at Desmond, as though fascinated.

"Oh, this is horrible, horrible!" she said, a break in her voice. Suddenly she gave the Balafré a quick, passionate look of rising fury. She began to curse him, so hotly that he stepped back a pace, and then checked her vituperation. "I'd sooner you had killed anyone, anyone, than this officer!" she cried. "You fool—"

The scarred man shrugged. "How the devil was I to know?" said he, impudently as before. "Orders are orders. So much a head, so much for dispatches and letters—well, there he is. And a good catch, by the sword-knot. A staff officer, eh, boys?"

Two or three of the men muttered assent. Again fell silence, hot and vibrant in the afternoon sunlight.

Desmond knew now why she had called it horrible. The carriage had come from the direction of the chateau, somewhere ahead. It was this woman whom Castries had been about to visit, as she now realized. Austrian? Not a bit of it. A pure Parisian, as her burst of passionate vituperation had betrayed. And what was more, the mistress of these killers.

Caution, wary habit, alertness, checked Desmond's fury. She was handsomely attired, too handsomely; beautiful, in a way, not as young as she might have been. Just the type of brazen actress to entrap the imagination of a young fellow like Castries, whose fancy would clothe her with youth and charms. Desmond perceived at a glance what she was, and somehow found a vague familiarity in her face. He had seen her somewhere ere this.

He knew, also, her business here. It flashed over him as that curious scene passed; astonishment, wild conjecture, bitter hatred flamed through his brain. Then, instantly, he slipped into his part. Monsieur Feufollet was far from dead—but he would be, if this she-devil guessed the truth!

"What's the meaning of this damnable business?" he demanded. "You recognized him, madame. Can it be possible that you are the lady we were going to visit—the Austrian lady of whom the poor boy raved? You, whose hired assassins have murdered him?"

Agitation leaped in her face.

"A mistake, a horrible mistake," she blurted. However, Desmond noted that her eyes were steady, poised, calculating. He took swift warning. "And who are you, monsieur?" she inquired in a silky voice.

"I? Jacques Duval of St. Malo, who else?" he replied readily.

"I'm spending a few clays in the camp, stacking up orders for honest Gonaives rum and Bordeaux wine. And now your damned assassins have killed the general's nephew and lost me my orders, curse you!"

SHE REGARDED him steadily. So much per head, so much for despatches and letters, the Balafré had said; Desmond knew what that meant, but she did not suspect that he guessed. He must not let her suspect. Meantime, he was trying to place that face of hers.

"You are well acquainted in the camp?" she asked slowly.

"*Diable,* yes!" he snapped. "With everyone in it, of course."

"Monsieur Duval, you must listen to me," she said quietly. "Yes; I am Countess von Brenner of Vienna, visiting relatives here. More correctly, I am occupying their house, as they are visiting in Brest. This young gentleman and you were coming to see me, yes?"

"Only to be murdered by your hired thugs," said Desmond angrily.

"Please! You mistake, monsieur," she said pleadingly, and a slight German accent crept into her words. "You do not understand. These men are not assassins. True, they've made a horrible blunder, but they meant well. Will you not listen to me?"

"I'm listening," he growled. She was playing for time, getting her wits to work. If only he could place her face, put a name to her! Then everything would be clear.

Clear enough, as it was. She paid these men. Others paid her. She was planted here, going to the towns around the camp, meeting officers, drawing them to her—and meantime these assassins of hers were at work. Payment for despatches, eh? Yes, the English would pay well for any documents, for information of any kind about this army which threatened their shores with invasion! But she was not English. She was pure French.

"Listen, please," she went on more quickly. "My relatives have given some of these poor homeless, wrecked men, shelter and food. Deserters, perhaps—but Frenchmen, and we believe in

Christian charity, monsieur. Threats have been made against me. Twice I have been annoyed, almost carried off, by parties of men from the army; you comprehend what terrible danger menaces a woman alone, in this district? These poor men set themselves to watch the roads for danger. I cannot absolve their crime, I can only excuse them. We must consult what is to be done about this frightful happening. You must advise me. Will you come home with me? I implore you, help me in this crisis! The afternoon is already getting late. I'll have poor Castries taken care of, and we'll decide what's to be done. Ride with me, monsieur."

A good enough story for a rough wine-merchant of St. Malo, thought Desmond; a good and well-baited trap for such an one, too. She was not a bad actress.

Actress! By Heaven, he had it now! To conceal the swift blaze in his eyes, he pretended to wipe sweat from his forehead, and then tucked away his handkerchief. His face cleared.

"Why, madame—Countess—why, of course!" he assented awkwardly. "I'll be glad to talk it over with you. A horrible thing, as you say; cursed if I know what's to be done about it. Can't bring a man back to life, that's sure."

She turned to the Balafré, who stifled a grin of comprehension and saluted her.

"Take care of this poor gentleman's body," she said. "Bring it to the chateau until we can decide what to do. See that you make no more such mistakes!"

"Understood, madame," the scarred rogue rejoined. "I'll take care of his horse, too."

The carriage was backed, turned, and started back whence it had come, with Desmond riding behind it, the road being too narrow for him to stay alongside.

Spies, killers, murderers of unsuspecting gentlemen! Desmond had no more oaths to waste; his brain was at work now. Luckily, she would not suspect him of having any papers worth getting—but she meant to have information out of him.

Well, she'd get it! And more than information, thought Desmond grimly. Payment for these diabolical murders. But first find out all he could, learn all he could!

La Delphine; he remembered now. The actress convicted of killing her lover, a year ago, sentenced to death, reprieved by the kind-hearted young king. Now she was in English pay, posing lamely and very poorly as a Viennese. Well, she could fool officers here and there, no doubt.

Not a bad notion, either, from the English viewpoint. If one of these old chateaux could be taken over by Cagliostro, up north, for some diabolical purpose, another one here could serve this murderess, this woman who hired killers.

Suddenly Desmond went cold. Jane Warr—was she directing all this deviltry? No, no, she was incapable of it! Constant was the man, or had been. It was his kind of work, all this. He had planned this, schemed it, perfected it. By heaven, he might be here on this very spot! If Jane Warr knew anything about the matter as a whole, she could know none of the details.

He caught words from the carriage ahead. The woman was speaking to her driver.

"Drop me. Then go as directed, and bring anyone who may be waiting."

Desmond caught the scrap of speech, wafted back to him, but at the moment passed it by without interest.

Yes, he could well comprehend that the murder of poor young Castries was a horrible mistake in her eyes. Had she only got him under her thumb and played him properly, she could have wangled all sorts of the most invaluable knowledge out of him, for he had been quite infatuated even after one meeting. Poor young fool! He had paid dearly for his inefficiency, thought Desmond.

Ten minutes later, he knew he had come slap upon the headquarters of all this devil's work directed against the Army of Brittany. Or at least, upon the headquarters of a large share of it.

CHAPTER XVI

ROGUES' RETREAT

THEY TURNED into the drive of a house with broken wall around the grounds. Not a chateau by any means; probably the old country house of some noble. Most of these great families hereabouts had a number of such places, gained by marriage or inheritance, seldom or never used. This was a pretty enough little house, solidly built of stone, half hidden amid a rank growth of trees and bushes, with crumbling stables in the rear. Desmond noted the details of the place at a glance.

As he dismounted and accompanied his hostess inside, Desmond was careful to show none of the graces of a gentleman. The situation was now all in the supple fingers of Monsieur Feufollet, the game was in his hand. He scorned to play his rough merchant's role with this unscrupulous creature, yet life and death hung upon it. More of a job for St. Vrain, he thought cynically. Well, play the game as St. Vrain would play it, then!

A man came running from the stables and walked his horse away. A servant opened the door, bowing. Little as Desmond knew of Breton peasants, he could see that these men were of a different strain. La Delphine, obviously, had well surrounded herself with such servants as the Balafré, outlawed men, army deserters or criminals.

Inside, the house was like death—dark, gloomy, chill. It was heavy with massive old furniture; the rooms were small and cramped, the architecture was of the simplest. This place was for use, not for display. However, the alleged countess led her guest into a sitting-room enlivened by the afternoon sun, and broke into a sparkle of talk. Her interest in Desmond, her flattery, her assumption of intimacy, were not badly done. When a servant had brought wine and spiced cakes and they were alone together, he pressed her hand warmly and made no mention of young Castries. Nor did she.

"Is is true that the army is really going to invade England soon?" she asked. "That a fleet is to be got ready at Brest?"

Desmond winked at her. He was putting down the wine as fast as she refilled his glass; good wine too, as he observed.

"Aye, and what a fleet!" he exclaimed. "I'm getting in touch with the right parties. I'm have an order there that'll make the other lads at St. Malo open their eyes! Fifty ships need rum and plenty of it."

"Fifty ships!" Her eyes sparkled, and she clapped her hands with delight. "Why, poor England will be overwhelmed! But from what I hear, the army is not in shape to move."

"Bah! That's all a blind," said Desmond, waxing garrulous. "They have twenty thousand men in fair shape to embark, and a dozen more regiments are being ordered to Brest from the south. Nobody knows it; a secret, you comprehend? All cavalry. The scheme—ah, what a plan it is! London will be captured in a week's time!"

"You know the plan, then?" she inquired eagerly.

Desmond grinned and helped himself to more wine. "I know everything, my sweet little chicken!" he declared grandly.

She was about to speak, when a clatter of hooves intervened. A horse and rider passed the window, the horse in a white lather of foam, the rider drooping wearily in the saddle. Desmond caught a full glimpse of that man's face, and started. Impossible! Why....

"Wait. I must hear more about this wonderful plan," said the woman quickly, and rose. "Excuse me for a moment, monsieur."

The moment she was out of the room, Desmond darted from his chair to the window. The new arrival was dismounting; yes, the same man! It was the Englishman Logan, who had driven Jane Warr on that ride south from Louvain. Then, as he staggered to the house entrance, Logan passed from Desmond's field of vision. Two men were coming on the run from the stables. One of them was the Balafré.

Turning, Desmond went to the door that opened into the

hall. It came ajar to his hand, and he listened. La Delphine was at the front door, talking with Logan. He caught the man's weary, hasty accents.

"I must see her, I tell you! She was to be here today...."

"Tonight," said La Delphine. "Very well. Balafré, take care of this man; food and sleep. When our visitor of tonight arrives, she'll want to see him."

Desmond regained his chair, his mind in a flame. She! Who other could it be, except Jane Warr? Coming here to this place— why, that carriage had been sent to meet her, of course! La Delphine had been on the way to meet her! So, after all, Jane Warr was behind this work of murder and deviltry. It was a stunning blow; he sat appalled beneath it.

La Delphine was slow to reappear. When she came, radiant and laughing, she was bringing another bottle of wine, and set it on the table at Desmond's elbow.

"A special vintage, my friend," she said brightly. "It's the last bottle in the bin, and worthy of such a visitor."

"Why, you're a proper wench!" cried Desmond. "Now, if I didn't have to get back to camp—"

"But you don't," she coaxed, leaning close to him, her eyes bright upon his, her breath coming fast. "It's a long ride, my friend; why not wait until morning? Stay and talk. Have pity upon a poor lonely woman who seldom sees anyone, much less such a boon companion as you! Stay, and dine, and make me happy!"

Desmond grinned. "Never refuse a lady! That's my motto."

"And what was this plan you were telling about? The one to capture London?"

"Oh, that! It's very simple! Land a heavy force of cavalry and a huge park of artillery, with infantry as a backbone only." Desmond invented as he went along. "Sweep the whole country with the cavalry—you see? Break up the English forces, sur- round London, take it! Once the city falls, England is helpless. Oh, there are a thousand details...."

HE POURED more wine. She opened the new bottle and filled a glass, and set it ready to his hand. Drugged wine, eh? She meant to keep him here, yes; she had something big now, and would make the most of it. She had information that would startle England!

Time passed. Desmond talked, evaded that drugged wine, although she pressed it upon him. True, his tongue thickened, his speech became more and more confused; but he evaded the finishing draught. He was not sure that it was not poisoned, in fact.

A knock. Desmond hastily loosened her hand, which he was pressing to his lips, and a servant came in. All the domestics here were men; a significant fact. No women around.

"Madame! The carriage is returning."

"Oh!" La Delphine gave Desmond a swift, sharp look, then nodded. "Very well. I'll be out in a moment. The room is prepared?"

"Yes, madame." The man withdrew.

Desmond seized the glass of drugged wine.

"To your health, most beautiful!" he exclaimed, with a maudlin laugh. "To your sweet eyes! Most beautiful eyes in Brittany. Most charming person—splendid woman. Kind sweet angel...."

"Yes, yes." She rose, cutting short his oratory. "Drink it, my dear friend, drink it, help yourself to the bottle! I must go to greet a visitor. In a moment I'll rejoin you, and we'll drink together."

"Aye, together," mumbled Desmond, waving the glass. "To your health!"

As she left the room, he was in the act of gulping down the wine. But, as the door closed, he lowered it from his lips untasted. A fireplace, with a wooden screen before it, was in one wall; going to this, he dumped out the wine behind the screen, put the empty glass on the table, and hurried to the window. He peered out cautiously.

His heart leaped. Jane Warr, by heaven! Jane herself!

A dusty carriage had pulled up. She had alighted, was greeting La Delphine coolly, distantly, authority in her air and manner. Sunset was at hand; the afternoon had ended. Hurt, incredulous, Desmond drank in the sight of her. That young and tender and joyous face, those lovely dark eyes....

"Oh, Jane, Jane!" The low groan broke from his lips. "You, behind these murders and foul deeds! You, so white and unsullied and gentle, to be drawn into such infernal work!"

At least, she was no intimate of La Delphine, who was humble before her, speaking volubly but low-voiced. Then, through the open window, Desmond caught her reply.

"Very well, in that case I'll remain for the night. But I must be off early and on my way north."

La Delphine spoke again. Jane Warr frowned slightly.

"What? A man—well, I'll see him in a few minutes. I must wash and fix up my hair a bit; the dust of these roads is terrible! I can't see anyone just now."

Frowning, Desmond sought his chair again. She had come to visit her hired agents, of course, pick up what information they had, and be gone again. At her door, then, lay the foul murder of poor Castries, and a dozen more.

Voices, steps in the hall, a pause. The door swung open. Desmond sat with his arms on the table, his face buried in them. He heard a light laugh from La Delphine.

"There's the fellow. Oh, the most magnificent information, I assure you! The whole plan of the headquarters staff, their strength, the new regiments coming—yes, I have everything! And in the morning I'll have more, but I already have the best of it."

"So!" More than a trace of scorn rang in Jane Warr's voice, as she looked at the humped figure. "This is how you do your work, is it? Well, I congratulate you on the results, at least. They've been remarkable. And if you really have this information it'll be splendid! What about despatches and letters?"

"A packet of them," purred La Delphine, quite missing any sarcasm in Jane Warr's words. "A whole file of official despatches to headquarters."

Those, thought Desmond savagely, would be the ones from Duquesne, whom Boufflers had mentioned as murdered and rifled. He sat quiet, fury alive within him; he could even catch a faint drift of perfume, Jane Warr's perfume. He remembered it acutely.

"Is your fellow there drunk?" came the question.

La Delphine laughed lightly.

"No—drugged. He'll sleep safely until morning. I'll get further details out of him tomorrow."

"Well, have that carriage ready for me by sunrise…."

The two departed.

Presently La Delphine came back into the room. She spoke to Desmond, shook him by the shoulder; he only grunted. Stooping, she began to rifle his pockets, with a mutter of satisfaction at finding his money. He had gold in a belt under his clothes, and his papers sewn into his waistcoat lining, but she did not find these.

"Take him to that little room upstairs," she said, as two men came into the room. "When you've left him, go and send in the man who arrived an hour ago; my visitor wishes to speak with him. Better take lights to her room, too. It's getting dark. Dinner in an hour."

The Balafré's impudent voice made assent.

Desmond was hauled out of his chair by the two men and taken stumbling from the room. Up a flight of stairs to an upper hall. Through half-closed eyes he noted all details as he went. On the walls, old rusty armor and arms, mouldy paintings, trophies of the chase. Near the stair-head was a tiny room bare except for an old broken bed. On this bed they shoved him.

"Go through him?"

"Bah!" The scarred rascal laughed. "Once she's done with a

sucker, no use looking; you won't find a sou. I'll get that fellow out of my room over the stable. You see to providing lights."

So the Balafré lived over the stable, eh? Desmond was glad to know it. He had not forgotten young Castries.

His door slammed and he was alone.

CHAPTER XVII

A PONIARD'S POINT

HE REMOVED his boots, went to the door, found it unlocked, and waited. The creaking floors resounded with footsteps, feet pounded the stairs. Presently everything was quiet again. The man Logan had been brought to Lady Warr's room, evidently. Desmond opened his door and looked out into the hall. Dark; not a light there, but from beneath a door came a faint glint.

Satisfied that all was safe, he stole out and went to the lighted door. A thrill surged through him. He could hear what was being said—the old wood was full of cracks, the huge keyhole was empty. However, he could see nothing through it.

"I tell you, it's impossible!" That was the man Logan, his voice filled with a curious desperation. "I can't stay there. It's the devil's own work, Your Ladyship!"

"Nonsense," said Jane Warr quietly. "Nothing of the sort, Logan. Merely trickery...."

"No, no! Worse'n that, Your Ladyship," the man broke in. "I saw him at work wi' that little girl. Like a corpse, she was, and him calling on Satan. No honest man could abide such doings—"

"You're a fool, Logan," snapped Jane Warr angrily. "Now listen to me. I know what the man's about; in fact, I've talked over the whole thing with him. Nobody is being hurt. No harm's being done anyone."

"Begging your pardon, but what's that little tyke a-screaming for, then?" said Logan sullenly. "I heard her a-screaming."

"What? Do you mean she was being hurt?"

"Well, I don't rightly know, but the devil's in that man, Your Ladyship!" Logan's voice took on a rasp of horror. "Two nights ago I was looking through the keyhole. That sad, lovely lady of his was in the room with him, and nobody else, but I heard voices talking, men's voices. And another time I had sight of a corpse walking about—I tell you, I just can't stand it! I came away and quit, that's all. I won't take chances with the devil, Your Ladyship."

"But the little girl?" persisted Jane Warr. "The child isn't being hurt, is she?"

"Oh, they treat her kind enough, but I've heard her a-screaming just the same."

Desmond, listening, was aware of red rage in his brain that blinded all coherent thought; he found himself quivering. They were talking about Cagliostro, of course, or Balsamo as he here called himself. The child was screaming, eh?

"Have you told anyone else about this?" demanded Jane Warr.

"No, Your Ladyship."

"Very well. You're a silly fool, but have your own way about it. After dinner I'll see you again and give you other orders. I can use you in St. Malo."

"Thank heaven for that!" Logan uttered devoutly. "Satan himself is in that house, I tell you. The very day I got there, I looked into a big box. It had a human head in it, a woman's head—"

"If you'd mind your own business you wouldn't get into trouble," Jane Warr broke in with cold anger. "Stop prying into things. Now get out of here and I'll see you after dinner."

Desmond softly went back into his own room. He left the door slightly ajar, flung himself down on the bed, and tried to still the rioting tumult in his brain. So Jane Warr was behind all this deviltry! No escaping it.

Screaming, eh? And he owed his life to that child, Celie. The nameless horror in Logan's voice re-echoed within his own heart; the man had been utterly sincere, utterly earnest. Not a man easily frightened, or he'd not be doing a spy's work in France. And Jane Warr had planned everything; whatever devil's plot was spawning, to whatever use the poor screaming child was being put, she was responsible. She had said so.

All the things Desmond had heard about Cagliostro rose before his mind, all he himself knew and suspected about the man. He clenched his fist, there in the darkness. He thought again of the child's wistful face with that queer faraway look— the face of Vergennes' daughter.

Well, he must make sure of the worst, make sure about Jane Warr being back of La Delphine. He shrank from this thought; he could not credit it. He must make sure, the first thing. Then, for the child. Thought of her tormented him afresh. Devil's brew, devil's work—what was going on in that old chateau of the St. Vrain family? Why would Cagliostro have taken that child from Paris, bought her from her people—to what infernal use was the poor creature being put? And the "sad, lovely lady" would be Cagliostro's wife. Desmond remembered those haunted eyes of hers, and shuddered.

A sense of something horrible, monstrous, incredibly awful, crept upon him.

The worst of it was that Jane Warr condoned it all, was behind it all. This quieted his gathering fury and left him stricken with the very hurt of it. He thought of poor young Castries, by this time flung in among the brush or buried in some hasty grave, and gripped his hands again until the nails bit into his palms.

Gradually his hammering pulses quieted, he got himself under control. He was drenched with sweat—not alone from the closed room. And as he lay staring into the blackness, another odd memory came into his head, and his brain clicked.

Stone stairs reaching up to heaven. Queer words, those which Cagliostro had uttered in Brussels! They came back to him as uttered: "The clashing of swords and the crying of dead men upon a vast stairway of stone reaching to heaven." They made no sense, but they left a frightful impression just the same. And now Desmond suddenly realized where he had known of just such a stairway. At Mont St. Michel. He had been there once.

FOOTSTEPS, VOICES; he came alert, listening. A rustle of silks. La Delphine was taking her guest down to dinner, a man had summoned them. The woman must have been some-where upstairs, probably had her own room here. Desmond heard heels clicking on the bare stairs, and the sounds receded.

And now—what? A dozen things beckoned; he forced himself to balance every course, to weigh each possibility. Today was Wednesday; why wait at all? Why not go on to the meet-ing-place and wait there? St. Vrain might show up ahead of time. Probably would, in fact. No use going back to camp—if he himself could do the work here. He could send word of this place, in case he failed. Once he had La Delphine nabbed and out of the way, all menace was at an end. She was the head of the damnable business, and would confess quickly enough when the police put her to the question.

Thus probing, fumbling, uncertain of his own course, Desmond decided to await what might happen; and meantime, he would head north if possible.

So Jane had gone down to dinner, eh? He could do with a bit of dinner himself; but he could also do without.

He stole quietly out of the room, cursing the creaky old floors, walking close to the wall to hit the less used boards. He paused at her door; it was unlocked. She had gone down with La Delphine and had not paused for security. With a low chuckle, Desmond stepped into the room, lit by a long candle burning on the table.

There was little to see. A cloak, a small traveling case, writing materials, half-finished notes. He peered at them, and laughed softly. Notes on the fantastic details he had given La Delphine. She might have these, and welcome! But there must have been

others, such as the despatches taken from the murdered
Duquesne.

He turned to the traveling case. Perfume, handkerchiefs,
toilet articles—nothing else. He stared at it, frowning. Then she
had those despatches on her person? Yet they must be stopped
at all costs.

Suddenly he picked up the case, eyed it inside and out,
studied it closely. So that was it—a false bottom! Now for the
secret. This was a matter of minutes only. Monsieur Feufollet
had used the same trick more than once.

He found the spring at last, and the false bottom flew open.

Raking out the packets of papers there, Desmond paused at
once, and trembled as he stared. Blood, dark and rusty over the
despatches—the blood of Duquesne, no doubt, for this was the
thick, heavy paper used for official documents. The sheer fury
that shook Desmond was almost past control.

It quieted by degrees. He cut loose all the letters and documents, thrust one into the candle-flame and carried it over to
the screened hearth. There behind the screen he burned them
all, saving only a single sheet of blank paper that he tore from
one. This he took to the table. He picked up a quill, dipped it
in the ink, and wrote briefly; his consuming rage dictated the
words.

> Congratulations, murderess. You are worthy of the people
> who serve you.
>   WILL O' THE WISP.

He thrust the paper into the secret compartment, closed it,
left everything exactly as he had found it, and crept out of the
room. In the hall, a candle-lantern was now burning, vaguely
illuminating the stairhead.

Desmond paused, cocking his eye at the wall. A weapon?
Here were a dozen to his hand. He selected one and took it
down. A poniard that must date from the time of the old reli-

gious wars, for it was fully as long as a rapier. Rusty, but needle-sharp.

He turned to the stairs and descended cautiously. The room in which he had talked with La Delphine was across the hall from the dining-room of the house; he was running practically no risk whatever. At the foot of the stairs he paused, found everything safe, and stepped over to the sitting-room.

Here a candelabrum was burning. On the table still reposed the bottle of drugged wine. With a grim smile, Desmond picked it up, and his glass with it. Then he went back up the stairs....

MEANTIME, IN the gloomy little dining-room, the two women were concluding their meal. La Delphine was over-dressed, voluble, affected in manner. Lady Warr, as the meal drew to an end, eyed her companion with increasing uneasiness.

"You have hinted at many strange things, madame," she said at length, and none too warmly either. "When I engaged you for this work, the last time I was in France, you were not at all certain that you would even be able to pick up a great deal of information. Yet you've turned in results that are marvelous. Tonight you've handed over information that is almost beyond price."

La Delphine broke into gay laughter that rang hard as steel.

"Yes, I've done well! If I had the same good advice always, I'd rise to the top of this profession, eh? These men of mine are superb assistants. That fellow Balafré is a merry rascal. Well built, too—you noticed him? He'd take any woman's fancy. And when he starts out, he brings home results, I promise you!"

Despite her involuntary wince at the vulgarity, Jane Warr's gaze held a vivid curiosity, and she voiced it.

"He brings results? That's odd. I could imagine," and her speculative accents held a touch of dry acid, "how you yourself might get results. In fact, you showed me one method. But you mentioned advice—whose advice? It's none of my business how you get the information, of course, but I certainly gave you no advice."

La Delphine positively grinned.

"No, you didn't," she rejoined. "And the less you know the better, like he said."

"Like who said?" demanded Jane Warr quietly.

"Oh, that fellow who got things started here and then went back to London—that queer Englishman. I forget his name. He had one wooden leg."

Jane Warr's face went white. "Constant!"

"That's the name. Queer that an Englishman should have a French name, eh?"

"Look here." Jane Warr leaned forward, her dark eyes troubled. "I want to know just what you're doing and how you do it—what sort of an organization you have, and exactly how you've collected all this information for us. Didn't I see blood on one of those packets? I want to know your methods."

"Oh, you do? Well, you won't; he warned me about you," said La Delphine defiantly. Then she softened, and reaching over, patted the arm of Jane Warr. "Come, come, dearie! I know you're a fine lady, an aristocrat. It's your job to pick up the information and pay for it; don't worry your pretty head over how it's got. You don't want to know about such things."

"I do," said Jane Warr quietly.

The other met her gaze and broke into an easy laugh.

"Well, you're not going to, so there! Listen, dearie. If you hadn't been coming, would I have wasted drugged wine on that St. Malo merchant? Not much. I might have entertained him upstairs and kept him talking all night long; a fine stout fellow he is? And the Balafré might have played him at cards or dice, and got him heavy in debt, and made him find out all kinds of things for us! We may do that yet. But what's it to you? Nothing at all, dearie. You're not concerned in such goings on. So let's go back and finish with everything the man told me. We haven't hardly begun yet! I'll tell you all of it and you can write it down. Eh?"

A look of acute distaste in her face, Jane Warr assented, and asked no more questions.

An hour later, what with voluble chatter while she strove to recollect all Desmond had said, La Delphine came to an end of her dictation, and Jane Warr welcomed it. Laying down her quill, she folded over the notes and thrust them into her traveling case, and nodded to her hostess.

"Good. I'll add a thousand francs to the payment—satisfactory? Very well. Now I'll turn in. I'm dead tired. Shall I see you in the morning?"

"At daybreak? Heaven forbid!" exclaimed La Delphine, with a laugh. "I haven't seen the sun come up in a long while, and never want to again! My driver has his orders, and will be ready. I'll have you wakened, and a morning draught prepared. Goodnight, dearie, and pleasant dreams!"

Jane Warr, with a sigh of utter relief, closed the door upon her.

La Delphine, however, was well pleased. She went downstairs, intruded the two men in the dining-room, and came back to her own room again. She was humming a gay, light tune as she entered, and crossed to the dressing-table against the far wall. She looked at herself in the mirror there, and chuckled, while her fingers worked at her gown.

"High time you were cashing in, my girl!" she observed. "Another month of this, and off you can fly to Brussels or Venice, with enough money in your stocking to cut a wide swath."

With a swift, lithe movement, she was out of her dress. As she cast it aside, she started, and stood staring down at a bottle and a glass on the dressing table.

"Devil take me! How did this get here?" she murmured. "Why—"

Something touched her naked back—something sharp. She shrank, looked up, and in the mirror saw Desmond standing behind her. The point of the long poniard touched her again as she swung around with a choked cry. Touched her, even drew blood to the white hollow between her breasts, so that she shrank again.

"Scream, La Delphine!" came the icy voice. "Scream, and I'll kill you as you killed your lover in Paris. No soft-hearted king here to pardon you, murderess! But, if you answer my questions, I'll not harm you."

At recognition of him, at these words which showed that he knew all about her, the woman was speechless and stricken. One hand at her mouth, the other at the poniard point, she stared from eyes dilated with horror. Her face drained of all color until it seemed old and yellow and shrunken.

"Where's Lady Warr going in the morning?" snapped Desmond. "Quick, curse you—speak!"

A sharp little cry, as the steel touched into her flesh again, merged with desperate response.

"To—to Hervé. Four miles away. Her coach is waiting there."

"Does she know what you're doing here? Does she give you your orders?"

"Yes, of course," she stammered.

This confirmation of his worst imaginings wrenched Desmond's very soul, drove him to an inflexible cruelty. His eyes glittered death at the terrorized woman.

"Pour that wine and drink," he commanded hoarsely. "Quick! Or, by heaven, I'll kill you as poor Castries was killed today, without mercy or pity—"

Her shaking hand went to the bottle.

"The wine—it—it was drugged...."

"I knew that long ago." The terrible smile of Desmond bit into her. "Quick...."

She poured and drank. At his command she poured again. One frantic protest broke from her. The poniard chipped a stifled cry from her lips, and she hurriedly emptied the glass.

MEANTIME, IN his room above the stable, the Balafré

and two other servants of the house were playing at cards, gaming for the money looted from Castries' body. A lantern cast its flickering light upon the table, on their faces.

"Who's driving the visitor to Hervé?" asked one, as they played.

"Andre. He's in bed snoring," said the Balafré, with his jaunty laugh.

"And you winning our money!" The third man spoke sullenly. "Mine by right. It was my shot that brought down the officer."

"Yours? Devil take you for a liar!" cried the other man. "It was my bullet took him through the heart and toppled him over! You couldn't hit the side of a house!"

The door of the room had slowly swung open. The last speaker glanced up, and a sharp cry escaped him—a cry of dismayed recognition.

It was drowned by Desmond's voice.

"Good boasting, murderers. Now do your boasting in hell this night."

He flung himself at them. One of those two men coughed and died, the old poniard through his neck. The second grappled savagely. Desmond struck him over the face with the heavy poniard-hilt, beat him away, evaded a knife, and ran him through the heart. But the Balafré, with the first glance, had darted across the room to pick up a rapier there.

And now, as the second man groaned and collapsed, the Balafré darted in. He showed no surprise; his scarred features were set in ferocity.

"Clever man," he jerked out, pausing in his attack. "Now you can discover about hell yourself...."

A deadly lunge ripped in. Desmond, with the long poniard almost as good as a rapier, caught the thrust and parried it. Surprise leaped now into that scarred face.

And into Desmond's as well. Another lunge, a riposte, and he knew that he was facing no bungler, but a very master of

fence. Confident, assured, deadly, the Balafré pressed him, striving to break through his guard. Only by the most desperate
agility could Desmond keep clear of that darting blade so eager
for his life.

A glitter of admiration sprang in the dark eyes.

"Ha! You're good!" gasped the Balafré. "Lucky you've no
sword there...."

He uncoiled with a long, swift thrust; but he had stepped in
a pool of blood. His foot slid. He lost balance and went hurtling
sideways, colliding headfirst with the stone wall. He fell in a
limp, inert heap.

Panting, Desmond came to the man, turned him over, shortened blade to end the scarred life—and paused. This brief and
savage fight for his own life had dulled his blood-lust. After
all, he had killed the two men who had actually murdered
Castries; he had their own words for it. And, whatever this
Balafré was, now he lay helpless, senseless.

With a grudging oath, Desmond flung down his old poniard
and picked up the Balafré's weapon. A good blade, this; well
balanced, well wrought. He frowned down at the senseless man,
still hesitant. La Delphine was drugged. With morning, or
before, this fellow would have sensed a trap, would fly. Well, let
him go. After all, the murderers were dead.

Desmond turned away. He took the sword-belt, buckled it
on, sheathed the rapier, turned out the light, and left the room.

Now there was other, and more bitter, work ahead of him.

CHAPTER XVIII

ARREST

MORNING IN the little town of Hervé, which
boasted a cobbled street and a good two hundred inhabitants.

The first early sunrise was striking level across the roofs and the swirling mists of bluish morning, when Desmond came downstairs and out of the inn. After only three hours of sleep he was still hungry for more. He stood yawning and stretching.

Clattering down the cobbled street came a squad of cavalry, twenty men and an officer, a foraging party from the army camp. Desmond snapped alert. He stepped forward and waved his arm. The squad drew to a halt, and he addressed the officer.

"Monsieur, I am Colonel Brian Desmond, on detached duty. Will you step inside and enjoy a morning draught with me? I'll be glad to have your men drink also, at my expense. I have something to discuss with you."

The end of this meeting was that Desmond and the officer sat in the tavern room together. When the officer had inspected the papers laid before him by Desmond, he glanced up with a smiling assent.

"Correct, M. le Colonel. I am of course entirely at your disposition. The signature of His Majesty is supreme. May I ask you to give me a note that will excuse me to my commander?"

"Gladly. First of all, I want one of your men to take a letter to the Chevalier de Boufflers at headquarters; courier service, at all speed. Here's the letter."

"Understood, monsieur."

"Next, I wish you to be ready with your men. I am about to send you north in charge of a prisoner—a royal prisoner, you comprehend, who must be treated with every respect, but watched carefully."

Desmond checked himself, rose, looked eagerly out the window. A carriage was just turning into the courtyard of the inn. It was the carriage of La Delphine. He pointed to it.

"Quick! Arrest the man who is driving; he's to be sent to M. de Boufflers with my note. That will take four of your men. The others will remain under my orders. When you've arrested that fellow, I want private speech with the lady in the carriage."

The officer saluted and went out.

Desmond watched and waited. Soldiers surrounded the carriage and the driver was hauled from his seat and pinioned. Jane Warr intervened heatedly from her seat; Desmond came out of the inn and advanced into the group while she argued. He caught her angry words.

"Here, then! Here is a safe-conduct for me. I demand that my driver be released!"

"The safe-conduct is canceled," said Desmond, shoving through.

Her eyes widened on him, a flash of color leaped into her face. Almost his heart failed him at the quick gladness in her eyes, the amazed delight in her look.

"Send the man as I've ordered," Desmond went on calmly. "The lady is under arrest, her safe-conduct confiscated. Give it to me. Then withdraw your men."

The officer obeyed. Desmond met the half angry, questioning gaze of Jane Warr, his blue eyes icy, his face like rock. She comprehended his manner and flushed more deeply.

"What does this mean?" she asked slowly, as the soldiers drew away.

"Haven't you looked in the secret compartment of your traveling case?"

She started slightly. "Why, no! I—how did you know about that?"

"Monsieur Feufollet knows everything," said he, coming close to the carriage.

She met his implacable cold gaze for a moment. A wave of emotion broke the rigor of her oval features; perplexed, pleading, she leaned forward, putting out her hands to him. Her gloves fell to the cobblestones, unregarded.

"Brian, I don't understand," she said softly, and he steeled himself bitterly against the warm intimate kindness of her voice. "What does this mean? What have I done?"

"Good God! What have you done—you can ask that?"

His voice trembled. He checked himself abruptly; he must

keep his head, allow no outburst, remain calm. He stooped and picked up her gloves, and then remained holding them as he met her bewildered eyes.

"You've done more than you know, more than you intended," he said slowly, his voice more icy than his eyes. He had himself in hand, now. "I loved you, Jane Warr. I looked up to you, I dreamed of you, I wove you in with the future and with my whole life. To me, you were the soul of honor and high woman-hood and loveliness. I loved you the more because you fought me, because you played the game as I'd play it myself, because you've come closer than anyone else to beating me."

"Well, Brian?" Her voice was soft with reproach, her eyes warm with tenderness. "And because—because I've done the work here you knew I would do—"

"No, by Heaven!" he broke out, then became cold again. "No, not that. I never dreamed you'd do what you've done, shown yourself lower than the low, until the blood of honorable gen-tlemen cries out to heaven upon your vileness and base crimes!"

She drew back, suddenly white and angry and yet incredu-lous.

"Do you realize what you're saying?"

"Too well, madame," Desmond said gloomily. "So well, that I think my heart and my life have broken with the saying it. By your own orders—I had it from the lips of that she-devil of yours, last night. Because I once loved you, because, God help me, I still love you, I'm not sending you to face a military court and a firing squad, as I could do and should do."

"What horrible thing has entered into you, Brian Desmond?" she demanded.

"The truth; and nothing could be more horrible," he said. "By your orders, a campaign of the basest murder has been set afoot. Gentlemen have been assassinated and robbed. Couriers, men serving their king and their country, have been trapped and killed. I don't speak of sabotage, of the ordinary work of spies, of obstruction. I speak only of low and dishonorable assassination, hellish work that the brain of a Constant must have planned and that you have carried out. Yesterday young Castries was shot down at my side, and I thank the saints that the man who did it has gone to hell; in a few hours more your whole cursed nest of assassins will be wiped out."

SHE STARED at him, growing whiter and whiter until her eyes were like two dark pools in a half-frozen river. Suddenly she burst into words.

"Oh! I must tell you—you must listen—"

"I must listen to nothing," and Desmond's voice beat her words flat like grass before the gusty wind of his cold fury. "Lies, lies, more lies! Murderess—do you understand? Murderess of honest gentlemen; murderess of my love and dreams and honor. War! I've warred and fought and lied and killed, but by the Lord I've never done a dishonorable deed or a shameful act, or soiled my soul with the dirt of assassination. I've never hired men to shoot down unsuspecting victims, or prison sluts to drug and drag down decent men to learn their secrets."

Her face was frightful to see. As she started *to* speak again, Desmond suddenly was aware of the gloves in his hand. A terrible laugh broke from him. He, too, was deathly white.

"Your gloves, murderess! They're stained with the blood of poor murdered men. Wear them, and dream of them!" And he flung the gloves into the carriage, and turned away.

He did not see that they had struck her across the face, for she had moved impulsively and swiftly. When he glanced back, he did see that she had fainted and was lying across the seat of the carriage, and at this he was glad.

He came to the officer, and thrust a paper at him.

"Here is a *lettre de cachet* filled in with the name of this woman. You will escort her to the royal chateau of Mont St. Michel and turn her over to the authorities there, to await the pleasure of His Majesty."

The officer saluted, looked into Desmond's face, and spoke gravely.

"Monsieur—you will pardon me. Perhaps you are not aware that those gloves struck her in the face? It must have seemed intentional—"

"What? Impossible!" Desmond swung around and looked at the carriage. "No; begad, I didn't mean that. I must apologize—oh, devil take it all!" His voice broke, as his heart was breaking in him. "I can't look into her eyes again. Give her my apologies. Take her away, take her quickly, quickly! By the saints, get her away from here before I change my mind and relent...."

He went staggering into the tavern, and like a madman called for wine and more wine, and downed it in huge drafts until the innkeeper gawked at him. His brain was burning, and the heart and soul of him were in wrenching agony; he was blind and deaf to everything around, and gulped down the raw red wine of the countryside until he fell to the floor retching and vomiting.

After a little he wakened to the ministrations of the grooms, and stumbled out to the horsetrough, plunging his head into the water. But when he blinked around, the courtyard was empty.

CHAPTER XIX

THE WOODEN LEG

TWO DAYS later, on the Friday, the Vicomte de St. Vrain dismounted in the courtyard of the White Horse Tavern, in the Breton town of Dol. With him were two Breton peasants, stalwart bronzed men under wide black hats, muskets over their shoulders.

St. Vrain was clad all in black now, making a somber and striking figure. Even the rapier at his thigh was black of hilt, his horse was black, and his long black hair fell about his ears, Breton fashion. When he passed through the streets, men crossed themselves and gaped after him.

He strode into the tavern and the innkeeper stared at him, slack-jawed.

"Come, man, wake up!" St. Vrain flung down a golden coin and gave his name. "I want your best private room, your best wine, your best dinner, and accommodations for my two men. I expect to meet a friend here today or tomorrow. Has anyone been asking for me?"

"St. Vrain?" The innkeeper furtively glanced down to see if this black-clad hand had a cloven hoof. Relief flooded into his face. "Oh, M. de St. Vrain—yes, yes! There was a—a gentleman here not half an hour ago. At least, I think he was a gentleman; but his manner was very singular. It was more like that of a madman."

"What?" barked St. Vrain angrily.

"It is true, monsieur. He had the look of a week-old corpse in his face. He drank two bottles of my strongest wine in five minutes, and never so much as staggered. He would not give his name or answer a question. He seemed to hear nothing. When he went out—"

"Went out? Where?"

"To ride to the hill above town, monsieur. He said he would return—" and the other hesitated—"when—when the devil brought him back. His very words, monsieur."

Amazement, anxiety, dismayed surmise, shot across St. Vrain's face.

"Desmond? Impossible," he muttered. "Yet no one else would have asked for me. What in the fiend's name has happened?" He lifted his voice in a shout to the grooms outside. "Hola, there! Don't unsaddle my horse. Leave him."

One of his two men came hurriedly into the place.

"Monsieur! Such a man as we have been searching for everywhere—an hostler says he has been here, is here now!"

"Eh?" St. Vrain's bitter, flaming eyes went to the innkeeper. "Is this true? Have you a one-legged man around here?"

"But yes, monsieur! Upstairs in his room. He is ill."

"*Diable!*" exclaimed St. Vrain. "His left leg gone at the knee? An Englishman with a wooden leg?"

The innkeeper smiled.

"No, monsieur, not at all. His left leg, yes; but he has none of wood. And not an Englishman either. He gets about with a crutch. He is one Michel Goebel of Strasburg, a pilgrim on his way to Mont St. Michel. He came here a week ago and was taken so ill that he could not go on to the Mont. The curé has visited him and examined his papers; he has a letter from the Prince-Cardinal de Rohan to the abbot of the Mont." The speaker tapped his head significantly. "A poor gentleman who lost his leg in the wars, monsieur. He is very gentle and harmless. A simpleton."

St. Vrain grunted doubtfully. "He wears a wig?"

"Oh, no, monsieur! He has long gray hair and a gray mustache."

"Not our man, then. No wooden leg either." St. Vrain drew a deep breath. "All right. Have the chamber prepared. I'll ride up the hill and see if this gentleman is my friend. Which road?"

"Straight up the street, monsieur. You cannot miss it."

St. Vrain strode out, mounted and departed, hurried on by perplexed anxiety.

He left the town behind and mounted the hill. Presently he came in sight of a horse and man, motionless; the rider sat gazing out across the sunset.

It was a view to strike into the dullest soul. Not the green Breton shores, with the gray smoke of hamlets rising here and there; not the wooded heights; not the wide expanse of the bay, reddened and glowing in the sunset light, but what lay there in the bay.

Here, rising sheer out of the water, was such a structure as men imagined only in fairyland, or in the wandering aisles of a dream. The Marvel—so it had been called for centuries past, and the name was fitting; nothing else in the world was like it. That human hands could have erected this glorious creation, whose walls and incredible flying buttresses and high towers lifted up and up as though reaching toward heaven, seemed impossible. In the sunset glow and at this distance, the ancient stones appeared like purest marble, tipped by a fleck of gold— the gilded statue of St. Michel rising above the highest spire.

Such was Mont St. Michel, once a Benedictine abbey and still inhabited by a handful of monks, but now a "royal chateau," the Bastille of the Ocean, a prison of which frightful tales were told. A prison from which there was no escape, except by death. The pilgrims who had once flocked here from all over Europe by the thousand each year, still came in feeble remnants. The Marvel still held its ancient treasure, a treasure so vast as to have no equal in France, gold and jewels donated by princes and kings and pilgrims of wealth. But for the past hundred and fifty years a royal garrison had held the Mont, and men had rotted there in the chill dungeons, and what had been a glori- ous symbol of God's mercy had become an accursed symbol of man's tyranny.

St. Vrain rode up to the motionless figure, and spoke. Desmond turned slowly in the saddle and gazed at him from burned-out eyes, and spoke in a lifeless voice.

"Oh, it's you."

St. Vrain was struck dumb. Desmond's garments were unkempt, torn, stained by dust and mud and water; it had rained on the way north. His square-shouldered figure now slumped in the saddle. Only by his voice could he be recognized, for his face was beyond recognition. It was masked by unshaven beard, haggard and drawn until it was like the visage of an old man. The blue eyes were lackluster. There was no life in this face. There was no life in Brian Desmond's heart, for that matter; he cared about nothing.

"*Mon Dieu!*" St. Vrain found tongue. "Are you drunk?"

"I wish it were possible," said Desmond. "I've tried; it can't be done."

Alarm leaped in the black, sinister eyes. St. Vrain drew his horse close, reached out, caught Desmond's shoulder in a quick, firm grip.

"Mon ami!" His voice was stirred, vibrant. "What's happened? What's done this to you?"

Desmond stared at him as at a stranger, then stirred a little.

"Eh? Oh, nothing, nothing. What news, St. Vrain? Any trace of that accursed Constant?"

"Not a single trace, comrade. Upon my word, he has dropped out of existence! He was not with Balsamo at all. That old Norman woman, I found, left the diligence at Rennes, and there wasn't a hint of her to be picked up. No sign of Constant anywhere about the chateau, either, nor in any villages that I've come through. I did pick up news of your charming Lady Warr, though. She was at the chateau, and should be back. Eh? Good Lord, man—what is it?"

Desmond fell into a fit of shivering as though an ague had seized him. He cackled out a hoarse, discordant laugh, and lifted his arm, pointing.

"She won't be back, St. Vrain. There she is—there! Look! In that fairy palace in the sea—an angelic vision outside, a hell-hole inside. Like herself, St. Vrain; and she's there where she belongs. I arrested her and sent here there."

A gasp broke from the other. "Desmond, have you gone mad? You couldn't do that. You couldn't have the heart—"

"I have no heart." Desmond looked at him blankly. "I have nothing. Nothing but a consuming thirst. My throat burns. Come along back to the inn."

He turned his horse, struck in his spurs, and the animal leaped madly. St. Vrain, in frantic alarm and bewilderment, followed.

THEY DISMOUNTED in the courtyard of the inn. The sun was down now. Like an automaton, Desmond accompanied St. Vrain and the innkeeper to the room up above, and there demanded wine. St. Vrain dissented.

"Enough of that, comrade. No more liquor now—"

A furious shout burst from Desmond, a torrent of oaths.

"Wine, d'you hear me? Cognac, Calvados, anything—but bring it! Anything that will burn out thought and memory. Wine, blast you!"

The frightened innkeeper scurried away.

Presently, with candles alight, with food on the table, with wine pouring down his unquenched throat, Desmond told St. Vrain everything. Not at once, but by fits and snatches. The two Bretons served them or stood in a dark corner like owls. St. Vrain got the whole story by degrees.

"I don't believe it!" he broke out hotly. "That woman, that angel? No, no! She could not have done these things. There was some mistake—"

Desmond leaped up, aimed a blow at him, lost balance, and gripped the table fiercely.

"You blackguard! Mistake? If you mention that word again, I'll put my sword into you—mistake, mistake!" He relaxed and dropped back into his chair, with a groan. "Oh, the word burns like fire! There's no such word, I tell you. It's impossible. That she-devil confessed to getting orders from her. There was nothing else to be done. I could not let her go, in honor."

"Devil take me, you could not," said St. Vrain, and swore a bitter oath. "This is a fine meeting! And I'd counted on such doings with you, comrade! Balsamo has my chateau, right enough, and I have him—have him like a flea, if he only knew it. I can show you everything that passes in those walls, Desmond. Everything!"

"Balsamo? Cagliostro, you mean," said Desmond dully.

"Or, more like, Satan in person," said the other, gloom in his face. "Come, comrade, for the love of Heaven wake up and be yourself! I'll put this magician in your hand, d'you understand? I'll show you everything. Didn't I tell you that an education in the galleys leaves nothing to be desired? Well, that's true—"

Suddenly Desmond shot up out of his chair again, hand uplifted.

"Silence!" The low word burst from him in a voice that chilled St. Vrain. So wild were his eyes, so suddenly aflame and distended with a light of madness, that the two Bretons crossed themselves in fear. "Listen, St. Vrain—you hear it?"

St. Vrain repressed a groan. "There's nothing, Desmond. Nothing."

"You lie!" cried Desmond. "His step—Constant! I know it, I tell you—the *tap-tap-tap* of his wooden leg!" He listened. Gradually his face dulled. "No, it's gone...."

He dropped into his chair again, reached for his wine-cup, and drained it at one gulp. When he tried to speak again, his tongue was thick and wandering. Presently his head was sunk, chin on chest; he was gone in a drunken stupor.

"Damnation to all women!" St. Vrain beckoned the two Bretons. They were no serfs, but independent, upstanding peasants who served him because he was St. Vrain; serfdom ran not in Breton blood.

"My friends," St. Vrain said slowly, "This man is bound for hell because he loved a woman. Well, help me to save him! Get him to bed. Fix up his clothes. Wash him, shave him. See that his horse gets attention. Eh?"

"Certainly, monsieur," said one of the two, brightening a trifle. A woman, eh? Well, that was different. One could understand things now.

When Desmond was in the big bed in the corner, the two men examined his clothes.

"These are terrible, monsieur," said one of them gravely. "They must be washed and dried and iron. We can cleanse them, and leave them before the cooking hearth downstairs to dry. They'll be ready by morning."

St. Vrain nodded. He went through the garments carefully; no money, no papers of any kind in the pockets. Nothing, in fact. The money-belt under Desmond's clothes was intact, however.

"Right. Take them down, then. And send up some warm water and soap. I'll shave him myself, poor devil! I've served my turn as barber often enough—"

He checked himself, with a thin smile. To Desmond, he might prate of the galleys, but not to other men.

LATER THAT night, with St. Vrain stretched out in the bed at his side, Desmond came wide and instantly awake. He started up, reached out, caught hold of St. Vrain.

"Listen!" he said. "St. Vrain—you hear it? Outside the door, in the passage!"

Sleepily, St. Vrain climbed out of bed, went to the door, and looked out.

"Nothing there," he said. "Thank Heaven you seem sane! How do you feel?"

"Like myself," said Desmond, in the darkness. And, in the morning, he wakened more like himself. The past few days were as an evil dream.

Yet all fire, all energy, was gone from him. He sat listless, while St. Vrain rang for a servant and summoned his two Bretons. Then he looked up, frowning.

"Did I waken in the night?"

"Aye, hearing things," said St. Vrain, and clapped him on the shoulder. "All's well now, comrade! We've work to do. No more liquor, eh?"

"Right. One more job," Desmond agreed. "Go after this Cagliostro, find what work he's doing. There's a traitor to nab, and then we're done. I'm done, rather. Make sure of this Baron Deaurevel—did I tell you about him?"

"After a fashion. You were rather incoherent."

Desmond grunted. "I don't wonder. Listen, then."

He described his visit to the camp, and what had happened

there, and what Castries had told him of the weekend party at the Chateau de St. Vrain.

"No doubt of it; Deaurevel's our man," said St. Vrain. "But pinning anything definite on him—that's something else. Hello! Here we are now."

The two Bretons showed up. One was despatched for the usual morning draught, the other for Desmond's clothes.

"Just what do you propose?" asked Desmond, forcing himself to the work in hand. "We cannot well walk in on this Balsamo, or Cagliostro—"

"Bah! I told you last night, but you don't remember it, comrade. That old house has secrets, and I know them. I can take you anywhere in the place. I was all through it the other day, and not a soul the wiser."

Desmond looked sharply at him. "You mean secret passages?"

"Of course. It was built during the religious wars." St. Vrain broke into a laugh. "If that imitation magician knew as much about the house as I know, he could produce results that would smack of real magic! At worst, we can see what goes on, and devil take me if I don't explain what happens! I knew two or three such fellows in the galleys, as I've mentioned before. Here's our wine—health and success!"

The morning draught put Desmond into shape, after a fashion. At least, it pulled him together, cleared his brain, restored a faint spark of his old energy. He sat with his head in his hands, while St. Vrain shaved and dressed. Then the other Breton, who had been sent for his clothes, came in.

"Well?" snapped St. Vrain. "Where are they?"

Desmond looked up. The man was empty-handed, stammering.

"Gone, monsieur! They were there last night. The people below are looking for them, but they have vanished clear away. And a horse is missing out of the stables."

"Gone? My clothes gone?" Desmond leaped up.

"Plague on them. I've an extra suit here," said St. Vrain. "There was not a thing in the pockets, anyway."

"But—good heavens, man!" Desmond stared blankly. "Everything was sewn inside the waistcoat. My papers, my authority, a blank *lettre de cachet*—"

St. Vrain uttered a dismayed oath. "And I never noticed them!"

"What did I tell you? Remember?" Desmond caught at his arm. "Constant was here, I heard his accursed thumping! That devil was in this very place, St. Vrain!"

"Monsieur!" eagerly interposed one of the Bretons. "You remember the man they told us about, the man with one leg who was here? The man who is ill in one of these rooms?"

A wild cry burst from Desmond, a cry of frantic comprehension, of indignation, of unreasoning dismay and anger.

"What? Here in this very place—you knew this, St. Vrain, and you did nothing? You didn't tell me—"

"Damnation!" broke out St. Vrain, with a snarl. "It was not the same man. This one is a sick pilgrim. He has no wooden leg but uses a crutch."

Desmond made a gesture and turned away. A hopeless despair seized him.

"That man was Constant. Well, forget it; I've no heart to fight."

St. Vrain uttered a scalding oath, caught up his sword, and darted to the door. As he swung it open, the innkeeper appeared, white and shaking with consternation.

"Gone! Your clothes, monsieur, my best horse, my hat and cloak—and the poor gentleman for whom I felt so much compassion. Gone, his score unpaid! Stolen away like a thief in the night! A thief indeed. All he left behind was his old clothes and his crutch. He must have worn the garments of this gentleman."

At sight of St. Vrain's countenance, Desmond vented a harsh and discordant laugh.

"He must have flown away upon wings, eh? More like, on his wooden leg."

"And the other one is gone, too," said the disconsolate inn-keeper.

"Eh?" Desmond swung around. "What other one?"

"Oh, the man who came in last night late and took a private room. The gentleman with the scarred face—"

Desmond stared, then threw up his hands.

"The Balafré! Birds of a feather, eh? Well, St. Vrain, let 'em go. Give me what clothes you have, and we'll be about our business. We still have Cagliostro to think about, and the child. Constant slipped out of your hands, as he's done out of mine. What of it? He's out of my life now."

"The devil's never out of one's life," said St. Vrain, with an oath of rage and chagrin. Then he sent his two Bretons to saddle the horses.

CHAPTER XX

THE SECRET WAY

"RIDE PAST? Faith, why not?" and Desmond shrugged. "We've nothing to fear here, and no one's interested in us. Look over the place, by all means!"

The Chateau de St. Vrain lay before them as they rode.

They were alone; the two Bretons had been left behind now, after a hearty meal in the farmhouse of one. It was early after-noon. The day's ride, the meal, had put heart into Desmond. His old gay smile was gone, his old abounding life was gone, but he was somewhat more like himself and intent upon the job ahead.

They rode slowly past the wall of the chateau, and the wide gates. A huge, massively built structure of stone, dark and gloomy with the years. Gloomily set, too, amid enormous dark

*St. Vrain's rapier
crossed with the
scar-faced rogue's.*

trees. No gardens, no pleasant glow of flowers, but a place of
ominous and savage appearance that had been built, and had
more than once served, as a fortress.

"Our man brought his own servants," said St. Vrain. "Rather,
his wife brought them. Not many, and apparently honest people.
A couple of women, three or four men; all from Rennes, I gather.
You've nothing against them?"

Desmond shook his head. "Nor against him, perhaps. I meant

one *lettre de cachet* for him, merely to make him talk later on. The other, I might have used for Deaurevel, but it's gone now. We'll see. Hello! Our guests are come. That's Boufflers—the big fellow."

He pulled down his hat, to avoid possible recognition. A group of officers were at the front of the house, about the figure of a woman; Desmond took her to be the Countess de Cagliostro—or the Signora Balsamo, as she was now become. He recognized Boufflers, Deaurevel and others. Long ere this, of course, Boufflers should have had his note, his prisoner, and have wiped clean the nest of La Delphine.

"No hurry," said St. Vrain complacently, eyeing the now alert Desmond with much satisfaction. "We've food and wine here. We'll leave the horses, come back on foot to a spot behind the stables, and then dive underground. The passage is clear; I've been through it already. I'll lay bare to you the secrets of every room in that house, comrade."

The prospect held a certain terrible fascination. Also, Desmond was now intent upon the rescue of the child Celie; this objective had roused him from his terrible despondency and had given him a purpose.

Once the chateau had dropped behind, St. Vrain turned into a bypath and halted at a spring among the trees. Here the horses were watered and then tethered. St. Vrain took the food and set off among the trees, and Desmond followed with the wine. Presently the wall of the park appeared before them, with a mass of stone farther on.

"The stables," muttered St. Vrain. "We may find our Constant here ahead of us, eh?"

Desmond shook his head. Constant, he was convinced, had nothing in common with Cagliostro in their affair. That westward trip in the same diligence must have been sheer chance.

St. Vrain halted behind the rear wall of the stables. Here was a door, which he opened and held back, after a careful look beyond. Desmond passed into the stables, and St. Vrain checked him instantly, turning to an apparently blank wooden boarding. He threw his weight on this, and it slid away to show a tunnel-like opening. On a shelf were candles, with flint and steel and a tinder-box.

Closing the way behind them, St. Vrain struck a spark in the darkness, puffed the tinder alight, and a candle flared up. He took this and led the way.

"Straight to the cellars," he observed. "And once there, no more talking."

"You picked that outer stable door-lock very neatly," Desmond said dryly.

The other vented his mirthless chuckle. "Noticed that, did you? Comrade, for the love of heaven rid your mind of this woman! Go back to work. You and I would be invincible together. With this bit of wire, any door will open to me, any lock; the galleys made a wonderful college. So it is in a dozen directions. With my knowledge and your abilities, we could milk all Europe dry for France! Think it over. The future is worth while."

"I have no future," said Desmond coldly, and St. Vrain plunged on with a sullen oath. Presently, when he paused before a massive iron-bound door, St. Vrain spoke again.

"And where do we go from here? Suppose we take action, make prisoners."

Desmond winced. "To Mont St. Michel, perhaps; I don't know. It depends. No, not there of all places! Lead on, lead on; stop prating about the future when there is none!"

SO DANGEROUS was his voice that St. Vrain said no more, but worked at the door and pulled it open. A dimly lit cellar lay before them, cavernous, heaped with debris.

A huge stone block in the foundation pivoted and showed a narrow little gallery with stairs winding upward. From his candle, St. Vrain lit a dark-lantern which was here, adjusted the slide, and sent the thin ray of light ahead of them. The air was good. Stooping, they crept up the stairs and came into a tiny square room.

"Headquarters base," muttered St. Vrain, depositing his bundle of food. "Down with the wine; right. Now we really get somewhere. Come along! Mind your head."

More stairs. Then a long dark little tunnel.

St. Vrain halted, reached out, slid back a little panel and peered through. Desmond waited. He had but one objective, the child Celie. Otherwise, all curiosity and interest had died in him.

"Blank," muttered St. Vrain. He went on farther to another little panel. He drew this back; then his hand moved in the lantern-ray, beckoning. Desmond joined him and looked into a room.

Baron Deaurevel sat sprawled in a chair, laughing gaily, talking with someone whom Desmond could not see.

"What I need is the money," Deaurevel was saying. "I've arranged it all with Boufflers. I put it into his head to demand that you summon up the daughter of Vergennes. He knows the girl well. He knows she's sick and dying. The rest is easy. Once he's convinced of your powers, he'll write Vergennes, and your game is won."

"So! Excellent, my dear baron." This was the voice of Cagliostro, affable, urbane, polished. There was a clink of gold. "Here is the sum we agreed upon. By the way, do you expect any couriers from Paris soon?"

"At the end of the week, yes," said Deaurevel. "Damme, Balsamo, you're a smooth one! So you really intend to fool Vergennes—pass off this girl on him as his daughter, get him under your thumb, eh? Pretend you can cure his daughter, switch this child on him—ha! It'd make a good comedy. What becomes of the real daughter?"

"That," Cagliostro's voice replied softly, "is not your affair, my dear baron."

"No?" The handsome, passionate face of Deaurevel contracted in a sneer. "Perhaps it will be, then. Careful! I know enough about you to send you to the scaffold!"

"Which would be very disastrous for you, my dear baron. Now you will excuse me, while I see to my guests. I think you'll find the sum correct."

A door slammed.

Desmond had heard this dialogue in stupefaction. Two diverse things tore at his brain. First, Deaurevel was the actual traitor, the man who had betrayed those couriers to death. Second, here was the whole scheme about the child Celie laid bare to him. An intrigue of the most damnable and impudent kind! To reach Vergennes, the prime minister; to pass off this child as his daughter—this child who looked so curiously like the real daughter! He closed the panel and turned abruptly.

"St. Vrain! There's the traitor. Is it possible to get into this room?"

"Yes. Not from here, however. From another point. The traitor, eh? You mean—"

"The sword. Here and now."

"Then, my friend, allow me the pleasure of doing it, while you wait here."

Desmond hesitated, then nodded. "Very well. And when it is done—"

"He will disappear magically, I assure you. I'll get rid of the body. Wait here."

St. Vrain departed. Desmond turned again to the panel, opened it, looked at Baron Deaurevel still sitting in the chair, and waited frowningly.

He wanted to think. Everything was coming clear at last. Boufflers would be convinced that he saw the daughter of Vergennes. This was also a sort of trial, no doubt. Boufflers knew the real daughter, and if Boufflers could be tricked, the game was won. Then to Paris, to cure the dying child. Substitute Celie for her, spirit her away, leave the waif—yes, but how, how? Celie could not be in the plot.

"Get Vergennes under his thumb, eh?" reflected Desmond.

"The minister of France a dupe for an English spy? What a game it would be! Well, it's doomed."

Abruptly, he heard St. Vrain's voice, cool and mocking, coming from the room. He saw Deaurevel leap out of his chair, pass beyond his vision. What happened there was hidden from him. He could hear a clash of voices, a clash of steel, and presently the mocking laugh of St. Vrain.

"So the devil flies away with you, my dear baron!"

A gasp, a fall. Then silence.

A F T E R A little, Desmond saw the lantern-flicker coming along the passage. St. Vrain came up to him, and spoke with sardonic gaiety.

"*Hola*, comrade! Well, our traitor is supping with his master in hell. Shall we go on to the next little scene?"

"On," said Desmond. "Clean up this whole damned nest while we're at it. Put this Cagliostro out of business—on!"

He followed St. Vrain. The latter presently halted at another panel, then drew him on to it. Desmond realized they were now at the end of the narrow gallery. He was looking across a handsomely furnished room. Here was Cagliostro again, now in full sight; and beside him was that lovely sad-eyed woman, his wife.

Cagliostro was speaking, but no longer affably.

"We'll be gone from here in another two weeks, I tell you. There's no risk. Don't be a fool, Lorenza!" His voice was harsh now, dominant and biting. "We go to Paris. I have the work there with Vergennes; but Paris is only a stepping-stone. Once finished with this affair, I'm ready to go after business in a large way. Strassburg is our goal. There we'll find fame, fortune, power!"

"And perhaps prison," said the woman mournfully. The two of them were speaking in Italian, which Desmond understood perfectly. Cagliostro frowned and began to pace up and down.

"Prison? For what? Be sensible, you little fool. This child responds perfectly; as a subject, she's marvellous, obeys every hypnotic suggestion I give her. A month in Paris, and I'm through. I don't intend to play with these stupid English forever; we'll do the work, collect our money, and move on. True, I don't want to linger here in Brittany, but it's well worth while. After Paris, Strassburg beckons! And at Strassburg, I'll give you a prince to handle. A prince, do you understand? One of the most powerful, silly, absurd men in all Europe, and the handsomest dupe you've ever managed—"

"No, no, Giuseppe! Not that!" The woman cried out in a burst of terror and anguish. "Not that, I implore you; don't make me do such work again, Giuseppe!"

"Silence!" snapped Cagliostro, and frowned. "I don't like this place any more than you do. I've had a presentiment, a warning of danger, from the start. But we must earn that money, do you understand? We need it; we must have it. With that safe in my hand, I can do all I've planned. Then, straight to Strassburg, perhaps returning to Brussels to finish the work there…. Stop your whining. Any other woman on earth would leap at what I offer her. Think of it—the great Louis de Rohan! I tell you, he's ripe for the plucking. Properly handled, I can play with him for months, for years!"

The woman turned, tears on her cheeks.

"Giuseppe, I implore you—"

Desmond closed the panel. He sent a growl at his companion.

"Decency sets a limit to this damned spying. That was Cagliostro and his wife; a scene of conjugal affection."

"Oh, I heard them, and I learned Italian in the galleys." And the dry, harsh chuckle sounded.

"Where's the child?"

"In a downstairs room. We're on the upper floor. Better leave her, until you're ready to vanish with her. Is that what you intend?"

"Why, I suppose so." Desmond was taken aback. Take the

child away with him? "Hold on, St. Vrain. If we do take her, what can we do with her?"

"Plenty of honest folk about here," said St. Vrain. "Leave her with them, pay them. She'll be happy, and bless your name. Eh?"

"Right. Excellent idea!"

St. Vrain, apparently amused, led the way back as they had come and then into a transverse gallery. Here, with gestures of caution, he halted, cautiously tested another and larger panel, and peered through a slight opening before pulling the whole thing back. Satisfied, he drew Desmond to the aperture. On the other side, within the room, hung a tapestry which concealed the gap.

Desmond put a finger through, drew the tapestry a little aside, and looked in upon the Chevalier de Boufflers and one of his staff, a major. The notion of spying upon such men was repugnant to him. He hesitated, as the major spoke.

"Well, monsieur! Another hour, and we'll be having our first taste of wonders, eh?"

The chevalier grunted in response, drew off one of his boots, and cursed it heartily as he examined it for a protruding nail.

With a gesture of distaste, Desmond was about to close the panel and pass on, when a name checked him, held him motionless.

"That Delphine woman." said Boufflers abruptly. "You say she poisoned herself? A pity. She should have gone to the scaffold. Ségur conducted the investigation; I had no chance to see him before we left camp."

"Oh, he told me about it, monsieur," said the major. "It was being written out in due form and attested, when I left."

"What was?" demanded Boufflers.

"Her confession. She talked, she told everything, before she died."

Desmond was frozen to the little opening. For an instant his heart stopped before the ghastly realization. In sending Jane

Warr to the Mont, he had condemned her to death. For La Delphine had told everything. This could only mean—

"Eh? Who was behind the whole thing, then?" Boufflers queried.

"English gold, of course. One of their spies, a man named Constant, had arranged the whole affair, had even instructed her what to do, how to act. She did not know where he is now; she has not seen him for some time. She turned over what papers and information she got to another English agent, a woman; I don't remember the name."

"What, a woman?" exclaimed Boufflers.

"A fine lady, she said; an aristocrat."

"No, no!" the chevalier broke out warmly. "I know these English. I can understand how a creature like La Delphine could do such things, but no English lady—"

"You misunderstand, monsieur," broke in the aide. "This lady knew nothing of the means employed. La Delphine made that quite clear. She had refused to let this lady know how she got results, for fear the flow of money would be checked. Bah! A shameful business, all of it! We, who should be fighting England, are fighting women...."

Desmond staggered. He drew the panel shut, then caught at the wall for support; his fists clenched spasmodically as he leaned against the cold stones.

A chill prickle crept down his spine, horror clutched at him, and a ghastly realization of the truth. Why, she had never known at all, had known nothing about it! La Delphine had lied to him, or more likely had told him what she thought he wanted to know. And he, against every dictate of his heart—good God! What had he said, what had he done!

A low, bitter groan was wrenched out of him. He slowly slid down against the wall, came to his knees, went forward on his face and lay there, his brain in a flaming, agonized riot of self-accusation, of remorse, of frightful and intolerable torment.

St. Vrain, who had also heard those voices and comprehended their import, stood in a silence more eloquent than words.

CHAPTER XXI

BLACK MAGIC

DESMOND LAY thus for a long while, his head in his arms, fighting down the emotion that shook and rended him; he was thankful for the darkness here. The memory of that last interview with Jane Warr, of his words to her, tortured him past endurance. Mistake! Mistake! The thought burned him like living fire. And she had been so sweet and tender, so innocent, so undeserving of his reproaches and vituperation! His own suffering was nothing to what she must have endured at his hands; this realization drew a low and terrible groan from him. Then he felt the hand of St. Vrain touching him upon the shoulder.

"Come. No talk here."

Desmond quivered. Talk! What good to talk? Suddenly a consuming fury took hold of him—a fury of impatience, of remorse, of frantic desire for action. He, and he alone, could undo what he had done. This was his task now; and he must abase himself before the woman he loved, the woman whose love he had spurned and wrecked. He must make everything clear to her, and then go. For him, there could be no forgiveness.

He scrambled to his feet. The lantern-ray shot forth, and he followed St. Vrain back to the little room where they had left food and wine.

"I understand everything, comrade." St. Vrain's hand fell on his arm. The harsh voice for once was low, soft, vibrant. Desmond trembled a little.

"Yesterday I thought—I thought I had passed the limit of suffering. It had only begun."

"There's no limit," said St. Vrain gently. "When you've lost everything, when you're in the galleys, chained to a bench, branded, lashed with whips—why, then you learn much about endurance. What now?"

"Get out of here," Desmond said hoarsely. "I've work to do. Get to Mont St. Michel, see her, find her, free her! Do you understand? Quickly!"

"And the child?" St. Vrain spoke gravely. "Wait a little. Time has passed, the afternoon is passing; we're about to discover what this magician is up to—"

"Devil take him! But the child—yes, yes." With an effort, Desmond forced himself to assent. "Is there any way of entering those rooms? Or can we hear and nothing else?"

"We can enter the lower ones, yes; downstairs. That's where he's up to his tricks."

"Then come along and get it over."

"First, wine and a bit of food. You may need it before morning."

Desmond fought back his burning impatience.

After a time he was following St. Vrain again, now upon the lower level. They halted, and St. Vrain spoke at his ear.

"Quiet. This is the little salon. We must reconnoiter."

After a moment he drew Desmond forward. Here were two small holes, at the height of the eyes. Desmond looked through them into a handsomely furnished little salon, almost empty. At one side was a chair, unoccupied. At the other, before a black curtain—the child Celie. Her hair was dressed and powdered. She was the image of Vergennes' daughter.

She sat in a chair, rigid, her eyes closed, apparently asleep. At first Desmond thought her dead; then he saw the bosom of her white toga-like dress move slightly.

From an adjoining room came the murmur of voices.

St. Vrain touched his arm, drew him urgently. Perplexed, alarmed, Desmond obeyed, stealing along the narrow little corridor behind the lantern-ray. St. Vrain halted again.

"The grand salon of the chateau," he murmured, and darkened his light.

A long, narrow slit opened in the wall to his deft touch. Desmond, beside him, looked into a large and very handsome room hung with several old portraits. The daylight was by this time fading away; besides, the salon windows were closed and draped. A single candle, burning on a massive carven table, illuminated the room dimly. On a stand burned a tripod of incense that curled up in grayish fumes. At one side of the table, by the candle, a sheet of paper was pinned to the table by an enormous dagger set into the wood. On the table were writing materials.

Boufflers and Cagliostro, alone, had entered the room and stood talking.

"This is the magic table of Isis, monsieur," said Cagliostro impressively. "I procured it in Egypt from the Grand Seigneur himself. It is one of the most remarkable objects in the world. Consider, now, that the forces of nature are about to assist us in the experiment; banish from mind all save the most solemn thoughts. Seat yourself before the paper yonder, while I exert the proper controls."

The chevalier, burly and frowning, seated himself at the table. Cagliostro went through incantations, with the most impressive gravity, and finally took the opposite chair. He gestured to a pointed stylus of ivory.

"Have the goodness to take that stylus, which writes invisibly," he said. "Write down what questions are in your mind—questions which you desire the spirits to answer. Do not waste their time with trifling matters. Nothing is beyond their scope, remember! If you wish to know the future, ask it!"

BOUFFLERS TOOK up the ivory point, and began to write on the paper before him. St. Vrain, with the ghost of his mirthless chuckle, put his lips to Desmond's ear.

"Clever, this; mechanical. A second paper below the first, coated with wax. When our man pulls open the drawer, the machinery works; the second paper comes to him under the table, sprinkled with black dust to bring out the impression—"

"You have finished?" said Cagliostro, when Boufflers paused. "Very well. Tear off the paper and burn it in the candle."

A groan broke the silence, another groan; a voice burst upon the room in a gabble of language that was perfectly incomprehensible. Startled, the chevalier ripped away the paper, staring around, and held it in the candle-flame. The black ashes dropped. Cagliostro opened a drawer before him and produced another sheet of paper, took up a quill, dipped it, and began to write.

"The magic squares are forming," he said, droning his words. Desmond, at a pull, drew away from the opening, while the droning voice went on. St. Vrain muttered again.

"You saw? This is mere patter while he reads the paper in the drawer. He'll go on from one thing to another—in the end, worm out everything he wants to know. Wait, watch!"

Desmond returned to the slit, fascinated despite himself. As for Chevalier de Boufflers, that redoubtable soldier sat with his eyes starting from his head.

"You question about the fleet at Brest," said Cagliostro. "You wish to know whether you will get to England. You wish to know what Madame de Sabran is doing at Paris, at this moment. Know, then!" and suddenly his voice lifted in a rolling vibration. He reached forward and tossed a pinch of dust on the tripod. A flash shot up, a cloud of smoke.

A horrible thing took place.

Something moved across the room, against the hanging tapestries there. A head appeared in the air; it took shape and form. From Boufflers came a low gasp. It was the head of Madame de Cagliostro, alive and breathing, the eyes moving! Even Desmond, warned as he was, stiffened to the sight and felt a cold chill run down his spine.

"Illusion!" breathed St. Vrain at his ear. "Wait."

"Speak!" said that head without a body. "Speak! We are commanded. We must obey."

"I obey," said another voice. Desmond's eyes turned. He started. There across the room, floating high, was another head—this, too, the head of Madame de Cagliostro. Desmond remembered what the man Logan had said to Jane Warr about a head in a box; none the less, he trembled. This second head was speaking now, was answering Boufflers' questions.

"The fleet will not sail—it will sail. I see it sailing in July. There is smoke and thunder on the ocean. The fleet comes back; it is doomed. You will never set foot in England. In Paris I see a woman with silvery fair hair, two little children at her knee. One of them she calls Elzear. She is writing to the man she loves—"

"It is she, it is she!" broke out the chevalier, sweat on his countenance.

St. Vrain quietly closed the slit.

"Now back to the other one; they'll go on to the child. You see, comrade? First the sucker is convinced of the supernatural. When he's well hooked, they pump him. One by one, these officers empty out their vapid brains. This fellow is an adept, certainly! I admire him. But now to see his work with the child."

They returned to the little salon. A low exclamation broke from Desmond when he looked into the room. The figure of Celie had disappeared. Then St. Vrain, laughing silently, pointed out to him that another black curtain had been lowered before her. She still sat in the chair, motionless, hypnotized, but invisible until the curtain in front of her had been parted.

"I'll end this damnable nonsense quickly enough," muttered Desmond. "Can we get into the room?"

"Certainly." St. Vrain indicated the lines of a secret door, a portrait set flush into the wall which would open at a touch. "We can step in at any moment. Ah! Silence, now. Here they come."

Cagliostro ushered Boufflers into the apparently empty room, with a running talk of spirits and powers. That Boufflers was completely under his spell, was obvious.

"You have demanded no easy thing, monsieur," said the necromancer. "You ask that I summon up, in the flesh, a child who is far away in Paris, and you want to speak with her! Well, I must warn you not to touch her when she appears, not to break the circle which I am about to draw around you. Here, be seated in this chair and I will begin the incantation."

Boufflers took the chair indicated. Cagliostro set incense to burning, took a wand from one corner, began to mutter spells and incantations, calling upon the names of angels and devils. He spoke the name of Marie de Vergennes; he commanded that she appear in the flesh. Upon the empty room floated a thin little voice of terror.

"No, no! You must not! Please let me go, let me go—"

DESMOND COULD see the girl, between the curtains. She did not open her eyes, but over her little body ran what seemed to be a ripple of quivering pain. Her features were convulsed. At the sight, realizing that here was some devil's work past his own comprehension, Desmond went cold as ice.

Suddenly he put his lips to the opening in the wall and sent a word floating upon the room.

"Listen to me!" he said in Italian. "Cagliostro! Pellegrini! Giuseppe!"

The magician started. He looked up, he stared around; he froze.

"End it," said Desmond. "Dismiss him. This is the spirit of the great Richelieu. What do you plot against the house of Rohan, Cagliostro? If you ever wish to see Strassburg, obey me, and do it quickly. Dismiss him. Bring that child back to life. Instantly!"

It was from Cagliostro that a low, startled cry now broke, for Boufflers heard the voice but did not understand the Italian words.

The plump features of the magician were distorted, pallid, fearful. He stared around with wide and frightened eyes.

"Obey!" ordered Desmond, with so stern and imperative a

tone that Cagliostro actually jumped. St. Vrain was chuckling delightedly.

The sorcerer turned to Boufflers.

"Monsieur—I—I beg of you, withdraw," he stammered nervously. "Something has—has gone amiss with my incantations. Withdraw, I implore you, lest something terrible happen to us all!"

"Loose the child quickly!" repeated Desmond, his voice quivering with fury. St. Vrain touched his arm, spoke at his ear.

"*Diable!* The fellow really believes in his own mummery, comrade!"

True. The aspect of Cagliostro was almost pitiable. Chevalier de Boufflers, striving not to display the fright that had come upon him, stalked out of the room and lost no time about it.

Cagliostro, his pallid features adrip with sweat, passed through the black curtains and shoved them aside. He went to the girl and laid his hand on her forehead. Desmond, watching, saw her become calm and placid. The rigidity passed from her thin body. He comprehended that she was in no danger, that she was not being hurt in any way, and some of his wild fury died out.

The girl opened her eyes. Cagliostro stepped back, and she was aware of him. A little cry of fright broke from her.

"No, please don't! I'm afraid—"

"Open," and Desmond nudged St. Vrain sharply. "You take care of him. Hold him helpless but don't harm him."

Under St. Vrain's touch, the whole panel slid open. Desmond stepped through the large opening into the room. His only thought now was for the child.

"Celie!" he exclaimed. "Celie! Do you remember me, little one?"

Her gaze found him, her eyes widened upon him. With a sudden convulsive leap, she was out of her chair, running to him, hurling herself at him.

"Oh! My monsieur, my monsieur!" she cried, flinging her

arms about him. Desmond stooped and gathered her against his breast. She clung to him, trembling, and he patted her head, with soothing words.

Turning a little, he glanced past her. Cagliostro was standing flat against the wall, his arms outspread. Before him was St. Vrain, black-clad, grinning like a devil. The point of his rapier touched the plump throat of the magician and held him motionless, not daring to move.

However, there was no longer any terror in the Italian's attitude. His dark, piercing eyes had perceived the truth. He was dealing with living men, and one of those men was well known to him. Even his dismay and consternation had passed. He was alert, shrewdly collecting himself, fighting for his life.

"Ah, Colonel Desmond!" he said quietly. "I made a great mistake in saving your life, there in Brussels."

"Aye, you did," said Desmond. He lifted Celie in his arms and spoke past her. "And now, Balsamo, or whatever you choose to call yourself, you're going with me. Your clever little game with M. de Vergennes has ended before it began. Did you really think you could make that man believe that this poor child was his own?"

"So you know everything," Cagliostro rejoined, and nodded. "Oh, yes; this child would not be harmed. No one would be harmed—"

"Never mind any soft talk or protests," snapped Desmond. "I'm in no mood for them. If you'd like a sword-point through the throat, you shall have it. Otherwise, you go with me, under arrest. We'll take you along with us. You'll be credited with the power of disappearing at will into thin air, when they come to look for you!"

The cackle of St. Vrain lifted on the room. Cagliostro looked from one man to the other, startled, alarmed, calculating.

"So it was your voice that interrupted me, eh?" he observed calmly. "And you spoke of Strassburg—ah! Secret panels, of course. You must have learned a good deal."

"Enough," said Desmond laconically. "Do you wish to accompany us, or to die here?"

The face of Cagliostro cleared. He shrugged lightly.

"I am immortal. You cannot kill me...."

"Oh!" exclaimed St. Vrain eagerly, and his rapier quivered. "Shall we test it?"

"No, no," Cagliostro said hastily. "I'll go with you—my life is safe, then?"

"Entirely," said Desmond. "That is, if you don't try to escape."

"Oh! As to that, I give you my word of honor, monsieur!"

"I accept it—backed by a stout cord about your arms, and your boots tied to the stirrups," said Desmond dryly. "After all, Cagliostro, I do owe you my life; therefore I give you yours, instead of killing you as you deserve for your intrigues against France. When I've finished my work, I'll set you free and give you three days to get across the frontier."

Cagliostro, freed of the sword-point, bowed.

"Two days, monsieur, will be ample," he said.

"St. Vrain, you bring him along, will you? As far as the horses, at least. Once he's secure, you can take Celie and put her in safety." Desmond turned to the child, lifted her, and kissed her. He smiled into her eyes.

"You hear, little one? I can't keep you with me now, for I've work and hard riding ahead. This gentleman will put you in safety with good honest friends, and later on we'll meet again. Will this suit you, my dear Celie?"

She leaned forward and kissed his cheek with a swift, eager peck.

"Of course, monsieur! Everything's all right now."

"Yes, everything's all right," said Desmond mournfully, "for you, at least."

"But wait, wait!" broke out Cagliostro. "Where do we go, then?"

"Aye," said St. Vrain. "Whither, Desmond?"

Desmond turned toward the hole in the wall.

"*Diable!* Why, to Mont St. Michel, of course! A night ride for you, Monsieur Cagliostro, but a magician shouldn't be afraid of the dark. Come on with him, St. Vrain!"

CHAPTER XXII

A PRISONER

WHEN THE tide went out, Mont St. Michel was accessible from the coast. It went out, as it came in, with almost incredible rapidity. Then, for miles and miles, the fairy mount was surrounded by glistening, gleaming sands. Quicksands of death, for the most part.

Morning at Pontorson, and the tide on the ebb; it would not come in again until noon.

In days not long departed, great swarms of pilgrims had flocked through Pontorson each summer. The inn here was a vast old labyrinth of a place, the ancient convent adjoining was still larger. The town itself was small, placed behind protecting hillocks of sand that ringed the shore, so that from here the bay was invisible.

By the road that wound in from the bay, came a carriage followed by an escort of cavalry. Two men rode in it, one in a black robe, one in scarlet and gold and white. About the inn yard were loitering half a dozen men of the *marechaussé*, the mounted force that policed the country; their officer was sitting in talk, in the tavern room, with a man who had one wooden leg and who wore a none too clean wig, and the clothes of Brian Desmond. The carriage, which had just come from the Mont, turned in at the courtyard of the inn. With an exclamation, the officer rose.

"Hello! Here's the commandant of the Mont now, and the

prior with him! I'll bring them in, Colonel Desmond. You must meet them, by all means."

The man with the wooden leg said nothing, but his gray eyes flashed uneasily. Here before him were the man who commanded Mont St. Michel for the king, the man who ruled the Mont for God, and the man who policed the roads of France.

As the three approached his table, he rose and bowed, with remarkable grace for a crippled man. The officer of police introduced him.

"It is a great honor," the man said composedly, "to meet such distinguished gentlemen. And, I confess, it's devilish convenient! I must ask you, gentlemen, to inspect my papers, so that I may speak freely. Here you see my commission, my powers of arrest, and a *lettre de cachet* which I trust is to be put into effect very shortly."

The police officer nodded. Dom Urban, a lean, harsh-eyed monk, seated himself. The commandant, Colonel Laroche, saluted the signature of Louis XVI and followed suit. Colonel Desmond's lackey, a lean brown fellow with a scar across his face, brought wine and served them. His master complacently regarded the three.

"Ha! Colonel Desmond? An opportune meeting indeed, monsieur," the commandant exclaimed. "We had just been talking of you. I spoke with the party of soldiers who brought us your recent prisoner. Most embarrassing, monsieur! We've written Paris for instructions, but now that you're here, you may perhaps take care of the matter yourself."

Colonel Desmond blinked.

"My—er—recent prisoner?" he repeated cautiously.

The lean prior nodded.

"Yes, Lady Warr," he said severely. "We don't receive female prisoners at the Mont. She should have been consigned to some convent. In fact, women are barred from parts of the abbey altogether. We've temporarily confined her in one of the cells of an empty block, while awaiting instructions."

"Lady Warr!" repeated Colonel Desmond in a tone of amazement. His pale gray eyes glinted suddenly. "Oh, yes, of course; of course. Messieurs, I pray you to pardon my ignorance of your rules. In catching these English spies, I've had to act rapidly, just as rapid action may impend at this moment." He turned to the police officer. "You're keeping watch on the south road?"

"Certainly, monsieur. Since last night I've had two men constantly on patrol."

"It's lucky, monsieur, that you have such extraordinary powers," Colonel Laroche said approvingly. "It's high time something vigorous was being done about these accursed English spies. Do I understand you are to send us another prisoner? This *lettre de cachet*, I see, is in the name of one Benjamin Constant."

"The most dangerous of them all; I'm hoping to nab him here," said Colonel Desmond, composedly adjusting his dirty wig. "So dangerous that I must ask you to place him in solitary confinement, keep him ironed at all times, allow him speech with no one. He is never to leave his cell for any reason."

The gloomy Dom Urban nodded as though he rather relished the prospect.

At this moment a horseman came pounding into the courtyard, flung himself from his saddle, and hurried into the tavern room. He saluted excitedly.

"The man, monsieur! His horse is quite lame, slowing his pace. We met him, I spoke with him. He called himself Colonel Desmond, as you warned us he might do. There's another man with him whose arms are bound. I didn't wait to ask about him, but rode on to give you warning. My comrade is riding in with them. We did not speak about arrest, of course."

The officer sprang up. Colonel Desmond, quite placidly and without excitement, checked him.

"As I thought, he has the effrontery to use my name. Well, monsieur! Arrest him; but further, tie him hard and fast, and gag him. Don't let him talk."

"Right." The other nodded assent. "And the man with him, the prisoner?"

"I'll investigate him when you fetch them in. Give him exactly the same treatment as the other—incommunicado, you understand? Here's the *lettre de cachet* for this Constant. Bring them here first of all—"

Dom Urban interposed.

"No, no; your pardon. Bring them direct to the Mont. Colonel Desmond will be there. We're leaving at once, to make arrangements."

The officer saluted and strode out, calling his men to horse.

COLONEL DESMOND regarded the prior in consternation, unable for the moment to find words. His scar-faced lackey, moving behind Dom Urban, caught his eye and made a gesture of impudent reassurance. The lean prior smiled and explained.

"You see, monsieur, Colonel Laroche and I were bound for an official inspection of the abbey lands and estates, here along the coast. This duty is imperative, as the annual report must go to the king within the week.

"However, we can drive back to the Mont and take you with us; you'll remain as our guest, of course. We can then return while the tide is still out, and go on with our trip. We'll be back in two days. By that time, you will have been able to make arrangements in regard to this Lady Warr. The sub-prior, Dom Clement, can give you full information as to the best convent in which to place her. I must really insist that you take her off our hands."

As he listened to this speech, as he caught a wink from his lackey, the features of Colonel Desmond cleared. A smile came to his lips, a smile only less terrible than the flash in his pale eyes.

"Oh, of course, of course! I'll be glad to take her off your hands," he responded cheerfully, and rubbed his hands. "I presume that my authority will not be questioned?"

Colonel Laroche cleared his throat, and motioned to the documents on the table.

"My dear monsieur, your authority is above question from anyone save His Majesty, God bless him! That is to say, regards these prisoners.

"It'll be simple to transfer the woman to the convent here, or to one at Avranches, as you prefer. However, we'd best be on our way. We must get back here to the mainland before the tide cuts us off. Leave your horses here and come with us; your lackey can ride with our driver. We have scant room for more horses out yonder. Ah, monsieur, it is such men as you, wounded, crippled, but ever indomitable, who have made France great among the nations!"

Colonel Desmond acknowledged the compliment with becoming modesty. At this point, the prior struck in.

"One thing—no weapons are allowed in the abbey, monsieur. If you'll be good enough to leave all your weapons here—not even a knife is allowed—the usual search will be obviated."

Once again Colonel Desmond looked slightly startled. However, he caught the eye of his scarred lackey, and assented.

"Oh, by all means!" he said. "If you'll excuse me for a moment, I'll put a few things together—eh? What's that, you rascal?"

The scarred lackey spoke with the greatest deference.

"Pardon, monsieur. There is the great waxen taper you brought from Rome, and the staff of the blessed St. Crispus which Cardinal Fleury gave you. You spoke of depositing this relic and the taper at the Mont."

"Oh, by all means! A good thing you reminded me," said Colonel Desmond. "Give me your arm. We'll have the bundle ready in no time, messieurs...."

Ten minutes later, indeed, a long bundle that might or might not have held the staff of the blessed St. Crispus was put into the carriage. The supposed Colonel Desmond, seated between the prior and the commandant, went rolling out of Pontorson. On the box, scarred of face and jaunty of eye, rode the lackey.

The expanse of gleaming sands broke upon their sight, with the Mont rising from the midst. The sands were dotted with folk—fishers seeking the peculiar shellfish that made the taverns of the place famous, some people coming in to the mainland, others going out to the island, loaded wagons ploughing along. For those who knew the perilous sands, there was no danger.

But for those who did not, there was death.

THE HORSES trotted fast, everyone saluting the gentlemen as they passed. The Mont had not only monks and garrison, but a population of its own, now largely turned to fishing, since the pluckings of pilgrims had grown scant.

As the carriage approached, the gaunt walls rose in blotches of old color, the rising details of the fortress below and the Marvel above became more plainly visible. Even Colonel Desmond stared blankly and amazedly at those spiring walls. Beneath the sheer precipitous face of the Mont, on the right, a wagon had halted on the sand. Ropes lowered from a crane, far above, were hauling up a net, heavy laden. The prior, seeing the visitor's interest, pointed to it.

"A swift and easy way of bringing up supplies to the kitchen," he said.

The gaze of Colonel Desmond, which seemed never to miss any detail, rested on the crane and ropes with interest, as Dom Urban explained how a drum and windlass operated the lift. That glorious architecture towering above meant nothing to him; practical details meant much.

Along the walls, below the abbey, flashed uniforms and muskets, and the scoured brass of cannon that commanded the sole approach, the only opening within this lower rim of massive stone. As they approached this one gate, Colonel Desmond spoke reflectively.

"Is it true, as I've heard, that you have an iron cage here, in which a prisoner can neither lie down nor stand upright? Now, that might be an excellent prison for this Constant."

"God forbid!" said Dom Urban sharply, giving Desmond a

glance of sharp abhorrence. "That cage is a foul and inhuman thing. It hasn't been used for a hundred years. We'll take good care of your man, never fear. Solitary confinement and chains -—what more could you ask?"

"Ah, but he's a devil!" And the so-called Colonel Desmond wagged his head.

Colonel Laroche grinned and nudged him in the ribs. "And St. Michel settled the devil's hash for him—eh? Trust us, my friend!"

The throng about the gates, fisher folk, inhabitants, soldiers, made way. The carriage drove in, and halted immediately. From this courtyard just inside the entrance, no horses could pass on. An open barbican at the right, portcullis raised, showed a steeply rising and narrow street that twisted about like a winding stairway.

As Colonel Desmond left the carriage, he looked back across the sand. A little knot of horsemen was just coming out from Pontorson, the sunlight glinting on steel. His gray eyes narrowed, and a look of satisfaction came into his heavy features.

"*Diable!* It's a climb for you, with one wooden pin," said the commandant. "I'll wait here. You'll not want me, Dom Urban?"

"No. I'll take Colonel Desmond above, and have Dom Clement receive the new prisoner," the gloomy prior replied, and glanced at Desmond. "Ready?'"

"Of course. I've managed worse than this." And Colonel Desmond stepped out. "Here, you lazy dog! Your arm, or I'll have you well thrashed."

His scarred lackey smothered a grin, and took Colonel Desmond's arm, supporting him.

The tortuous, narrow little street wound up between old shops and houses and taverns, to the chapel. As they went, Dom Urban pointed out the landmarks—the famous Licorne inn, the house where the wife of Bertrand du Guesclin had lived and studied the stars, the old cannon left behind by the English, after their fruitless siege of the Mont centuries ago.

Then, at the chapel, Dom Urban uttered an exclamation of satisfaction. Here was Dom Clement approaching, a lean dark figure like himself. As the rule of silence observed by the monks above did not hold good here in the town, the prior and sub-prior were soon engaged in rapid conversation. Colonel Desmond was introduced, orders and arrangements were per-fected.

Standing a little apart with his lackey, the false Colonel Desmond looked ahead. Here the street ended in an enormous curving flight of stone stairs, the full width of the street, with platforms and benches where one could rest. On the right, rose the tops of the ramparts. The curve of these stairs went up to the abbey defenses to the left—great massive towers—but they did not end there by any means.

"*Diable!*" observed the scarred lackey softly. "This is an ad-venture, my honest colonel! You've handled things admirably. How long do we remain?"

"Two days, no more," said Colonel Desmond, uneasily eyeing the lofty towers and pinnacles above. "We may leave tomorrow. And Lady Warr goes with us. I've a score of my own to settle with this lady."

"Excellent!" The lackey chuckled. "A charming piece of goods, that woman. You may count on me to lend you full assistance, my dear master."

The pale gray eye of his master rested on him, with a thought-ful nod.

DOM URBAN made his farewells, and scurried off below to get off with Colonel Laroche. Dom Clement took his honored guest in hand and led the way slowly up those curving stairs toward the twin towers beyond.

"This ascent is called the Outer Degree," he said. "These days, we don't man the upper defenses here; except at night, the gates are left open. The defenses of the lower walls are held by the garrison, merely a nominal matter."

"But your prisoners, with such lax methods, might escape," said Colonel Desmond.

"They know better." And the sub-prior laughed. Then, as they toiled up the curving stairs, he pointed through the open entrance of the towers beyond. "There's the Great Inner Degree. Luckily, monsieur, you don't have to climb it all."

Luckily, indeed. Colonel Desmond stared, and so did his lackey. Through this entry of the abbey buildings, which towered up on either hand into the sky, ran the Great Inner Degree— now steep naked rock, now incredible stone stairs, now platforms for rest. It ran up and up, to end at the platform before the abbey church far above. From below, however, that ascent seemed to have no end at all. It was like a vast stairway reaching up to heaven.

"Is it your pleasure to seek rest in your room, Colonel Desmond?" asked the sub-prior. "I must receive the two prisoners when they come, and some arrangement must be made in regard to the second person. Dom Urban said there was authority for only one—"

"With your permission," said Colonel Desmond blandly, "I'd like to be present when you receive them. I must ask you to permit them no speech whatever, but allow me to visit them separately when you've assigned them to cells. When I investigate this second person, I will be able to decide his disposition. I may take him with me, as well as Lady Warr, for incarceration elsewhere. Until they arrive, I have no need of rest. Perhaps I might have a word with Lady Warr, indeed?"

"As you like," said the sub-prior. "I'll give you a monk for guide. By the time you've spoken with her, the others should be here."

Colonel Desmond was curious, and asked many questions as they toiled on. He learned that the abbot of this place was usually some court favorite, the appointment being purely nominal. The prior was the actual ruler.

Without mounting the Inner Degree, Dom Clement led

them through a doorway into the towering structure on the left. Here were the abbatial chambers, the hospice for pilgrims, and on through, the cells for the royal "guests," not unpleasantly situated along the high point of rock below the loftily mounting walls of the abbey church.

To these cells a silent black-clad monk presently led the false Colonel Desmond, who stumped sturdily along with his lackey supporting him. Jingling his huge ancient keys, the monk led them into a corridor, halted, and pointed silently. Evidently he had no intention of himself looking on the face of the woman prisoner, which quite suited Colonel Desmond.

Leaning on his lackey's arm, Colonel Desmond halted before the one occupied cell. The monk unlocked the door, and then drew back and away, after a curt knock.

"Enter," said Jane Warr.

She stared at them in utter blank incredulity. All her effects were here; she looked quite her usual trim, poised self; but her features were drawn and haggard. So struck was the man who posed as Colonel Desmond by the change in her face that for a moment he could not speak.

"You!" she murmured, drawing back.

"Yes, as you perceive," he rejoined, in English. "So your ladyship got me dismissed the service, eh? And here you are, put away safe. You'd like me to help you, no doubt."

Her bewilderment was acute. "But I don't understand—you're not a prisoner?"

Ben Constant smiled composedly. "Not much, Your Ladyship. I've nipped Monsieur Feufollet at last, and now I've come for you. Say the word, and I can get you out of here, and you can fix up things in London for me. Tit for tat, Your Ladyship. Eh?"

Her eyes widened on him. "You—you've killed him?"

"Better than that," said Constant with relish. "But never mind him. Do you go away with me? Is it a bargain?"

She stared at him, and shivered a little. "No!" she cried

sharply. "No! Oh, you evil creature, you horrible beast—no! I'll make no bargain with you. I want nothing to do with you, now or ever again!"

"Very well, Your Ladyship. In that case, you'll go anyway."

Now she saw the Balafré, realized his presence, for the first time. She started.

"You? You here, with him—"

"We are old friends." And the Balafré bowed, with his jaunty, impudent air. "We are enjoying a very pleasing adventure to-gether. And with your company, madame, the adventure prom-ises even better."

She looked into his eyes, shivered again, and then swung on Constant furiously.

"If—if this is all real," she said in English, "I don't understand it. I can't believe it. Get out! Both of you, get out of here!"

Constant laughed softly and obeyed. The Balafré bowed again, regarded her greedily, and with a mocking smile, followed the one-legged man.

IN THE abbatial quarters, hung with ancient tapestries, gloomy with massive old furniture, the sub-prior regarded the two prisoners and their escort. He glanced at the *lettre de cachet*, and entered the name of Benjamin Constant in his books. Gagged, bound, the two prisoners had nothing whatever to say.

Dom Clement omitted the usual lecture given new prison-ers.

"You, Monsieur Constant, are relegated to solitary confine-ment pending the pleasure of His Majesty," he said dourly. "I warn you that if you make any effort to speak with the brother who brings your meals, you will be punished by three days of bread and water. You are to be ironed, and to remain ironed. However, we are not cruel here. Instead of riveting irons upon your arms and legs, we employ more humane and modern ones that lock. In case you do not accept your situation as the orders of His Majesty should be accepted, we will place you in one of the ancient dark dungeons and rivet you in the old irons. I trust this is satisfactory, Colonel Desmond?"

The false Colonel Desmond helped himself to a pinch of snuff. His pale gray eyes rested complacently on the blue eyes of the prisoner, which were icy cold.

"Oh, it is quite satisfactory," he said placidly. "Any insubordination in this fellow must be met with the strictest discipline."

"As to the other prisoner, here—"

"I'll interrogate him privately in the next room, if I may."

"By all means, monsieur."

So the false Colonel Desmond, presently ensconced in the great chair of the absentee abbot, found himself alone with the bound but no longer gagged Count de Cagliostro. He regarded the prisoner with open curiosity.

"Come, monsieur! Your name?"

Cagliostro gave it without evasion. He was helpless and bewildered, with a certain nameless terror in his deep eyes. He had not the faintest notion why this one-legged man should be addressed by Dom Clement under the name of Colonel Desmond, and he did not care. His own situation was all that interested him at the moment.

"Hello, hello! This is lucky," and Ben Constant whistled softly. "You're the great magician. I've heard of you, a good deal about you, in fact. Once these monks find out who you are, monsieur, do you know what they'll do?"

Cagliostro made no response, but a trickle of sweat came out on his forehead. Constant winked at him.

"Well, they'll burn you as a sorcerer—that's what. The old laws against sorcery are still in effect. These silent, black-clad monks would like nothing better than to hold you to trial, and they could do it."

The terror at the back of Cagliostro's eyes deepened. Entry into this place, for him, was like entry between the very jaws of hell. Constant chuckled.

"I see you don't relish the prospect. Well, I've nothing against you. I can order your instant release. You can be given a horse down below, and be gone. In fact, I strongly advise such a course. If you keep your tongue between your teeth, you can get away a free man—but remember, only if you're silent. Being a magician, of course, you can make this action worth my while?"

Cagliostro brightened. He was well aware that he would lose his money in any case, and here was at least a chance to lose it to some purpose.

"I have five thousand francs in my pocket, in banknotes," he said quietly.

The pale eyes of Ben Constant glittered avidly.

"Good! What pocket?"

The bound man told him. He heaved up out of his chair, stumped to the prisoner, and next moment had the money and was stuffing it into his own pocket. Then, calling in the guards again, he sought Dom Clement in the next room.

"There's no harm in this fellow," the false Colonel Desmond told the sub-prior. "It seems that the prisoner Constant was trying to extort money out of him. I recommend that he be taken below, given a horse, and turned loose at once before the tide comes in. Place the horse to the account of His Majesty, of course."

"Very well, monsieur," said Dom Clement.

"And perhaps I shall leave tomorrow with Lady Warr," went on the other thoughtfully. "It might be as well."

"Oh, that's impossible until Dom Urban returns, monsieur," said the sub-prior. "You see, the order of release must bear his signature; I have no authority in such a case. But you will be quite comfortable here, and he'll be back the day after tomorrow."

The false Colonel Desmond reflected on this, and agreed. He could do nothing else.

So it happened that, before the tide came rolling in with such rapidity that not even a galloping horse could outrun it,

Cagliostro spurred away from the Mont as from the gates of hell itself.

His lessening figure disappeared. The figures dotting the sands were gone. Off to seaward, a slight glitter of water appeared. Here and there on the vast expanse of sands, water glittered elsewhere. The sands seemed to vanish, to be abruptly turned into water. Then, suddenly, there were no more sands at all. Waves and rolling masses of water were sweeping in, beating about the lower walls of the Mont, glittering on for miles. This, in fact, was not unlike a lesser miracle. Anyone trapped on those sands when the tide came in was a lost soul.

The alleged Colonel Desmond, enjoying a belated but hearty nones meal in the refectory of the monks, naturally saw nothing at all of this miracle. Nor did he see anything of the lone pilgrim, clad entirely in black, who just reached the shelter of the Mont before the tide came in and closed off all communication with the mainland.

Very lucky for this pilgrim, said those who welcomed him down below. The guards took his arms, since no one was allowed to bear any weapon into the abbey above. Then he was sent on to enjoy the hospitality of the monks and to finish his pilgrimage.

CHAPTER XXIII

"STAIRS TO HEAVEN"

THE REAL Desmond, no longer gagged, but clogged with heavy chains locked about wrists and ankles, stared from the barred window of his cell—stared out across infinity, it seemed. These cells faced the land. The island below was all shut out of his sight. He could see the sweep of water and the far coast, nothing else.

The sun had gone down into the ocean. Soon the tide would follow it and the sands be bare in the darkness.

For Desmond, this day had been one of torment to steel the soul. Suddenly arrested, bound, gagged, and led here; the scene of ghastly realization when he looked into the eyes of Constant and comprehended everything; and this cell. The silent, black-gowned monk who brought his meals; the threat against him if he uttered a word. He was helpless, utterly helpless. Constant had made good use of those garments with the papers sewn into the waistcoat lining! Easily enough found, for Desmond had replaced them carelessly after his arrest of Lady Warr.

And somewhere here in these walls, Jane Warr—unfound, unseen, nothing explained. This hurt more cruelly than anything else. He had counted upon gaining a complete confession from Cagliostro and then releasing the man, ordering the release of Jane Warr and if necessary getting its confirmation from Paris—and this plan was wrecked.

His own plight was of no great moment. St. Vrain would come sooner or later, explanations must ensue, and ultimately he would be freed; even if he were held here incommunicado, it could not last forever. But Jane Warr! His whole soul cried out to reach her, to correct the frightful wrong he had done her. And he could not.

From somewhere, he could hear whinings, screams, the voices of men; he shivered. The chief use for *lettres de cachet,* these days, was to confine lunatics, members of great families who were wanted out of the way. The prisoners here were largely of such nature. And amid such a crew, he had placed Jane Warr. The thought made him writhe again.

There was no one around. No guards were stationed up here. Once the cells were locked for the night, the prisoners were left alone; the monks, who held the Marvel, had no reason to stand guard. Desmond knew that his own cell was away from the others. A bare handful of prisoners were here, where in the old days dozens had been accommodated.

Darkness closed down gradually, and the stars blazed out. Later would be a moon, round and full and high—but not yet.

With a *clank-clank* of his irons, Desmond flung himself on the miserable wooden bench that served as bed, and gave way to utter despair. A sound of men's voices chanting came faintly to him—the monks singing in the church up above, that topped the Marvel. With a groan, he cursed the lot of them, and chiefly Constant.

Wearied in mind and body, he finally dozed off in uneasy slumber.

A sound reached him. He opened his eyes, sat up, swung his feet to the floor. His cell door was shut and locked, but the grilled opening in the center was left open for ventilation. The sound came again. Desmond rose, went to the door, and pressed his face against the opening.

He could see nothing at all in the obscurity outside, but after a moment he heard the sound once more—a faint, cheerful whistle. He had heard St. Vrain whistle like that. St. Vrain? No, impossible! Yet for this man anything seemed possible.

The whistle died out. A volley of curses came from some prisoner, and then a lunatic yammering. Once again Desmond caught the whistling. He thrilled to it. His pulses hammered fast.

"St. Vrain!" He lifted his voice, not too loudly. "St. Vrain!"

"Easy, comrade."

Then it was real! Desmond could scarce believe that he had heard aright. A wild desire seized him to burst into shouts, into tears, into a whirlwind of emotion. The voice reached him anew.

"Where are you?"

"Here, here! I don't know where." Desmond fought for control of himself, and gained it. "No one else near me."

"Go on talking, comrade—but softly. Hello! These must be the cells. An empty block?"

"Yes. Are you really there, St. Vrain?"

"Aye, comrade. I have it now! Can you hear me better?"

"Yes. This way, here, here!"

Desmond's choked voice was guide enough. A blacker mass moved in the blackness outside his cell. Then St. Vrain was close by, in front of him, touching him through the opening!

"Thank God," breathed Desmond. "It's like a miracle."

"Oh, miracles are simple things once you understand them." And the harsh chuckle of St. Vrain seemed like music. "Still, there's plenty I don't understand in all this. When I got to Pontorson, the town was buzzing with news of the arrest of two men. I figured things out, after a fashion, when I heard about the one-legged man and the lackey who had a scar on his face. I was all ready to come on after you, when back from the Mont appeared our friend Cagliostro, riding as if the devil was at his heels. I came along, asked questions, and acted accordingly. I'm a pilgrim, you see, lodged up here in the hospice for pilgrims, and the rest is nothing."

Desmond drew a deep breath. "But you're here! How did you find the way?"

"*Diable!* I knew every inch of this place when I was a boy, every rat-hole! I got my schooling from the monks, and was here for weeks at a time. As soon as I get this lock picked, I'll have you out of here. Then over the lower wall and away. The tide's out and we can make it safely."

"No," said Desmond, hearing the other at work on the lock. "Does Constant know that you're here?"

"I took no chances, but played sick and lay hid all afternoon. Of course, you can go to the monks, if you prefer, and tell 'em your story with me to back it up—"

"No," repeated Desmond. The word came like a blow. "First, Jane Warr. Then Constant; finish him once and for all, if I have to use my bare hands to it! That is, if you can get me out of these irons."

"Riveted on?"

"No. Locked."

"Bah! That's nothing! In the galleys, we had 'em riveted on for life."

Desmond's spirits were rising high now. True, locks were nothing to the right man. He himself, had he been free, could have walked through this whole abbey.

"There!"

THE DOOR swung open, and St. Vrain caught him in a swift, strong embrace. Now for the irons, no simple matter in this obscurity. While St. Vrain worked at them, the two talked together. Once he comprehended that Desmond was savagely resolved on a certain course, St. Vrain shrugged and gave up all argument.

"Very well. Suppose we get this woman of yours free; suppose I get her here. What's the use, beyond your clearing up matters with her?"

"That must be done."

"And then Constant, eh? And after that, escape—if we're still free. All right. But I can't bring her here. She's in one of the lower cells. And you'd best not go there with me; it's danger-ous. See here! We need weapons, and I can get them. Then I'll get her. Will that do you?"

"Of course, but—"

"No buts, then, for the love of Heaven! Come along and follow me; walk softly. Here we are—a pleasant sound, eh?"

The irons clicked; Desmond's hands were free. Presently St. Vrain had mastered the other lock. A moment afterward, they were out of the cell together.

When they had a glimpse of the eastern sky, Desmond saw that the moon was just rising, round and glorious. Then he plunged with St. Vrain into the depths of masonry and the sky was shut out.

Where he was, Desmond had no slightest notion or care. St. Vrain's knowledge of the place was no idle boast. They passed through corridors, endless stairs, and great empty rooms—a slow and tedious matter in pitch darkness. When at length they emerged again into the open air, it seemed to Desmond that they were at the bottom of a well. St. Vrain laughed softly when he said as much.

"Why, so we are! There's the Great Inner Degree, as they call it. The moon is getting high already; we've wasted a lot of time. Here's the entry at the towers—gates closed but no guards. The guardroom is just to the left. I'll get in there and locate some sort of a weapon. No hurry. As long as we're going to be fools, we'll make a good job of it. Wait on this bench."

"You know where Constant is quartered? And the Balafré?"

"Aye. Not fifty feet away, in the guestrooms of the abbot. But I'll have to get your woman out of the cells, unless you want to be sensible."

Desmond chuckled. "No. Let's be fools all around, as you say!"

The other slipped away and was gone.

Free, then! Desmond went to the bench and stretched out, looking up at the strip of stars overhead, almost closed out by the towering walls. Free—everything else wiped out and forgotten, except this understanding with Jane Warr, this settlement with Constant and the Balafré. He laughed a little. There would be a sad awakening for the monks and the commandant here, when the truth became known!

He turned and looked up the Inner Degree. It was clear enough in the starlight and the reflected moonlight. He had been once before in this place, for a brief visit, and had climbed these enormous stairs to the platform and the church high above. Now, as he looked up the sharp incline of rock, up the successive flights of enormous stairs, a memory came back into his mind—the words of Cagliostro. Something about dying men and stairs going up to heaven. So Cagliostro had been turned loose, eh? Well, nothing mattered now. Let the man go.

Something stirred and moved in the darkness. Then St. Vrain, almost invisible in his black garb, drew into focus.

"Here—a couple of old rapiers that'll serve our turn," said he. "Last chance—do the work now and see the woman later?"

"No."

"You stubborn devil! All right, then." And with his dry, mirthless chuckle, St. Vrain slipped noiselessly to a doorway in the towering wall, and disappeared.

MORE TIME passed—an interminable time. Everything was dark and silent in the buildings around and above. The moon had by this time risen high; her bright light struck on the upper platforms, and the reflected radiance banished the obscurity of the lower ascent. Silent and white and beautiful, the lines of the Marvel drifted up and up into the heavens, more impressive from here even than from a distance.

Desmond stirred at last. The stone walls, reaching up on either side, caught and made louder a dim murmur of voices. St. Vrain returning—no! A sudden thrill shot through him.

"I tell you. I feel stifled! I don't like this place. I'm out for air."

"Aye. But wait. Don't go unarmed." That was the voice of Constant—the composed, calm, deadly voice Desmond knew so well. "Never mind. Take no chances."

Going out? Where were they? Impossible for him to say. Speaking at an open window, no doubt. Close by, according to St. Vrain.

Instinctively, Desmond left his stone bench and drew back against one of the side walls. The rapier in his hand was an ancient one, long and heavy, poor of balance—but at least a sword. If St. Vrain would only come now, with Jane Warr....

Ah! A door in the gloomy wall swung shut. It was just past Desmond; toward the upper rise. Two figures showed for an instant—then the accursed sound, the *tap-tap-tap* that had haunted him so long. Constant and the Balafré! They were going up the steep slope, away from him....

Like a hound let loose, Desmond hurled himself after them. His heels rang on the naked rock. An oath, a low exclamation of amazement, of startled recognition—for the moonlight was reflecting down this well of stone, lightening the gloom. He saw the Balafré whip out a sword: and face around at him. Constant went stumping on up the sharp slope toward the first flight of stairs, in frantic haste.

"Ha! No slipping this time!" exclaimed the Balafré.

Desmond checked his rush.

"Your life and freedom, to let me at him. Yes or no?"

For answer, the scarred man sent in a lightning thrust. He was grinning wolfishly. Desmond barely parried it, and the blades clung and clashed, slipped in and out. Desmond's hurried brain cleared; a master swordsman, here. He drew back a pace, with an oath of exasperation. The other was at him with a plunge, and had the advantage of higher ground to boot. So fierce was the attack that Desmond went back and back.

"I have him! Come and take him!" panted the scarred man.

Constant was at the steps. He swung around. At this instant, Desmond's heart leaped. St. Vrain's voice came to him in a sharp exclamation.

"Ha! Let me have him, comrade! After the other!"

An oath of dismay from the Balafré. He disengaged, leaped backward, then turned and ran for it. Desmond had a glimpse of St. Vrain, a cloaked figure behind him, and heard the voice of Jane Warr uttering his name. He disregarded it, and with St. Vrain at his heels flung himself up that steep slope. Savage exultation rioted in him. Here was the end, here and now—no escape, no evasion this time! No matter what happened, even at the worst, Constant could not leave this spot alive—and knew it. He had turned again and was hopping nimbly up the steep flight to the first platform.

"Look out," panted Desmond to the man beside him. "He's a master."

St. Vrain laughed harshly and threw himself forward. The Balafré, on the steps, whirled and awaited the attack, went up another step, engaged the blade of St. Vrain. Desmond circled them, intent only on that figure ahead. Swift as a flash, the Balafré leaped sideways, tripped Desmond neatly, kicked St.

Vrain in the face, and was gone. St. Vrain and Desmond fell, collided, and came up with hot oaths. The mocking laugh of the scarred man rang out from ahead. He had a good lead now, with Constant stumping along but now less nimbly.

The dark silence of the abbey walls, towering to either hand and above, was ringing with voices, hoarse breaths and the click of heels. Furious as he was, St. Vrain checked his oaths to save breath. The savagely steep climb was telling on them all.

Up the stairs now. Desmond saw Constant well in the lead, on toward the next flight, with the Balafré beside him. They gained the stairs beyond, and the scarred man paused, Constant went on. More moonlight now, a point of silver light striking down upon this next platform. Desmond, sobbing for breath, caught St. Vrain's word.

"Easy! Wait."

He drew back. St. Vrain plunged on, as though to attack the Balafré, and suddenly halted. Planted on the stairs, the scarred man taunted him. St. Vrain rested, coolly, and made an unexpected leap to the side. He swung on the Balafré, who was only one step above him now, and the steel clashed. Before Desmond could pass, a short, sharp yelp broke from St. Vrain. The scarred man leaped backward, blood on his face, and then was up half a dozen steps and facing around afresh. St. Vrain and Desmond came at him together, and for one mad moment he fought them both, with a slashing and furious burst of agility that disregarded all rules of fence. Here, his superior height served him well, until of a sudden he was free of them and dashing up again.

On to the next platform, where moonlight struck down, and in the moonlight the Balafré faced around once more, gulping frantically for breath. Desmond was first up and at him, engaging his rapier on even ground, driving in with burning lungs.

From the shadows beyond came a sharp cry. Something moved there.

As though warned by that cry, the scarred man leaped aside

and away. Desmond saw something flash in the moonlight, and desperately writhed from its course. A knife—and another! Neither struck him, but he heard a thudding *"whick!"* a short, vicious sound. A cry burst from St. Vrain. The latter, clutching at his breast, fell forward and lay quiet across the moonlight.

CHAPTER XXIV

ACROSS THE SANDS

WITH THIS, a stark and frightful madness came upon Desmond. St. Vrain dead—the last in that chain of murders by the knife! That death-cry echoed up and up between the walls. Desmond forgot his lungs, his aching legs, everything. He hurtled forward, found his way blocked by the Balafré, dashed sword and man aside, and went straight at Constant.

The latter was toiling up the steps beyond, as Desmond came for him. Warned by a hoarse cry from the Balafré, Constant turned about, and halted. His arm swung. Desmond recognized the motion, and at the swing of the hand, darted to one side. The cast failed. And now Desmond was leaping up again, his blade ready for the thrust. Constant, unarmed, was there before him....

Unarmed, but not helpless. As Desmond lunged at the figure above, the wooden leg flew out, struck his blade, knocked it aside. And then the man came down, full at him, grappling him, dragging him down, rolling with him down the stairs, down and ever down. Desmond still gripped his blade, however, as they struck on the platform below and the grip of Constant was broken by the shock.

And, an instant later, as Desmond came to one knee he found the Balafré upon him with rapier stabbing down. He parried that thrust in desperation, came erect—and the other stepped back, spent. So was Desmond, for that matter—lungs heaving, sparks flying before his eyes. A glance showed Constant scuttling up the stairs again. As Desmond instinctively turned to follow, the Balafré drove in. The moment of rest was ended.

Desmond engaged. Nothing for it now, but to settle one before he could get at the other. His nerves steadied, his wrist steeled. Fool that he had been to spare this ruffian, that night in the stables room!

A glimpse of the dark motionless figure of St. Vrain, across the platform, sent fire through him. He met the scarred man's attack and gave thrust for thrust, with a ferocity that sent his opponent backward, They fought into the patch of moonlight, across it into the lesser obscurity beyond.

Suddenly the scarred man gasped. He had flung off his garments to his shirt, and now blood started on the white linen. He made a last convulsive attack, and Desmond met it with steel wrist, and then he gave ground rapidly. Desmond pushed after him. Back into the moonlight, now, with fear printed in the scarred, panting features.

Then Desmond had him, and sent the thrust home, and wrenched loose his blade.

With a cough and a groan, the Balafré staggered. The sword fell and clattered as his fingers were loosened. He staggered again, lost balance, and went back into the shadows with a crash.

Knowing his steel had gone to the heart, Desmond paused not to watch, but swung around and panted upward. Somewhere beyond and ahead was his quarry. There was nothing to stop him now, he thought with fierce exultation. Not bursting lungs nor failing legs could withstand the driving urge of his will.

But Constant had a far lead on him. As he plunged upward, Desmond suddenly realized the man's purpose. Sanctuary, in the church high above!

His pace redoubled. He gained rapidly, so rapidly that at the last mounting flight up into the moonlight, he was not six feet behind that stumping, frantically toiling figure. Constant loosed his cloak and hurled it, struck Desmond across the face, gained a fraction of a second, and emerged upon the topmost platform.

The high church doors, off to the right, were closed.

Desmond was up, out on the platform, and breaking into a last spurt, when his foot slipped and he went down. Up again, unhurt, gasping curses, to see Constant disappear around the angle of the walls. He followed, to find only shadow and blankness.

THEN BEGAN a frantic and wholly mad pursuit, only a trifle less mad than the flight of this man who faced certain death. By daylight, it would have been an impossibility. By moonlight and shadow it was fantastic in the extreme.

Whether guided by instinct, or by some knowledge he had picked up this day, Constant doubled, darted forward, circled back—now by the fairy cloisters behind the church, now across an open roof expanse, now at last into a doorway and down a corridor. Desmond followed, with the *tap-tap-tap* to lead him on, but more than once went amiss. Only when he followed into the corridor, was he certain of his man.

And then, somehow, he missed the track again. He emerged into full moonlight, on a patch of roof, with battlements before him. It was empty. There was no sign of Constant anywhere.

As he stood panting, gulping air into his lungs, Desmond heard the faint *tap-tap-tap* from somewhere. And it was below him. He looked about frantically, and suddenly caught another sound, a *whir* and *burl* as of rope going out about a drum. It came from below, yes, but not from inside the walls. Rather, from outside them! Constant…?

Desmond staggered to the parapet. Dropping his sword, he pulled himself upward and craned forward. Below him was nothing.

He peered down at this vacuous moonlight until it cleared, and his gaze pierced the gulf. Once focused, everything was brilliantly clear and distinct. He was on the side of the Mont facing the coast; directly below him was a huge beam jutting forth. He craned over a little farther—and suddenly he comprehended.

Like a spider on its web-thread, the figure of a man was descending the sheer face of the rock. Constant, on the rope that wound out from the crate! This was the huge jutting beam. There was a rattle and rumble of turning drums or winches, as the rope went out. One look told Desmond that any pursuit or interference was hopeless.

The noise ceased. The rope was ended. The man was down.

Constant was there below, on the sands that gleamed and glistened in the flood of moonlight. One instant he turned, shaking his fist as though aware of Desmond watching him. Then he struck out swiftly, away from the Mont, pegging along toward the distant line of the coast.

The moonlight revealed his figure clearly enough. Somewhere down below, a guard shouted out, and then another. They were frantic cries, cries of warning, but doubtless Constant misinterpreted them. He moved the faster.

Abruptly, for a moment, he halted. Desmond's gaze caught a moving glitter, off to the left. After an instant he realized what it must be. The moonlight struck upon water, over there. The tide was coming in. His gaze went back to the figure below.

Constant leaped into motion. No longer walking now, he went ahead in great awkward strides, hopping over the sands, flinging himself desperately forward. Desmond, from above, perceived how useless it was. The sheet of water was spreading and advancing with terrific rapidity, in utter silence. Desmond was fascinated, motionless, staring down.

Waves suddenly swirled where sand had been. Still that figure went plunging forward, up and down, with its enormous, ungainly hops. Then, all at once, it ceased to move. Water was creeping in around it, water that seemed to be rising and coming up fast. In reality, it was the man who was going down.

He had struck a quicksand.

Still his figure lingered there, dark against the sheen of the waters. The waves crept and broke around him. Desmond had one sharp glimpse, real or fancied, of the man struggling there, his arms upflung frantically—then nothing was in sight except the bursting whitecaps of the waves.

The tide was in.

BY THE time Desmond managed somehow to retrace his mad course, the whole abbey was in wild turmoil and uproar, like a beehive all abuzz.

When he regained the platform again, weary and spent, he found Jane Warr kneeling and at work over the figure of St. Vrain, in the shaft of moonlight. She gave him no word or look until her task was finished. Then she rose and staggered a little. Desmond caught her.

"Thanks. It's all right," she murmured. "He—he'll not die, Brian."

"Praise be for that!" said Desmond, with a long breath.

Her hands clung to him, and she sighed. They were both oblivious of the glittering lights, the growing tumult of shrill voices. All these things would reach them in due time. For the moment, they were alone.

"Jane, dear, I've much to tell you," Desmond said quietly. "Apologies, heartache—oh, the shame of it all! I'm so bitter sorry—"

But Jane interrupted him.

"Never mind." She pointed to the motionless St. Vrain. "He told me. That is, he told me enough. Oh, dear Brian, let's forget it all, forget it all! There's nothing I don't understand. It's all over and done with. But what's going to come of it now, this night, tomorrow? What's ahead of us?"

He bent his head, and kissed her.

"Why, just that!" and his old gay laugh rang out. "We'll send to the army, to Boufflers and others who know me; we may even send to Versailles, to convince these monks. There's no haste. In any case, Will o' the Wisp is dead, his work's done, and if you'll say the same about Jane Warr, it's a bargain."

"Thank Heaven, my dear," she answered softly. "Yes; I shudder to think of it all, when such things can happen, such mistakes, such terrible enmities. You're worth more to me than everything else, and if you'll not be an enemy, then I won't—"

"Glory be!" exclaimed Desmond. "Those are the happiest words I've ever heard! And now look!" He turned her in his arms and pointed to the spiring summit of the high church above. "D'ye know what that is, my dear?"

"That? What do you think it is?" she demanded, smiling.

"An elegant place to be married, begad!" said Brian Desmond.

H. BEDFORD-JONES

BEDFORD-JONES IS a Canadian by birth, but not by profession, having removed to the United States at the age of one year. For over twenty years he has been more or less profitably engaged in writing and traveling. As he has seldom resided in one place longer than a year or so and is a person of retiring habits, he is somewhat a man of mystery; more than once he has suffered from unscrupulous gentlemen who impersonated him—one of whom murdered a wife and was subsequently shot by the police, luckily after losing his alias.

The real Bedford-Jones is an elderly man, whose gray hair and precise attire give him rather the appearance of a retired foreign diplomat. His hobby is stamp collecting, and his collection of Japan is said to be one of the finest in existence. At present writing he is en route to Morocco, and when this appears in print he will probably be somewhere on the Mojave Desert in company with Erle Stanley Gardner.

Questioned as to the main facts in his life, he declared there was only one main fact, but it was not for publication; that his life had been uneventful except for numerous financial losses, and that his only adventures lay in evading adventurers. In his younger years he was something of an athlete, but the encroachments of age preclude any active pursuits except that of motoring. He is usually to be found poring over his stamps, working at his typewriter, or laboring in his California rose garden, which is one of the sights of Cathedral Cañon, near Palm Springs.

Bedford-Jones has written stories laid in many corners of the earth, but among his most popular tales were the John Solomon stories which started many years ago in the *Argosy*.